SUMMER AT FORGET-ME-NOT COTTAGE

HELEN ROLFE

Boldwood

First published in Great Britain in 2023 by Boldwood Books Ltd.

Copyright © Helen Rolfe, 2023

Cover Design by Alexandra Allden

Cover Photography: Shutterstock

Every effort has been made to obtain the necessary permissions with reference to copyright material, both illustrative and quoted. We apologise for any omissions in this respect and will be pleased to make the appropriate acknowledgements in any future edition.

A CIP catalogue record for this book is available from the British Library.

Paperback ISBN 978-1-80415-536-3

Large Print ISBN 978-1-80415-537-0

Hardback ISBN 978-1-80415-535-6

Ebook ISBN 978-1-80415-539-4

Kindle ISBN 978-1-80415-538-7

Audio CD ISBN 978-1-80415-530-1

MP3 CD ISBN 978-1-80415-531-8

Digital audio download ISBN 978-1-80415-532-5

Boldwood Books Ltd
23 Bowerdean Street
London SW6 3TN

For my family, the only people I'd want to share a cosy cottage with...

1

Morgan Reese never thought she'd come back to Little Woodville, let alone be here for so long. She'd come here to be with her mum Elaina, intended it to be for a month, six weeks at most, before she loaded up her car and drove the long journey up to Edinburgh to join her fiancé Ronan. And yet here she was seven months later, still in the quaint chocolate-box village in the Cotswolds.

She closed the front door to Forget-Me-Not Cottage behind her, and lightly cradling a spring bouquet, she locked up before heading out into the sunshine. Every time she did this – made her way to the end of the path, went through the little gate at the end and turned back as she pulled it to and flipped the little latch into place – she was reminded that nothing would ever be the same again. Her mum was gone. And Morgan wouldn't trade the time they'd spent together for anything. Not even for Ronan, the man she'd promised to spend the rest of her life with.

Forget-Me-Not Cottage had had its name for a long time before Elaina moved into it with her two daughters, Morgan and Tegan, and on the border of the front path were the charming blue blooms with their yellow centres, a feature that came and went with the seasons and had done ever since they'd arrived. Elaina had kept the tradition going despite not being much of a gardener. That was what Little Woodville was like really, in a nutshell; people respected the village for its inclusivity, its welcome, its character, which included little touches like the appropriate flowers if you owned a residence with a particular name. Morgan hadn't always appreciated the special touch the forget-me-nots added but she did now it was almost summer and the little flowers added colour to the front garden of the cottage, both beside the path and in the bed below the front window where Elaina had insisted on planting more.

Morgan headed across the village green and down towards the high street, aware of how different her surroundings would be when she eventually left Little Woodville for good. Rather than thatched roofs and the closeness of a smaller community, the city of Edinburgh was busy, diverse and had an eclectic mix of buildings. She'd only been twice, both times with Ronan to visit his family, but it was a move that she'd agreed to and that had excited her for a time. Now, she felt unsure, but she suspected that was the grief talking, the unwillingness to accept that this part of her life was behind her. And a lot of it had to do with how busy she was dealing with the practicalities, including getting her mum's cottage ready for sale and wading through all the stock Elaina had collected for the market stall she'd run in the village as a hobby and a source of extra income.

When she reached the high street, she turned left, crossed the road and made her way over the small, humpback bridge that straddled a shallow stream. She paused at the top, smiling. She remembered this place well. She'd played Poohsticks on more than one occasion with her mum and older sister, Tegan. And on the occasions their mum had let go of some of the tension she tended to carry with her, it had been fun. But those times were few and far between. Tegan and Morgan didn't always get the fun Elaina, the one who wanted them around her for company. What Morgan and her sister had had more often than not was a stressed mother working long hours both as a secretary and at a supermarket to make ends meet since their dad walked out and never came back. Morgan remembered school uniforms being bought two sizes too big so they lasted, never being allowed to buy school dinner like their friends, not having family holidays apart from two short camping trips to Norfolk when a lot of their friends went further afield, not having much time when the three of them simply enjoyed one another's company. Morgan had written to their dad to tell him that Elaina had died and he'd sent a sympathy card, but that was the extent of his involvement, and neither Morgan nor Tegan longed for it to be anything else.

She walked on and when she reached the other side of the bridge, she turned left and meandered on until she came to Snow-drop Cottage. She felt herself mellow as she opened the periwinkle gate with its white plaque depicting the name of the residence. At least she'd have some company today. It had been a couple of months since her mum died, then there had been the funeral, the wake, the empty days afterwards, even though Ronan had asked her to go back to Scotland with him. And now she was nervous because although she'd been here enough times for dinner, she'd usually had her mum at her side and she really hoped she didn't let her emotions get the better of her if well-meaning friends expressed their sympathies today.

Late spring held a promise of more fine weather to come, with summer just around the corner, and floral notes scented the air around the cottage that was illustrative of quintessential England. This was the sort of home that reminded you of the beauty the country had to offer with its thatched roof, and ivy creeping across the front walls. Between January and March especially, visitors were drawn to Little Woodville and the impressive display of snow-drops. Snowdrop Cottage was one of the places to see them at their very best, with the idyllic cottage showing off snowdrops that surrounded the front and to the side. Then, as you drove on and turned into Snowdrop Lane, you realised how the road had got its name because in season, on either side were swathes of the dainty, white flowers nodding their heads in welcome.

Sebastian Hadley owned this stunning cottage, a piece of Little Woodville's character, named after the flowers that grew around it in abundance. But it was Belle, Sebastian's girlfriend and business partner, who answered the door.

Belle held open her arms. 'Welcome back to Little Woodville.' She embraced her friend. 'Again.'

'I've only been away for a couple of weeks this time,' Morgan laughed. She'd been up to Edinburgh to see Ronan, a far less melancholy trip than the one she'd taken right after the funeral. She'd got more of a feel for the city, been able to open her eyes to so much more of it.

'Well, you were missed.' Belle made an elegant hostess with her long, dark hair wound up in a chignon, leaving her fringe hanging loose.

When Morgan had come home to the village to look after her mother, Ronan had taken the job he'd been offered in Scotland. They'd agreed it was for the best that he forge ahead with what they'd both planned together. And it was definitely a savvy career move: the next step up in his career as a financial planner with a generous relocation package. The last thing Morgan had wanted when she knew her mum needed her was for him to stay in England out of guilt. She knew it would make her feel terrible too and she'd had enough to deal with at the time back at Forget-Me-Not Cottage. But Ronan missed her, given she'd been left behind in England for far longer than either of them had anticipated. And she'd missed him, so after he mentioned yet again that it was crazy how long they'd been apart, she'd headed on up to Edinburgh for a surprise visit. And in truth, it had been good to go there again, to get away and really take a look at the new life that was waiting for her. She'd felt comfort being back in his arms too because she hadn't been to stay with him since right after the funeral when he whisked her away from it all.

'It's so good to have you back,' Belle smiled. There was a time when Belle had been away from the village for an extended period before returning for family commitments long before Morgan, but it was something they had in common, and after they got chatting on more than one occasion when Morgan visited the Bookshop Café, they'd struck up a friendship that Morgan had come to value.

'It's really nice to be wanted.' Although Morgan knew it made it more difficult because this was only temporary. Slowly, without realising, the embrace of the village had grabbed a hold of her and already she knew it would be hard to let go. She'd assumed everyone would have realised that when her mum died, she'd get sorted and then move on with her own life. But either people in the village had forgotten or they were just being their usual welcoming selves and not making her feel as though her time was up.

'For you.' Morgan passed Belle the bouquet she'd held out of the way when the hostess welcomed her. She might not live here with Sebastian just yet, both of them having decided they didn't want to rush things, but it always felt like it was her home too.

'They're beautiful. Thank you.' Belle leaned in to inhale the scent of freesias, tulips and roses, a brightly coloured arrangement perfect for the season. She indicated for Morgan to hang her denim jacket on one of the hooks behind the front door as Sebastian appeared from the kitchen at the end of the hallway, arms outstretched to welcome their next guest.

The cottage was as gorgeous inside as out. To one side of the hallway was a lounge with a wood burner in situ, the once-was dining room was on the other side with an open fireplace and a casual set-up of a big reading chair and a coffee table and a comfy sofa. During the dinners she and her mum had been to, talk at the table had often centred around the changes the cottage had had over the years, how it had evolved sympathetically and still held its character.

'Go through, everyone's waiting,' Sebastian told her, green eyes that spoke of kindness twinkling as he welcomed her.

'Am I late?' she wondered.

'Not at all,' said Belle. 'And you're not the last either.'

When Morgan and her mum Elaina had first come here for dinner, Elaina had explained the history of these gatherings as well as the background to the cottage. The cottage had originally been owned by Belle's gran, Gillian, but Sebastian had been the tenant for a while. He'd ended up buying the cottage and Gillian was now living in a residential care home. Sebastian had continued the tradition Gillian had started by making dinner for anyone in the village who wanted or needed the company. Gillian even came along to some of the dinners as she didn't want to miss out and whenever she was here, as she was today, you could tell how proud she was that Sebastian had kept them going.

Elaina and Morgan had joined in with the dinners several times over the last few months when Elaina was up to it. They weren't always on a weekend, they weren't every week necessarily depending on people's commitments, but they happened with regularity. At first, Morgan had thought her mum needed companionship and that was why she insisted they came along, but with Elaina constantly feeling the need to apologise for derailing her youngest daughter's life, Morgan began to suspect the real reason behind it was that her mother wanted another chance to remind

Morgan of the village that had once been her home, the love and friendship that was still here if she could open up to the possibility.

'Something smells good,' Morgan declared as they went into the kitchen, a bright space with windows at the back. She smiled in greeting as everyone called out their welcome to the latest arrival.

'Roast chicken with all the trimmings.' Belle pulled a vase from a corner cupboard and filled it with water as Sebastian took his station at the Aga. 'It's still officially spring, we can get away with it; soon it'll be summer and nobody will want a roast.'

'Speak for yourself,' Gillian called out. 'Sebastian is such a good cook, I wouldn't say no to any of his meals and I bet nobody else would either.' Belle's gran was already in situ at the smooth, wood table in the charming kitchen with wooden cabinetry that suited the cottage down to the ground. Belle gave Morgan's arm a reassuring squeeze before she opened up the flower arrangement to put the blooms into the vase.

Local teacher Anne arrived next, followed by Barbara, who did a lot of work at the church.

Gillian patted a chair next to her. 'Come sit down, Morgan. It's good to see you again, how are you keeping?' Gillian might no longer be a resident of the village but she'd never stop caring. She understood Morgan and Elaina more than most, as just like Morgan and her mother had endured a bit of a strained relationship for a time, Gillian had had the same with her own daughter Delia. Belle had given her a brief story of what had gone on without breaking confidences, but Gillian and Belle's mum Delia were lucky; they'd patched things up before it was too late and were in regular contact, even though Delia and Belle's dad lived in Ireland now.

Knowing their story when Belle shared it had made Morgan value her time back in the village all the more. What had been an alteration of her own life's plans had given her and her mum the chance to get to know one another again. They'd never had a huge falling out, but their difficult relationship had been as a result of Morgan growing up feeling that Elaina didn't really have time for her or Tegan. Sometimes, the girls had felt in the way. And so leaving for university hadn't come soon enough for Morgan and then she'd joined the workforce as a journalist and had never moved home permanently again. Tegan and Elaina had mended bridges a long time ago, which Morgan suspected had a lot to do with the fact that Tegan had kids and wanted their grandma to be a part of their lives, but Morgan hadn't managed to reach the same stage with their mother until she came back this time.

Morgan accepted a glass of water that Betty from the bakery had poured for her. 'Thank you, Betty. And I'm doing okay, thanks for asking, Gillian.' She smiled inwardly. Sometimes at these gatherings it was hard to get a word in edgeways even when you were directly asked a question but rather than it being a frustration, it was all a part of the tapestry of Little Woodville.

'You know that everyone here is looking out for you, don't you?' Gillian pointed out.

'We are,' chimed in Jeremy, adding his two pennies' worth. Jeremy, in his seventies, was a close match in age to Gillian and a lively, friendly character. 'Otherwise we'll have Gillian to answer to.'

Gillian's glance of agreement proved he was correct.

Morgan noticed Belle looking over at her gran fondly as she commanded a presence in the cottage that had once been hers. Belle had also told Morgan how much she'd missed her gran when her mum had taken her away from the village and how being in her life once again had made it whole. It sounded like such a dramatic statement, but the emotion layering Belle's voice when she'd told Morgan that had been clear, and Morgan got it because she felt the same way about her mum.

It was hard to contemplate leaving all these people behind when she eventually went up to Scotland. Sometimes, living on her own in the cottage, it was easy to forget she was going to be married. She had a wedding to plan and had so far done nothing. But she would, soon. Ronan had proposed after only one year together and saying yes had come naturally. And he'd always made it clear he wanted to move back to Edinburgh, his birthplace. He'd mentioned it the first night they got talking in a cocktail bar, introduced by a mutual friend, and you didn't mention that sort of thing to a girl you'd only just met if it wasn't what you truly wanted as part of your life's plan.

'Coming here without Mum is a bit weird,' Morgan admitted to everyone, although she felt less emotional than she'd expected. Instead, she felt comfortable.

Trevor, a man similar in age to Jeremy and Gillian and a good friend of Gillian's, was the last to arrive at Snowdrop Cottage amidst many jokes that he lived the closest and should really have been there first. And once they were all seated – it was a bit of a squash in the kitchen but cosy – Belle and Sebastian delivered platters, bowls and plates to the table, the roast dinner laid out like a magnificent feast. Conversations battled to be heard, laughter rang around the table, the entire room filled with a welcome warmth.

'Any plans to go back to the Snowdrop Lane markets?' Belle passed Morgan the gravy boat.

Little Woodville was host to the Snowdrop Lane markets once a week, every Saturday. If you turned right out of the front gate to Snowdrop Cottage and kept walking, you'd reach Snowdrop Lane before too long. And a couple of hundred metres up the lane was a wide-open expanse bordered by Snowdrop Woods. It was in that open space that the markets were held and Elaina had had a stall there for years. Morgan, during her time back in the village, had helped her out and stepped in to run it solo on the days her mother wasn't up to it.

'I should do it soon, I know that much.' Morgan pushed a piece of stuffing onto her fork and ran it through a puddle of gravy. Ronan had asked the same question, although he'd suggested she do the speedier option and sell everything on eBay. 'Mum accumulated a lot of stock – she was forever buying things that caught her eye.'

'Probably the best way to do it,' Anne approved from the other end of the table. 'I have to buy things as I see them or I forget.'

'The trouble with Mum was that she collected things way faster than she sold them. She was always fretting she'd miss out on a bargain and already I know it'll take weeks to shift everything.'

'You'll have it done in no time at the markets,' Gillian assured her.

'Elaina was a lot of fun,' Barbara declared. She was a jolly woman who always had time for whoever wanted a chat. 'I remember being at the markets when she sold Jasper's wallet by mistake.'

'I haven't heard that story,' said Morgan as laughter erupted. And rather than feel a wave of grief, she had a curiosity to know more, to glean as many extra details about her mum as she could. 'How on earth did it happen?' The murmur in the room also begged the question about the wallet belonging to the market manager.

Barbara explained, 'Elaina had a near-identical one priced up and for sale, beautiful Italian leather it was, but when Jasper was helping her put up the sign at her stall that morning, his wallet must have fallen out of his pocket right next to the one she had. And Elaina sold it.' To gasps, she responded with an animated tale of how Elaina had chased after the man when she realised she'd sold someone's actual wallet. 'I thought she was going to rugby tackle him to the ground.'

Morgan was pleased she hadn't. But she loved the story and the amusement and applause the tale got.

Barbara, arms supporting her bosom beneath a lightweight, grey jumper, continued, 'She swapped it with the other one and when Jasper saw the commotion, that was when he realised he'd lost his wallet. He bought her the biggest bunch of flowers he could find on Hildy's flower stall – bright pinks, purples, yellow. He was so relieved to have it back.'

Peter, Betty's husband, wondered, 'Didn't the man realise it was on the heavy side when he bought it?' He thanked Anne who was sitting next to him as she picked up his herringbone cap that had been knocked from the wooden finial on his chair and put it back in position. Morgan wondered if he ever went anywhere without his cap, apart from the bakery, of course.

'Maybe Jasper, like the rest of us, doesn't use much cash any more,' Sebastian suggested. 'Perhaps the man thought the cards inside were fake.'

'You do get those fake cards when you buy a purse or wallet,' Anne agreed, fork poised in the air.

Gillian leaned closer to Morgan and said, 'Bet he didn't think they were fake. Bet he was cursing your mum for catching up with him when he'd almost got away with it.'

'I'll bet he was too,' agreed Morgan with a feeling of mischief as the banter at the table continued and she and Gillian fell into an easy chat.

'I remember your mother at one of these dinners telling us about a beautiful silver antique tray she'd sold at her stall.' Gillian cut into a roast potato and its heat curled into the air. 'She sold it to a young boy. Thought it would be a gift for someone. And then that evening she found him using it to sledge down the sloping part of the village green.'

Morgan burst out laughing. She could imagine her mum thinking that was terrible, and wishing she'd sold it to someone who'd appreciate it more. Elaina had always loved finding hidden treasures at bits and bobs shops or, more recently, because that's all she could cope with, online. And she'd always imagined the sorts of homes the items would end up in, who would be the new owners. It was the reason Morgan couldn't just pack everything up and get rid of it. Her mother would've wanted all of the things she'd chosen to be sold at the stall and so that was what Morgan had decided to do. Tegan had agreed too, which meant a lot because there'd been a tension between them on the day of the funeral and Morgan didn't want anything else to add to it.

Both Tegan and Morgan were executors of Elaina's will and had so far managed to deal with everything over the phone or via email as they ploughed through the tasks the best they could. But tomorrow, Tegan was coming back to the village again for the day and an overnight stay, leaving the farm she ran with her husband Henry in his capable hands. The sisters had always got on well enough, saw each other when they could, but Morgan got the impression there was something Tegan wasn't telling her. Or was it just grief creating tension that might simply pass in time?

Morgan tuned back into the conversation around the table as they ate. Betty and Peter talked about their travel plans in autumn to see family, Barbara complained about the amount of work that needed doing in the churchyard to keep it tidy and Sebastian assured her he'd be over to take a look soon. With the Bookshop Café on Little Woodville's high street, his new venture, he was no longer the caretaker at the school but he still took care of the grounds around the church, which Morgan had noticed were immaculate.

As voices filled the kitchen, Morgan caught Belle's eye and they shared a giggle each time either of them tried to speak and gave up because it was too hard.

When the meal came to its conclusion, Morgan helped clear the table and scraped plates into the compost with Belle's help. They could hear Jeremy and Trevor talking about their late wives, first dates, romantic gestures.

'Imagine being so in love with someone that fifty years isn't enough,' Morgan sighed wistfully as she overheard Trevor. She piled the final plate onto the stack beside the sink.

'Surely you feel that way about Ronan,' said Belle.

'Of course.' They were engaged, he'd welcomed her into his family and they were all such wonderful people. His mother was quiet and kind with a touch of class, his father polite and clever. She'd be a part of a clan, a phrase they used often when talking about family, and she quite liked it.

Sebastian came up behind Belle and wrapped his arms around her waist. 'Think we can go the distance? Fifty years?'

Belle turned in his embrace to put her hands on either side of his face. 'Definitely. Think we'll be doing these dinners in fifty years?'

'Not sure, maybe someone else can be the chef, we'll be the guests.'

Belle flushed when Sebastian patted her on the bottom. They were a lovely couple – together romantically and in business – and they were both well and truly on the same page. It felt an apt way to think of them when they owned and ran the Bookshop Café in Little Woodville.

Jeremy was talking about how much his wife had enjoyed coastal drives in Devon.

Morgan leaned closer to Belle as they listened in. 'Jeremy nearly ran me over yesterday,' she confided so only Sebastian and

Belle could hear. 'I was crossing the high street and he came out of nowhere.'

'Doesn't surprise me,' said Belle as Sebastian took over loading the dishwasher with what he could squeeze in. 'You've got to have eyes in the back of your head when he's on the roads.'

'He really should think about stopping driving altogether,' Sebastian agreed as he picked up more cutlery, 'but try telling him that. He thinks he's quite capable of local drives, nipping down to the high street and back, tells me it's not like he goes on any main roads.'

'Hardly the point,' Belle whispered.

'Maybe I'll have another quiet word with him,' said Sebastian, raking a hand through messy, dark hair. 'Probably best done over a pint at the Rose and Thatch.'

'You're a good man.' Belle planted a kiss on his cheek and despite their guests, it was as though it was the two of them in their own little world.

Morgan wondered – had she and Ronan ever been like that? Maybe at the start. Perhaps the key was that these two didn't live together yet, whereas she and Ronan had begun sharing her flat pretty quickly after they got together. Maybe they'd leapt right into domestic life and missed one of the most exciting steps. But she supposed the end goal was the same. Being together.

'I need to rest my voice.' Belle hooked Morgan's arm as she led her from the kitchen along the hallway.

Plenty of people were still here but Morgan needed the fresh air and a bit of peace now, so a walk home would do her good.

'I didn't get to talk much, my voice is fine,' Morgan laughed. 'You were an excellent hostess, by the way, kind of like a permanent fixture.'

Belle rolled her eyes at the teasing. It was nothing she hadn't heard before because she was always here at the cottage, despite keeping the flat above the Bookshop Café.

But if Morgan was a betting woman, she wouldn't mind guessing that it wouldn't be long before Snowdrop Cottage became Belle's permanent address too.

2

———

Nate Greene filled a trolley at the supermarket. He was visiting Little Woodville all the way from Wales, but he knew that if he went to his dad Trevor's place first before he came here, his dad would likely insist that he saved his money rather than restocking his elderly father's kitchen cupboards. And Nate couldn't do that. He was staying the entire weekend and he had no intention of letting his dad cook for him or fund all the ingredients. He threw in a couple of packets of his dad's favourite biscuits and another big box of tea bags.

Nate drove on from there to the village he'd grown up in, his dog Branston, aptly named after his favourite sandwich accompaniment, in the passenger side of his pick-up. But when he pulled up outside his dad's place and knocked on the front door, there was no answer.

'Great.' He looked down at Branston, who was already sniffing around the doorway. 'What seventy-five-year-old man is out gallivanting at 8 p.m. in the evening?' The spaniel gazed up at him as if pondering the same.

Nate went back over to the pick-up to get Branston's lead. He doubted his dad would be too long – he was probably at the pub or a neighbour's place – so they'd have a decent walk, which they both needed after being stuck in traffic for so long. The perishables – the milk and the cheese – would be fine in the truck now that the sun had gone down and darkness wrapped the Cotswold village.

Nate had grabbed a torch as well as the lead and set off towards the village high street, but the long way round. It was a walk they were both familiar with, down the country lanes, and once they'd tackled those devoid of a pavement, he let Branston off the lead. He was well-trained and, no longer a puppy, he was usually predictable and well-versed at coming to heel.

They cut through the churchyard and emerged onto the high street at the far end. From there, they walked along and through the main drag of the village, the Rose and Thatch pub like a warming beacon at the top of the village green to his left. He'd always liked it in the country pub, with its friendly clientele and staff, and he knew his dad did. Perhaps they'd have a chance for a cheeky pint this weekend. There wasn't always time given Nate usually had to get back to his plumbing business in Wales, with client demands always high. Leaky toilets and faulty piping rarely had the decency to let him have an extended time off unless he made special arrangements.

Branston trotted along beside him, stopping to sniff at the odd shrub or patch on the pavement, lifting his nose in curiosity as he detected different scents on the air, and they continued all the way to the very end before they crossed back over when the pavement ran out before the road led its way out of the village. Coming back down the other side towards Little Woodville's centre again, he stopped when he saw the Bookshop Café and peered in the window. Sebastian and Belle had done well. This place was once a photography studio but that had been some time ago and it was now a far cry from what it had once been.

Nate didn't know Belle more than in passing but he remembered Sebastian and had bumped into him enough times at the Rose and Thatch to be friendly. It would be good to catch up with him again if he got a chance. Perhaps he'd come back in the daytime to check out the Bookshop Café properly on his next visit, bring his dad for cake and a coffee or mug of tea or a light lunch of soup if he'd read the menu inside the front door correctly. It looked like the café was at the rear, but he couldn't see all that well now that it was dark, even when he tried to shine his torch through the glass. And he didn't want to trigger any sort of alarm.

They walked on. Sebastian was in business with his girlfriend and Nate wondered how it would feel to be that secure with someone.

For some people, it worked out.

Maybe one day it would for him too.

He passed the bank, the little post office, and headed towards where they'd turn and go over the humpback bridge. It was as they got closer that there was enough light from the nearby streetlamps to see a figure on the bridge lift something that looked like a stick in the air as if she was going to throw it.

That was it. While Branston was obedient, he was still a dog, after all, and at the sight of a potential stick, off he went.

Nate swore. He broke into a run. 'Branston!'

He rounded the corner and while Branston emitted a low growl, a woman bent over in front of him, her thick, chunky knit cardigan almost down to her knees flapping around her and getting in her way as she engaged with his dog in what could only be described as a tug of war over what was definitely a stick.

Nate held back before commenting. The battle was a bit of fun to watch. 'He'll win, you know,' he said eventually.

The woman turned and as she did, must have lessened her

grip, because Branston triumphantly ran towards Nate, stick in his mouth.

Nate bent down to stroke Branston as he obediently came to his master's side. To him, this would've been nothing more than a game, but when Nate looked up, the woman seemed upset. 'Are you all right?' She said nothing. 'It's only a game,' he tried to joke.

She didn't say anything, but her eyes filled with more tears. Shit. He wasn't great with women, he'd been told by one he didn't have an emotional bone in his body. He wasn't sure that was entirely true, but he knew how easy it was to say the wrong thing when emotions were involved. He walked closer, took a clean tissue from his pocket and handed it to her.

Her voice wobbled when she thanked him and added, 'Don't mind me, I just got a bit emotional standing here. It brings back memories, that's all. And I know it's only a game...'

Branston trotted up to her as if he understood and Nate muttered, 'I'll be damned,' when the dog dropped the stick at her feet.

That got a laugh as she crouched down and put her face close to Branston's, her hands fussing his cheeks, not worrying that she didn't know the dog. 'What's his name?' She looked up at Nate. She had glossy, mahogany-coloured hair in a slightly off-centre parting and rich, dark-brown eyes almost the same colour.

He was momentarily lost for words. 'Branston,' he managed. She'd obviously been oblivious to Nate calling him moments ago.

She focused her attentions back on the dog. 'Well, hello, Branston. I'd be happy to throw a stick for you, but I think the green is a much better place to be playing than here near the road.'

'What were you doing, anyway? It's kind of a bit dark to be throwing sticks.'

She stood up tall again, stick in hand, Branston looking up at her then down at the stick as though waiting for action. 'I can see well enough with the streetlamps. And I was playing Poohsticks. Not really the best time, but I just felt like it. It was hard to resist when there was a stick in my path.' When she smiled, it sent all kinds of sensations fizzing through his body.

'Wait a minute, did you say poo sticks?' He pulled a face. He hoped Branston didn't have any of the remnants around his mouth. 'That's kind of disgusting.'

She began to laugh. 'Pooh with an H, as in Winnie the Pooh.'

He shook his head. 'Still don't get it.'

'Really?'

'Really.' He liked the way she didn't know him and yet talked to him as though she did.

'You've never heard of it?'

'Can't say I have. Tell me more.' He wanted to keep her talking, this woman he'd met quite unexpectedly.

'You can play Poohsticks from any bridge over running water, so this location is perfect. Each player has to drop a stick on the upstream side of the bridge and whoever's stick first appears on the downstream side wins the game.'

'Neat.'

She frowned. 'Are you making fun of me?'

'Not at all, promise. So can I play?'

'Now?'

'Why not?'

She looked around. 'Well, it's a bit dark to find another stick but how about you give it a go with this one we have?'

'Sounds good to me.' He took the stick when she handed it to him.

'I usually hold it high up in the air and drop it but you don't have to, I only do that because my nephew always insists I do it and it's a hard habit to break.'

'So kids love this game?' he questioned, his eyebrows lifting.

'Kids and adults alike,' she smiled before warning, 'Watch out for cars when you run across.'

Nate put Branston on the lead. 'He'll run with me otherwise.'

'Give me your torch and I'll wait with Branston over the other side.'

Just like that, as though they weren't strangers.

Nate waited for them both to cross, then he leaned over and as the moonlight cast its glow across the surface of the stream below, adding to the light given by the streetlamp, he dropped the stick, saw it hit the water and begin to travel beneath the bridge.

Looking both ways in case any cars were coming, he legged it across to the other side and sure enough, as he leaned over and the girl shone the torch down below, the stick, moments later, made its way out.

'Yay!' she cheered, probably the way she cheered for her nephew.

But he appreciated it. 'My first game of Poohsticks at thirty-eight, eh?'

'Better late than never,' she shrugged. 'I'm Morgan, by the way.'

'Nate.' He held out a hand for her to shake after she handed him the torch. 'It's very nice to meet you, Morgan.'

'Likewise.'

When he checked his watch, he realised it looked a little rude. And he didn't actually want to leave. 'I'm conscious of the time because I'm visiting my dad. He wasn't home when we arrived, but he should be now, or at least soon enough.'

'Your dad lives here?' She seemed to realise something. 'I thought you looked familiar. I think we may have gone to the same high school. I was a couple of years behind you from memory.'

'Are you sure? I think I'd have remembered you.' He really could do with a filter sometimes rather than making it obvious he thought she was attractive.

'I didn't hang around the village once I was done with school. I went to university, got a job and didn't come back all that often.'

'That makes two of us.' She was smiling again and he liked that. 'What's so funny?'

'I can't believe you grew up here but never knew how to play Poohsticks.'

'Me neither, although the woods were more my domain than the stream.'

'Snowdrop Woods are pretty impressive in whatever season.' She was fussing Branston but flipped back to the start of their conversation. 'Who's your dad?'

Branston had already fallen for her and was sitting beside this woman as though he didn't want to be taken away. 'Trevor. He doesn't live too far from here.'

'I know Trevor,' she beamed. 'I've just been with him for dinner, as it happens.'

'Ah, the legendary dinners. I should've known. I'm a bit earlier than he was expecting me.'

'Your dad has been going to the dinners for years. He's lovely. And he's been really supportive lately, particularly at the funeral.'

'Ah, you went to Elaina's funeral too. Dad told me all about it. Sad. But it sounds like most of the village were there; she must've been popular.'

She nodded. 'It wasn't ever the way I'd have described Mum before I came back here, but now I've realised how many friends she had, what a part of the village she was. I guess I didn't always see it when I was younger.'

Shit. He'd put his foot right in it, not realising it wasn't just any funeral; it was her mother's. 'Me and my big mouth. I apologise and I really am sorry for your loss.'

'Thank you.' She barely met his gaze, preferring to focus her attentions on Branston.

Nate felt for this woman, he really did. Because he'd been through it himself, losing his mother. The funeral had been draining, emotional; he knew what it was like with well-wishes and kindness that you couldn't feel because you were so numb. He and his dad had scattered his mum's ashes at the foot of the grand old oak tree in the garden at his dad's home, aptly named Oak Cottage.

'Is that why you came home?' he asked. 'To be here for your mum?' He didn't remember her, but then again, he'd been away for some time and his visits didn't always involve socialising too much, given they were usually quite rushed, with a business to get back to.

'Yeah. It's what you do, isn't it? Put family first.'

There was no disputing that Morgan was an attractive woman. He'd never had a particular type. Perhaps that had been his problem all along. But right now, aside from the aura of sadness around this woman, she was ticking a lot of boxes. Listen to him. She was grieving and probably after a sympathetic ear rather than a man lusting after her, and if the sparkling ring on a very important finger was anything to go by, she was already very much spoken for.

'It is. It's what I'm trying to do, anyway,' he said.

'Then Trevor is lucky. But he's all right, isn't he? He certainly seemed in good form earlier.'

'Good to know. But I worry about him all on his own. I wouldn't mind knowing he's somewhere where he has people looking out for him.' Why was he telling her all of this? Probably because he hadn't really spoken with anyone about it until now, least of all Trevor. 'I'm his only family and I live far away. Too far to get here quickly in an emergency.'

She looked as though she understood exactly where he was coming from. But she added, 'You know he won't ever leave the village, don't you? I can tell because Mum was the same way.'

'I just want what's best for him.'

'You might have to be the one to move,' she teased. Although was it teasing? Or was she being totally serious? He wouldn't mind betting it was the latter.

He smiled. 'You know, you might be right.' He fussed Branston on the head. 'We'd better get going, see if Dad's back at the house and not panicking that we've disappeared into the night.'

'Me too. It's getting late.' She gave a shiver and it was almost instinct to want to put his arm around her and warm her up.

'Thanks for the introduction to Poohsticks.'

'You're welcome,' she grinned. 'I'll be having a word with Trevor about never teaching you that as a young boy.'

'Maybe I'll see you around.'

'Maybe,' she said as he and Branston turned to make their way to the opposite side of the humpback bridge. He looked back to watch Morgan walk away, but she'd already gone. Probably not a bad thing because he couldn't deny she was attractive, that given half the chance he wouldn't mind getting to know her better. And given his track record, that could only lead to trouble. It usually did.

Nate and Branston plodded on. Even in the dark, the village was pretty and he could see why his dad wouldn't want to leave it behind. But Nate still worried about his dad being on his own. And right now, he had a plumbing business in Wales, a business he couldn't walk away from just like that. It wasn't practical long-term for his dad to be all alone. And last week, when a bungalow had come up for sale three doors down from Nate's house, it had caught his eye because it would be perfect for Trevor. And then Nate would be around to look after him and never let anything happen to him.

Because that was his biggest fear: not being there when his family needed him.

3

Morgan was Belle's first customer of the day at the Bookshop Café. Having bypassed the books, she'd gone straight to the café at the back and clasped her hands together in front of her. 'I'm hoping your pancakes are on the menu?'

'Always. And a portion of pancakes, coming right up,' Belle smiled. 'I thought your sister was coming down today.'

'She is, but she'll be a while and as I'm making lunch for us, I thought I deserved a treat first thing.'

'Too right. Coffee too?'

'Yes, please.'

As Belle set about getting everything ready and making the batter, Morgan told her what she and her sister planned to get through today. The list was extensive, but they'd do as much as possible. 'She's staying over, which is great because I reckon we'll be shattered after doing this. And with the kids in tow, it won't be as quick as we'd like.'

'Wow, she's bringing the kids?' Belle was busy cracking eggs into a well in the centre of the bowl of flour. Without any other customers yet, it gave them a chance to chat. And just by the nature of the environment, a cosy café and a front of shop full of books, Morgan felt a sense of calm.

'She has to. The farm can't look after itself so Henry will need to focus his attentions on that. And it's easy enough for us to have the kids playing nearby in the cottage. It's great to see them too, I don't see them enough.'

Belle had taken the carton of milk from the fridge and a measuring jug too and as she poured, Morgan mentioned she'd bumped into someone on her way home from last night's dinner at Snowdrop Cottage.

'Who?' Belle clearly thought Morgan was going to mention a local she knew as she whisked the pancake mixture with enthusiasm, but her focus changed when Morgan said the name Nate.

Belle's whisk paused but not for long as she wouldn't want the lumps. Her body turned partially towards her friend. 'Trevor's son Nate?'

Sebastian came over and grabbed the coffee in the thermos Belle must have made for him earlier. He didn't miss the opportunity to give his better half a peck on the lips. 'Great guy, hope he pops in here.'

'Is he...?' Belle asked Morgan when Sebastian left them to it and she finished making the mixture. She wiped her hands on her apron, giving her friend the full force of her attention. She'd met Ronan, said she liked him, but the mischievous glint in her eyes now suggested she might be lining up for some gossip.

'I went to school with him, actually,' said Morgan, nodding at the suggestion of lemon and sugar as Belle found the appropriate additions to Morgan's order.

'Oh, no...' Belle scrunched up her nose. 'Was he a total tool, one of those people you hope never to bump into again?'

Morgan chuckled. 'Not at all. He was a couple of years above, he was popular with the girls in his year.'

'And in your year?' She deftly sliced the lemon into wedges, unable to keep the amusement from her voice.

'I shouldn't have mentioned bumping into him.'

'And yet you did. The plot thickens.'

'It does not. I thought you might know of him, that's all. He seems to be worried about his dad being on his own.'

'Trevor?' Belle got a frying pan ready to make the pancakes and added a little bit of oil to its surface. 'Nothing to worry about there; he's got friends around, he's happy. Although I get where he's coming from.'

'Me too.'

Belle smiled at her kindly. 'It's good that he cares. Sounds like a nice guy to me.' She added, 'Don't worry, I know you're taken.' But she whispered, 'Nothing wrong with looking at the menu, though.'

'Belle Nightingale,' Morgan giggled. 'What are you like?'

'She's terrible,' Sebastian called over, 'and I heard every word.'

'Oops.' Belle pulled a face at Morgan. 'I thought he was at the front of the shop.' Instead, he'd been neatening up the books on the table closest to them but slightly out of sight. 'Love you,' she called out to him, slipping into her more professional persona when a customer came in through the front door.

As Morgan waited for her pancakes and coffee, she couldn't help but let her thoughts slip to Nate, the stranger she'd met on the top of the small, humpback bridge. They might not have had long together, but even in the dark, she'd recognised his expression – one of concern, worry – because she'd been feeling the same emotions herself, like rolling waves that built up and crashed down whenever they felt like it.

At least it appeared Nate and his dad got on well enough. Trevor had never said anything to the contrary. Morgan felt sure they'd sort it out between them, but she knew that much like her mother didn't want to leave Little Woodville – she could've asked her to do so until she was blue in the face and she never would've backed down – Trevor was the same. Morgan wondered whether it was like that no matter where you lived; you wanted the familiar, especially when you were at your most vulnerable. Or did Little Woodville work a certain magic and make anyone who came here never want to leave?

This wasn't where Morgan had lived as a little girl, but her mother had moved here when her marriage ended and her daughters were already teenagers. Since Morgan left home, her visits back here had been scant. She was working hard in her career as a journalist and then as a freelance writer, building up contacts and delivering pieces on time. And with a boyfriend who had work demands of his own in his corporate role as a financial advisor, life was busy. She and Ronan often spent their weekends heading off to the country for a break or going into London for fancy dinners. But Morgan and Elaina kept in touch over the phone often when that was all they could manage.

Shortly after she and Ronan got engaged, Ronan had moved into Morgan's flat that she owned. He'd rented out his three-bed townhouse so they could make a good income and give them more towards a deposit for a joint property purchase up in Scotland, something they'd only so far managed to look for online. They'd visited Elaina once to tell her the news they were getting married and she'd congratulated them, hugged each of them in turn, but every time Ronan talked about Scotland, Morgan had seen her mum trying to disguise something. She wasn't sure whether disapproval was the right word. It might have been fear of the unknown, worry perhaps that her daughter wanted to go so far away. But in her phone calls home since that day, Morgan had been sure to let Elaina know, indirectly, that this move wasn't about getting away from her mother the way it might have been when she left for university. This was about new jobs and possibilities, excitement, a new life and a marriage.

It was when Elaina phoned three times in one week that Morgan began to suspect something might be up besides wanting to talk to her daughter.

'Mum, you've called me already this morning.' Morgan set her pen down on top of her notebook next to her laptop. 'Did you forget?' She pretended to be amused but she wasn't; she was worried.

Elaina's voice wasn't the usual upbeat tone when she blurted out, 'I need help.'

'Mum...' Morgan's voice wobbled. 'What's wrong?'

'I'm sorry, love. I've panicked you,' Elaina said gently. She'd been stoic when the girls were younger; she'd rarely showed much emotion, being a single mother whose job was to deal with the practicalities, leaving little room for much else.

'You have panicked me. Tell me, Mum.' As Morgan probed, Ronan turned to look at her quizzically from his place beside the stove, where he was stirring a splash of red wine into the beef stew. Ronan had taken on the cooking as he loved being in the kitchen and with her flat being small, the kitchen was also the dining room and her place of work. Life simply carried on around her.

'I have weak bones,' her mother offered. 'Osteoporosis.'

She knew what it was in basic terms but not much else. But as her mum began to talk about her diagnosis, what had been going on over the last year or more, Morgan realised she'd missed it. The clues had been there. She'd assumed her mother was a little clumsy, fracturing her left wrist a few months ago, then her right one, then the hip pain that she often mentioned but dismissed as nothing much to worry about. She'd looked fine when she and Ronan had been to give her the news that they were engaged, but again the signs had been there – the insistence that she hated the Le Creuset dish she'd always adored, instead serving a casserole in a much lighter Pyrex dish she had Ronan take out the oven for her, the take-away pizza she'd insisted on getting for dinner the evening Morgan visited on her own. Since when had her mother ever got takeaway anything? Never, that was when. Her mother had been covering up what was going on, from her and she expected from Tegan.

'Morgan, are you there?' Elaina must have taken a break from explaining and waited for a response that hadn't come.

'I'm still here, Mum. I'm just a bit… well, I didn't know.'

'Neither did I, how could you?'

'You said you needed help.'

'I find the easiest of things difficult,' Elaina admitted. The vulnerability wasn't what Morgan was used to and it almost made her crumble to hear it in her mother's voice. 'And the doctors can't fix me.'

'Have they given you medication? To stop it progressing?' Morgan turned her laptop away from her. Life had been so simple moments ago when she'd been in the depths of going through interview transcripts with experts and preparing to work on a free-lance article about email marketing tips and what to avoid.

'They have, but I'm… well, I'm scared.'

Morgan gulped. To hear her mother say those words was confronting, the honesty not something she'd grown up with. 'I know, Mum.'

'I'm scared to bend down, worried I'll trip on the stairs, even picking the cat up isn't without risk.'

She was panicking; Morgan could hear it in her voice.

'Morgan, I don't want to be a burden, but I don't want to be put in a home and forgotten about.'

'Who said anything about you leaving Forget-Me-Not Cottage?' But she was right; if she wasn't managing now, what would happen further down the line? Morgan looked over at Ronan. She thought about the job he'd landed in Edinburgh, the interview she'd already had for a job herself.

Elaina's voice came out small. 'I'm not coping. I have painkillers and medications but… well, I have to be really careful.'

'So you don't trip over or fall, is that what you mean?'

'Well yes… but it's simple things like opening a tin of baked beans for my lunch. My wrist… well, it could easily break again.'

'It's that bad?' Morgan, her head resting on her hand, closed her eyes. This was far worse than she'd thought. How had her mum kept it hidden for so long?

'I'm afraid it is.'

Morgan looked up and Ronan could tell something terrible was happening. She'd felt all the colour drain from her cheeks as the conversation continued. It didn't bear thinking about, the way Elaina's wrist, her hips, her spine, anything could fracture so easily and she'd lose her independence just like that. Morgan had heard of osteoporosis as the silent killer and rather than reading about it here and there, now it was staring her right in the face.

'Mum, have you looked into getting some home help? Someone to come in and do daily tasks like cleaning and cooking, that sort of thing.' She didn't know enough about the condition to make many more recommendations.

'It would be nice, but it would cost.' Elaina had always been careful with money. She lived a basic life, very little in the way of luxuries bar the odd meal out and a fancy bubble bath as a treat. Other than that, Elaina had been content to live her life in the village she'd fallen in love with as soon as they moved there.

'I'll look into it for you.'

'I'm worried I won't be able to cope in my cottage, Morgan. What if… what if I can't get up and down the stairs, what happens if I can't even use the shower myself?'

'Are you being careful getting in and out?' The shower was at least free standing in the small bathroom alongside the bathtub. Squashed, but adequate.

'I am.'

But she was terrified of something happening and nobody being there, Morgan could tell.

They spoke a while longer, Morgan taking the call into the bedroom. She just let Elaina share her worries, the fears she had, some of the pain she was in, although Morgan suspected she was still dialling down how bad that was. Her mum was fearful of having strangers come to her house too, citing some terrible stories she'd read of elderly people being robbed and having their most treasured possessions mysteriously go missing. Her mum was getting ahead of herself, but Morgan got it. The loss of independence was the thing she most feared out of everything, never mind the pain and the inconvenience and the change of routine she had.

'What's going on?' Ronan asked, pouring her a glass of wine when she finally emerged from the bedroom.

She sat at the table and he rested a hand on her shoulder as she filled him in on what her mum had told her. 'She's scared, she's on her own. I told her I'd do some digging, find out costs for someone to go in and cook, clean, do odd jobs. A carer, perhaps.'

Ronan sat down next to her. 'Is she at that stage?'

'I think she might well be. And if she's not, soon she could be.' Morgan's voice shook and he pulled her close. When he let her go, she took his hand in hers. 'She asked me to come home for a while until she can organise some help.'

'Back to Little Woodville?' He swigged his wine. 'What about Edinburgh? We're all set to move.'

'I can't just abandon her.'

'But she's not...' he harrumphed and scraped a hand through blond hair that stuck up in a way it really shouldn't.

'She's not what?'

'You've never been overly close, Morgan. You said it yourself when we first got together.' He went back over to the kitchen area.

'We weren't close when I was younger, no.'

'Nor when you were at university or when you first started work.'

She bristled. Things changed. And she and her mum seemed to be doing all right these days. They weren't the closest of mothers and daughters, but it had been enough and they were getting better every time they spoke. She felt the bond keenly now her mum had been so honest with her, sounded so vulnerable. 'She's my mum, Ronan. What would you do if it was one of your parents?'

He attended to the pot on the stove, gave the contents a stir and tasted what was inside before leaning against the benchtop, wineglass back in hand. 'You're right, I'm being unfair. It's just that this job interview you had, it was promising, right?'

'Very promising.' She couldn't disagree. She'd been freelancing for a while now and although she loved it, she'd interviewed for a position as a content editor for a media brand, an office position with a steady income that would be reassuring if they were setting up home together in a new city. And she really did want the job; the people sounded amazing, the role varied enough to capture her interest. There was a strong possibility that she'd be asked for a second interview, too. But did any of that matter if her mum needed her?

'Ronan, I think this is something I might need to do. I'll be with Mum, help out, keep looking at what help we can get her and then I can come to Edinburgh.' And if her job opportunity completely fell through, then so be it.

'Are you saying I should go before you do?'

'Of course, you've got work lined up, I don't want you to give that up, not for me and not for yourself.' She went over to him and snuggled against his chest as he wrapped his free arm around her and kissed the top of her head. 'The sale on this flat is underway so that's sorted, we don't have that to worry about. And this arrangement isn't ideal, I admit, it's not what we planned, but it's the only solution short term.'

'Why didn't she ask Tegan to go home?'

Morgan pulled back. 'Come on, that's not practical. Tegan has the farm, she has kids.'

'So because we don't, we have to change our plans?' He'd put his wineglass down none too gently and was pulling out bowls ready to serve the dinner.

'Don't be like that, Ronan.'

'I'm not annoyed at you.'

'But you're annoyed she's asked it of me?' He said nothing. 'You're annoyed that Tegan isn't the one to go back to Forget-Me-Not Cottage? Tell me, Ronan. I don't have the energy for guessing games.'

He stopped midway through getting out the cutlery and dumped it on the benchtop. 'It's just I was looking forward to our fresh start, together.'

She took both of his hands in hers. 'And it'll happen, we just need to wait a while, that's all.'

He sat down at the table again and pulled her onto his lap, nuzzling at her neck. 'I'll miss you.'

'I know. Me too. But it won't be forever.'

That night at the flat, she'd been too exhausted to ask herself how it had worked out that somehow she was comforting Ronan rather than the other way around. She'd told herself he was just gutted they weren't forging ahead with their own plans. He'd gone to Scotland without her and she'd moved to Little Woodville as soon as the flat was sold. She'd missed him a lot but with her own freelance writing to keep up with and her mum the focus, she'd soon got into a new routine here in the village. She'd done whatever she could to help at Forget-Me-Not Cottage – jobs around the house, driving her mum to medical appointments, making sure Elaina was careful and safe in her cottage, running the market stall with her some weeks.

She'd made a few enquiries for cleaners, home help, but they hadn't found many suitable candidates – either they were too pricey or they didn't have any availability. And slowly what had been a life change and a bit of a burden had begun to be so much more for Morgan as she spent time with her mother and in the village. She and Elaina had begun to forge a new relationship, much better than ever before, and they'd enjoyed one another's company. Her mother had become a precious gift she wasn't ready to lose. She missed Ronan, she told him she was still midway through organising help for her mum, but in truth, she hadn't been ready to leave it all behind and so she'd taken her time. And then her mum had died of a sudden heart attack, making the decision to leave and head up to Edinburgh an easy one. Or so she'd thought.

Full from her pancakes at the Bookshop Café, Morgan headed back to Forget-Me-Not Cottage, where she made up the bed for her sister, another for her nephew and set up the travel cot for her niece. And when her phone rang and she saw Ronan's name and picture on the display, she felt guilty but she pressed decline. She'd call him later when she had time to chat for longer. But right now, she had too much to deal with.

Tegan had arrived absolutely shattered from the drive. She had dark circles under her eyes and after she'd put Morgan's two-year-old niece Lily down for a nap – she hadn't slept in the car much at all and was beside herself with tiredness – Morgan had set her sister up with a mug of tea and a pointed her in the direction of the bread and the toaster should she get hungry before their lunch.

She'd then insisted she take her four-year-old nephew Jaimie out to burn off some of the energy he'd had to keep at bay on the long journey that had started at the crack of dawn. It was either that or let him terrorise Elaina's cat Marley, who'd taken one look at the new arrivals at the cottage and bolted upstairs to hide under Morgan's bed. Tegan had offered to take the cat once Morgan made her move up to Edinburgh; perhaps she should point out to Marley that it was time he got used to the liveliness of her sister's household and its habitants.

'Again!' Jaimie begged after he'd leant over the honey-coloured stone wall on one side of the humpback bridge. He'd run across the road with Morgan's supervision to see the stick he'd dropped on the other side and into the stream pass beneath.

'That'll have to be it,' Morgan told him. 'Your mum and I have plenty to do back at the house.' Morgan had done her best to make a dent in everything that had to be done but despite having lived in the cottage for a while, even she'd underestimated the extent of what there was to do. The formalities of their mother's estate were pretty much in hand but even they took time from both girls, mostly Morgan. Then there were the things that should be simpler – paying utility bills, making sure home insurance was all covered – but when you had no idea where to start, it was yet another daunting task to add to a pretty huge pile.

In her will, Elaina had left Forget-Me-Not Cottage to the sisters and they'd always said that they'd sell it. But to do that they had to clear it out, tidy it up, clean it thoroughly and with only one of her, Morgan knew she had her work cut out. So far, she'd tackled the shed at the bottom of the garden because she'd needed to access it for the lawnmower and gardening tools. She wasn't much good at gardening, but she could do a basic job with the small patch of lawn. It was a nice space too and as soon as the spring weather had arrived, she'd taken to bringing a book out there to sit and read on the bench at the foot of the garden.

'Come on, you,' she urged Jaimie again after he'd ignored her and gleefully bent down to pick up another stick as though it were a piece of treasure to discover on the footpath. 'Maybe Mum will bring you out again later on.' She'd better be careful what she promised, though, because knowing Jaimie, he'd remember what she'd said and drop her right in it with Tegan. Morgan was glad her sister was here now, it was good to have the moral support, but Tegan seemed so exhausted, she would probably be far more appreciative of a hotel spa break than coming here to sort out their mother's cottage. Mind you, Morgan could do with one of those herself.

As Jaimie insisted on readying another stick to play the game, Morgan thought about Nate. The handsome villager she remembered from school. Not that she'd ever had anything to do with him – she'd been shy back then, she probably wouldn't have spoken to him even if he'd come up and said hello, which was something the higher years never did with the lower, like it was totally uncool or something. Nate, with his deep brown eyes and broad chest, had been wearing one of those leather bands around a tanned wrist which she'd seen when he reached out to pull Branston back towards him. And it was good to know he'd come to see Trevor because, just like her mum had been, Trevor was on his own. She wondered – was he lonely? He always seemed chipper enough, but you never could tell. She would've said her mum's request for help was purely out of necessity until she got here and realised that actually, despite the friendships she'd built in the community, Elaina was still a bit isolated when it was just her in the cottage with Marley for company.

She waited for Jaimie to lift yet another stick up high, ready to drop. It was a big assumption to think that Trevor might be the same as Elaina, that he needed his son with him the way her mum had needed Morgan. But Morgan knew better than many the guilt of not being here enough, not making more of an effort to repair a relationship that wasn't entirely broken but could've been made so much better a long, long time ago, giving them so many years with each other. Years she could never get back.

'Come on, Jaimie. It really is time to go.' And she'd have to be firm; he was pushing the boundaries, something her sister was always referring to when it came to the kids. It was times like this that Morgan really understood what that phrase meant.

But the little boy had no intention of listening and had already dropped another stick. He turned to dash across the other side of the road without her say-so at the very moment Jeremy's ruby-red Robin Reliant reached the top of the bridge.

Morgan's reflexes were good enough that she grabbed Jaimie by the hood of his bodywarmer just in time. Jeremy had slowed and gave her a wave, which sent his car across the wrong side of the road before he righted it again.

Morgan pulled Jaimie against her. 'Are you all right?' She released him and looked at his face to make sure he was still in one piece, as though she couldn't believe it otherwise.

'I'm fine, Auntie Morgan.'

'Don't do that to me again.' She exhaled hard, pulling him into another hug before looking him in the eye. 'You have to think every time you cross a road. Stop. Look. Listen.' Those words were drummed into every kid. And you never forgot them. Unless you were over-excited like Jaimie clearly was. He'd had a fun time down here with some freedom, and sensibility had gone out of the window.

'I'm sorry.' His bottom lip wobbled.

She touched his nose gently with a finger. 'You're in one piece. I want you to stay that way so I can watch you climb those trees in the woods again and play more games of Poohsticks. Promise me you'll do that.'

'Yes, Auntie Morgan.' He giggled when she cuddled him again overly tight and lifted him off the ground.

'Do you know that crazy man?' Jaimie asked her when she put him down. 'The man in the funny car.'

'He's not crazy,' she admonished and under her breath added something about it being time he surrendered his driver's licence. His attention to his surroundings was questionable at best and taking a hand off the wheel to wave was something she hoped he didn't do too often. 'That was Jeremy. You've met him before.'

'At the wake-up?'

'The wake,' she corrected and chucked him under the chin before, hand in hand, they started to walk back over the bridge.

The wake: the final part of her mother's farewell. When she'd floated through the day on autopilot and barely remembered much at all, soon realising that when someone died, normal life carried on. Morgan hadn't really appreciated what that would be like. The seasons came and went even when you lost someone. Elaina had died on Valentine's Day, when the snowdrops were out in abundance around Sebastian's cottage. Not long afterwards, the first heads of daffodils had emerged and sighed against a breeze and everywhere you looked in the village, it was gradually coming to life again, green and colourful, the air fresh with the scent of new blooms once spring came along. Life didn't pause when you were up against it; the wheels kept on turning. There were fathers who could've been better, children who needed teaching about road safety, there were strangers who'd never heard of Poohsticks, a nephew who loved his auntie, a sister who seemed to be holding onto much more than she was telling Morgan.

'Make sure you take your muddy shoes off at Grandma's house,' Jaimie instructed as they walked, him doing a little jump every now and then as though this still wasn't enough activity for him.

Morgan looked down at her ankle boots, which had a good coating of mud on the edges. It must've come from Snowdrop Woods, where she'd taken Jaimie first so he could climb trees. It was a kids' paradise in there; he'd loved every second and run off some of his never-ending energy, although clearly not enough as he was still wired. Perhaps that was what kids his age were like. Morgan had no idea.

'I promise I will take my shoes off,' she assured her nephew.

'Grandma never let us keep our shoes on,' he continued, as though needing to prove his point. 'Lily did sometimes but I always told her not to.' It was clear that with his fifth birthday looming, he had already assumed the hierarchy of age and taken on responsibility for ensuring his younger sibling did things the right way. It had been similar for Morgan. With Tegan being the eldest, she'd always thought she was in charge.

Morgan tried to scrape off some of the mud from the edge of her shoe on the grass nearby. It felt like such a shallow thing to be doing, worrying that her shoes were dirty, that she might bring mud into the house, when they'd lost her mother. But at the same time, as the sun ducked behind the clouds and made her shiver, she felt a warm sensation inside her because had Elaina been with them today, it would've been her mum's exact concern too. Jamie had nailed it.

They headed back towards the high street and crossed the road to cut across the green which sloped up towards the Rose and Thatch as well as the odd bench dotted at the top of the grass. Elaina Reese had made her home in Forget-Me-Not Cottage. There were a few enormous houses on the same side of the street as well as the smaller, quaint, chocolate-box cottages like Elaina's. With period features and a courtyard garden, Forget-Me-Not Cottage had three bedrooms, each of modest size, and an inglenook fireplace that seemed almost too big in proportion to everything else. There was no porch above the front step, so both Morgan and Jaimie took off their shoes and left them on the mat inside the front door.

'Did you have a good time?' Tegan held her arms open for her son as he raced down the hallway to give her a hug. She looked less tired and less stressed than she had earlier. Perhaps the tea, some toast and the rest while her daughter slept and her son was otherwise engaged had been the best remedy.

Jaimie talked at a hundred miles an hour about the woods, the games of Poohsticks, the almost getting run over. The last one had her sister's eyebrows raised.

'He's exaggerating,' Morgan assured Tegan. Although she hated to think what might have happened had she not grabbed his hood. 'Promise,' she added to her sister's stern expression.

Tegan unrolled Jaimie's car mat in the lounge in front of the fireplace. She had the same dark hair as Morgan, but whereas Morgan's flowed freely in loose waves, Tegan had hers tied back in a ponytail at the nape of her neck.

Jaimie sank down on the floor with his bottom on his heels and began raiding the box of cars. Lily was still asleep upstairs and over a mug of tea each, the sisters got on with some of the admin they had to get through.

Once they'd made good progress, Morgan's tummy rumbled so much, she couldn't put lunch off any longer. 'Let me get the food ready,' she suggested. Jaimie had already come through twice and Tegan had managed to placate him by giving him a slice of bread the first time and a small packet of ham, cheese and crackers the second. 'If it's all set up, it doesn't matter when Lily wakes up or when Jaimie gets hungry, as it'll all be waiting for them. It's a help-yourself cold lunch, I hope that's okay?'

'Of course it is.'

'Thanks for driving down, Tegan.'

'You don't need to thank me. I always intended to be here to help; it's just challenging to get away.'

'I know.'

'There's so much to do.'

Morgan harrumphed. 'You're telling me. Every time I open another cupboard or drawer, I'm reminded of how little Mum ever threw away.' She took out the quiche and the sausage rolls and when Tegan asked whether she'd been cooking, shook her head. 'They may look homemade and they kind of are, but courtesy of Betty's bakery, where everything is fresh and tastes like it's from a cosy cottage rather than a business.'

'Mum always loved going in there.'

'You haven't seen what else I got for us,' Morgan grinned, tilting her head in the direction of the fridge.

Tegan was right on it and checked each shelf, finding the treat on the bottom one. 'Is that Mum's favourite cheesecake? I didn't spot it when I used the milk for a second cup of tea earlier. If I had, you might not have come back to a full cheesecake.'

'Leave it in there for now or it'll get hoovered up.'

Tegan laughed. 'Yes... by us.'

They laid out the rest of the food between them. They made up sandwiches, adding cucumber minus the peel that both kids would be happy with, they cut the slices of quiche and kept the dessert out of sight.

'There's another two boxes of those French fancies in the cupboard,' Morgan told her sister.

'I hate those.'

Morgan cut the last of the sandwiches she'd made into four triangles. 'Me too. But they were in the cupboard, got to be used up. It wouldn't feel right to throw them out. And the kids will love them.' Their mum had insisted on buying French fancies when either of her girls visited, thinking that somehow the bright colours made them delicious. And neither of them had ever told her the truth. They'd simply extolled the virtues of Betty's cheese-cakes every time so that Elaina would be more likely to serve one of those.

As they finished getting the lunch ready, Tegan asked about Morgan's trips to Scotland. 'You've been up a few times now, is it feeling like somewhere you might soon be able to call home?'

Morgan thought about it. Home. She didn't feel that way yet, but then she and Ronan didn't have a place of their own in Edinburgh so maybe that was a part of it. He was renting and keeping an eye on the market for the time being.

Morgan told her sister about the hilly capital, the long walks she'd taken, the rain that had hammered down on some days, the stunning architecture and the winding streets. 'It's a beautiful place,' she said.

'I'll have to go some day.'

'You'll visit?'

'Try and stop me,' Tegan smiled, although it didn't quite reach her eyes. 'Have you guys looked at anywhere to buy?'

She shook her head. 'Not yet, but I'm sure the right thing will come up soon. We don't want to leave it too long.'

Tegan put some crisps into a bowl on the table but only added half a packet so the kids didn't go mad. Morgan picked up the pork pie she'd got from Betty's and cut it into portions.

'I like being back in Little Woodville.' Tegan's words took Morgan by surprise.

Morgan turned to her sister. 'Do you miss it?'

'Kind of.' She wiped crumbs into her palm and tipped them into the sink. 'But I think it's more Mum that I miss.'

'Me too. And you love where you live now, don't you?'

'I really do. It's so peaceful, well, maybe not on the farm, but at the end of the day when our work is done and we're tired, the kids are in bed, the wood burner is on. There's nothing like it.'

Morgan wondered if she'd feel like that about Edinburgh some day. Would she and Ronan be content of an evening sitting in front of a fireplace, sipping wine and sharing a cheese board, happy in one another's company in a big city where they both worked and wanted to stay for good?

'Ronan is very patient.' Tegan filled up a kid's sippy cup with water ready for Lily when she woke. 'He's waited a while for you to join him. He's very understanding.'

'He is.' But Morgan had never thought they'd be apart for this long when she'd told him of course he should go. And she'd never predicted or admitted to him just how much she felt a part of this village now. Maybe she always had been and had simply forgotten. And maybe she was getting anxious about going to somewhere different. Was it always the way? she wondered. Was it inevitable that new jobs, new places to live, a move away from the familiar came with a ton of giant butterflies that stopped you in your tracks? Perhaps this was how she was supposed to feel. How everyone felt in the same situation.

And yes, Ronan was understanding, but his patience was starting to wane. Morgan had felt it on her most recent visit. They'd bickered about the fact she wasn't there with him on a permanent basis yet and even to her, it had sounded a bit like she was dragging her feet when she listed all the things that still had to be done. And she couldn't be annoyed at him for wanting her there. It had been their plan for a long time.

They were engaged to be married and had promised one another a future.

4

Nate had made a sumptuous breakfast for him and his dad and then he'd taken Branston out for a long walk mid morning, leaving Trevor at home to rest. Or so he thought.

He turned at the sound of a vehicle, a ruby-red three-wheeler shunting onto the driveway, almost touch parking behind his grey Ford Ranger that doubled as a work truck as well as everyday transport. This would be Jeremy; there weren't many red three-wheelers in these parts, or any parts, for that matter.

'Dad?' He watched his dad push the passenger side door wide open.

'Son, I'm sorry.' His dad waved a hand over at him before unfolding himself from the confines of the tiny car. He gave Branston a pat as the dog bounded over to him. And after a brief greeting from Jeremy to Nate, the driver of the three-wheeler reversed off the driveway with a delightful toot-toot of the horn.

Both men waved Jeremy off as Nate asked, 'Where did you get to?'

They let themselves in the front door. 'I got restless and

thought I'd have a walk after all. I bumped into Trevor and we had coffee at the Bookshop Café. He offered to bring me home.'

'Nice of him.' Although he wasn't sure about the safety of the mode of transport. The car looked as though it wouldn't take much to blow it off course or topple over.

Branston was wagging his tail and nuzzling Trevor as though reminding him that they only had a limited time together. The dog was doing his best to trip one of them over in his excitement.

Nate got another wave of nostalgia once they stepped inside the house. He wasn't sure whether it was the smell of laundry drying on an airer in the dining room, or perhaps a lingering smell from cooking that reminded him of being called in for his tea when he was little. People said all houses had a smell and he didn't necessarily believe it, at least not until he visited his dad. And this visit had taken too long to come; he'd left it almost three months and the last one as well as the one before that had been quick stops in Little Woodville, less than forty-eight hours each. His own life had got in the way, but he'd finally pulled his head out of his arse enough to come and see what was what.

'Did you eat at the Bookshop Café?' Nate asked his dad.

'I didn't. Trevor is off to the pub now and eating there so he wasn't interested and to be honest, I'm not even hungry yet. I think I'm still full from the dinner last night and the breakfast you made us. An old man like me can only fit so much in, you know.'

His dad had form when it came to not eating properly. After Nate's mum died, Trevor hadn't been the best at looking after himself. Nate had helped out while he lived here but he knew Trevor had slipped into bad habits for a while when he left. When they talked, his dad insisted those habits were history, but Nate sometimes needed to see these things with his own eyes.

Nate had a sudden thought about the driver of the three-wheeler who had almost touch-parked his car with Nate's and then driven off the drive at a speed that probably needed reassessing along a country road. 'I assume Jeremy won't be drinking at the pub.'

'Who's the parent here?' Trevor couldn't leave Branston alone. He was running his hand along the spaniel's rich brown coat over and over again. 'There's no need to make a fuss. He might have a half pint but that'll be it. I know Jeremy. And remember it's important at our age to keep up a social life.'

'Are you sure he should drive even after a half? I mean, is it even legal?'

'The beer or the car?' His dad always looked younger when he smiled like he was doing now as he took out two mugs from the cupboard and a couple of tea bags from the caddy. 'He'll have plenty of food to soak it up too. He's not a tall man and not particularly big built; I think he must have hollow legs, the amount he can eat.' He flicked the kettle on to boil. 'And as for the car, well, it's legal, roadworthy, but a few of us in the village are trying to make him aware that he's not the driver he once was. But that sort of thing needs to be dealt with delicately. Any loss of independence is a blow, son.'

This was exactly why Nate had come and wanted to do so more frequently. His dad was getting older, no denying it, and for now he might be fine living alone, but he wouldn't be able to forever. When Nate's mum had been alive, they'd had each other. One of them on their own was a whole different story. Sure, there was a village high street and other residents, but Trevor's house was tucked away, surrounded by trees, nobody to hear him if he yelled for help. Part of Nate coming here was to really see for himself how his dad was doing. So far, Trevor seemed content, he definitely ate well if the tales of the dinner last night up at Snowdrop Cottage were anything to go by, and he had a social life to rival Nate's own what with trips to cafés and the pub.

'I'm sure it is. Just stay safe, Dad.'

'I will, don't you worry. And he's good company is Jeremy. Likes a bit of a chinwag and I need that.'

Nate was well aware he could've come more often or called more times than he did. He'd let his own life get in the way, which was all too easy to do when you had your own business. There was no shirking responsibility and he'd never liked saying no to anyone who wanted to book his services. He supposed it was a good situation to be in: too much work rather than too little.

When Branston settled by the back door longingly as though he hadn't had enough fresh air, Nate asked whether it was all right to let him outside.

'Son, make yourselves at home for the weekend. I love having the both of you here.'

'Cheers, Dad. I'll leave the door open.' Before the garden continued around to the front of the property, there was a hedge, so there was no danger of the dog sneaking through the trees and wandering into the road.

While Branston was outside, Nate got the milk from the fridge. Funny how you could be away from a place for ages and when you were here, it was as though you'd only been away for a matter of days. 'I'm sorry it's taken me so long to visit again.'

'You've got your own life, I understand. When your mother and I were your age, we had you to keep us busy, we did a lot of walking, we travelled. It was as though we couldn't sit still half the time. I don't think we spent much time with my parents or at the in-laws.'

Nate liked hearing about his parents' lives when they were first married and when he was little. He couldn't recall much of it himself, being taken to Europe when he was too young to remember, and then when he was old enough to have some memories, only snippets came to him.

'Well, I should've got here more often.'

'You're here now. And I'm glad.'

It wasn't only a case of being too busy either. It was also that Nate had been a bit of a mess. The job in Wales had been a gift at the right time, exactly what he'd needed. He'd left the village after his mum died to find something new, to pull himself together, and it had worked. He hit the ground running with his work and then went into business on his own but when it came to his personal life, he was screwed.

Nate had dated Carys for almost nine months – wild party animal Carys who was out for a lot of fun, which she got, and promptly took a job on a cruise ship, leaving him behind. Which he wasn't all that sorry about. Next had come Susan. Susan was sensible, worked hard studying medicine, and they saw one another when they could fit each other in. He was happy but he wasn't as on his toes as he'd thought; he'd rocked right back on his heels because after working hard in his plumbing business to pay his own mortgage off, he'd found himself paying off the hefty sum Susan had borrowed from a loan shark. He hadn't had the conscience to walk away and leave her to it, leave her with a debt that could've endangered her. The thanks he'd got for helping her out was her dumping him for a junior doctor because apparently they were 'on the same wavelength.'

His most recent relationship, which ended almost six months ago, had been going well, or so he'd thought, until he found himself caught by the scruff of the neck outside the pub one night and a fist ready to punch his lights out. Sheena had been married and although she and Nate had been seeing one another for a year and had even had a week in Spain together, she'd never once let on. And her husband clearly hadn't seen her being at fault, only Nate. Nate had steered clear as soon as he knew and on the grapevine in the form of local gossip at the pub, he'd heard Sheena and her husband were still very much together.

Sheena was one of many women who'd come into Nate's life and somehow he'd never managed to get it right. And he was more than a little embarrassed. He'd had the best marriage to aspire to. His parents had been together for fifty years and he couldn't even manage a respectable percentage of that time.

Nate looked at the coaster he'd set his mug of tea on. 'New?'

'Thought it was about time. We had those free cardboard ones that were handed out at Christmas, but they were a bit worse for wear.'

'These are nice.' He lifted up the sea-green, china coaster for closer inspection. 'Mum's favourite colour.'

'That's why I bought them. I found them on Elaina's market stall.'

He immediately thought of Morgan again: the sadness behind her eyes, the loss he unfortunately understood all too well. 'Was it a nice funeral service?'

'There was a good turn-out and it was very pleasant, given the circumstances. Most of the village came and then went to the wake at her little cottage behind the village green to say their final goodbyes. The daughters both moved away a long time ago, not sure why they never came back. Morgan, the youngest, is here now, though. She's a nice lass.' As he chatted away, Nate noticed the shoulders his dad had once carried him on as a little boy were so much smaller beneath the grey, lambswool jumper these days. It was just another reminder that nothing lasted forever.

'Was it sudden, Elaina dying?' A question he wouldn't ask Morgan when he barely knew her but felt he should ask now in case he bumped into her again.

'It was, in the end. Heart attack.' He sipped his tea. 'I'm only glad her daughter was with her for a time and that she was in the home she loved.'

Was that a hint? Nate suspected it was. A while back, they'd talked about getting his dad into a residential care home. He had a good friend who loved it where she was. 'Who's the lady who comes here every Christmas and you have mince pies?'

'Gillian?'

'That's the one. She's in a residential care home now, isn't she?'

'She is, although she comes back to Little Woodville when she can. She was at the dinner last night.' He chuckled. 'You know she still likes to think she made it happen between Sebastian and Belle.'

Some things about the village he knew from his own time growing up here; other parts came from his chats on the phone with his dad or during visits to Little Woodville. 'The Bookshop Café looks impressive.'

'Oh, it is, you should get in there if you can. Sebastian and Belle are a good match in life and in business.'

'It's good she still gets back to the village. Gillian, I mean.'

'I don't think she'd have it any other way.'

'Does she like it where she is?' He got his focus back to part of the reason he was here, thinking about how he could best help his dad long-term.

'She does. But everyone is different, son.'

Nate might have talked about the idea with his dad, but he'd always met with resistance and it was difficult to know how hard to push.

'Let's go back to talking about the markets,' said Trevor.

'We weren't talking about the markets.'

Trevor indicated the coaster. 'We were, kind of.' He set his mug down. 'You never put your trading licence to good use. The workshop is still full of your things.'

Last year, his dad had been talking about Nate sorting through his things in the workshop which had originally been a garage before it was converted for Nate to make items out of wood to his heart's content. Nate had ignored his dad at first, given he didn't want to set foot in there, but had then altered his thinking, decided perhaps it was a good idea to finally get rid of everything. And so, with his dad's encouragement, he'd applied for a trading licence for the local markets with the intention of selling the entire contents of that workshop if he could. And then he'd gone back to Wales, the licence had eventually come through with six months' validity and he'd done nothing with it since. Nothing except avoid the issue, that was.

'Your wooden pieces would go down a treat at the Snowdrop Lane markets,' Trevor went on, 'you mark my words.'

'Maybe.' He'd been making things out of wood ever since he could remember. But he hadn't set foot in his workshop since his mum died and even though he'd applied for the licence, that was a whole lot different to actually sorting through things and bringing them to the public's attention.

Trevor brought the biscuit tin over.

'I thought you weren't hungry.'

'I wasn't. I am now,' he said matter-of-factly.

'You shouldn't eat so many, Dad. Let me make you a sandwich or something.'

'No need.' He proffered the tin in Nate's direction. 'And a couple of biscuits with a cuppa is fine.' He pulled out two Hobnobs. 'You make out I never cook. I'm not bad now, you know.'

Trevor had never done much in the way of cooking before his wife Ruth died six years ago. She was always in charge of the kitchen; it was her place, she said. It had been her mission when Nate was growing up to keep him fed and watered, something she'd carried on well into his years as a young adult as though he needed her to make sure he didn't wither away. When Nate lived close by and visited frequently in his early twenties, he'd have homemade snacks on demand, meals even when he didn't need them, she'd send him away with food to put in his freezer as if he wasn't capable of making anything himself.

'So no more tins of tuna or bread and butter?' That was what he knew his dad had had day after day for dinner when he was first on his own because he'd laughed about it. Nate hadn't seen the funny side and had cooked for him whenever he was here. This morning, Nate had insisted on making them both scrambled eggs on toast with a side of spinach, tomatoes and mushrooms. It made him feel better to know that he could at least look after his dad the best he could while he was here.

'I still eat both, but not all the time. Remember, Gillian taught me a few things after your mum passed – I can make a mean vegetable soup, a good chicken casserole, fish pie and I can even do mince pies. Gillian went through the recipe with me. Betty's from the bakery are wonderful, but I wanted to be able to do them for myself. And now I can. If you visit again this Christmas, you're in for a treat.'

'Just try to keep me away.' Nate loved being with his dad for the festive season, cooking up the big turkey dinner. They were often invited to Snowdrop Cottage but with Nate home so rarely, Trevor liked to have it just the two of them if he was and then catch up with friends and neighbours over afternoon teas or a drink at the Rose and Thatch. Nate had never been able to stay long over the Christmas period; people still needed plumbers, and he'd hated the year there'd been so much snow on the roads that he couldn't get here. He was only thankful that Trevor had been embraced in the warmth of everyone at Snowdrop Cottage for Christmas Day itself, and the pub for Boxing Day. Trevor had had plenty of company right up until New Year when the roads had cleared enough to allow Nate to make the journey safely.

Branston wandered in from the outside but they left the patio door open for the fresh air.

'It's a shame I don't have a jar of mincemeat now,' said Trevor, 'talking about mince pies has got my tastebuds going.'

'Mine too,' Nate laughed.

'I even make the pastry from scratch.'

'Mum would be very impressed.'

'You know, I think she really would.' The moment settled between them. 'You still appear to enjoy cooking if that breakfast was anything to go by.'

'I don't mind it at all.'

'I see the joy, kind of. But I'll admit a lot of the time I do it out of necessity. Because I don't want to wither away.'

'I don't want that either.' Because when he'd arrived here, he'd had a discreet inspection of his dad's kitchen cupboards and the fridge and there hadn't been many supplies at all, so it was lucky he'd come prepared. A half-empty packet of pasta sat miserably at the back of one cupboard next to gravy granules, a jar of unopened jam and a bag of rolled oats. In another, he found herbs and spices and suspected most of them were out of date. And the fridge, while it did have a couple of kiwi fruits and a bag of carrots, that was about it. Before Nate left this time round, he'd go back to the supermarket and get more pantry staples, leave enough fruit and vegetables for another week, and sneak in some cleaning materials and washing powders too, the things that were more expensive.

If his dad was to live near him in Wales, he'd be able to make sure his kitchen was always filled with fresh ingredients. They could shop together, go to the independent greengrocer near his home for the best products. Nate could cook for him, perhaps teach him some more dishes. Nate could do his cleaning for him. His dad was certainly managing here. But the fact was, he was living on his own, and one minute Nate felt reassured, the next he was panicking that he was too far away should his dad suddenly need him.

'Dad, I was thinking, how about I visit for a bit longer next time?' They had to talk but Nate didn't want to upset his dad. He needed to tread lightly, think before he spoke and made suggestions. Even if he was doing it out of love, his dad might not appreciate it if he thought he was trying to swoop in and take control.

'I don't expect you to come again soon.'

'Well, I'd like to. I was actually thinking I could come back next week and stay for a month.'

'A month? You'd take that long off work?'

'I haven't had a decent stretch of time off for a while; I'm due. And I know another reliable plumber who could take on some of my work. I could do a few jobs around the house – two of those cupboards in the utility room need fixing, the doors have dropped. And didn't you mention replacing the shower unit?'

'It's old, it's about time. But no rush.'

'I'll do that too; you should have a decent shower. I'll order another one online, have it delivered here. And I drive the van around anyway, most of my tools and plenty of the bits I need for the business and DIY jobs are already inside.'

'If you're sure? I don't want to be any trouble.'

'You're never trouble, Dad. Perhaps we could do some sorting out too. I know for a fact that if you don't know what to do with something, you open up the loft hatch and push it inside. Lord knows what's up there.'

Trevor began to chuckle. 'Guilty. I used to do it when your mother wasn't looking.'

'She always knew,' Nate laughed. 'We joked about what we'd find up there if we ever looked.'

'Your mum hated holding onto things we didn't need. Every new year, she'd do what she called a "winter clean". Never a spring clean, she was more interested in the garden or filling the house with flowers by then.'

His dad didn't have to say that the winter clean ritual had stopped when his mum could no longer cope with it. Her Parkinson's had progressed and even the little things had become harder for her.

'I also know you still have some of my old toys up in the loft. I'm in my late thirties; I'm pretty sure I've grown out of them.'

'I kept all of your *Thomas the Tank Engine* track and engines.'

'In case I wanted to play with them again?'

'No. Course not.'

No, he meant that grandchildren might have played with them, but Nate hadn't even managed a relationship, let alone anything else. He wouldn't mind settling down one day and having a family, but so far, it felt out of his grasp.

'You could sell the track and trains on eBay, Dad. Make a bit of money. People go crazy for that stuff.'

'I don't need the money; I'd rather keep my memories. And really, there's no rush. I'm still here, so is the loft; it can wait. I'm more interested in what you're going to do about the market stall.' He got no response from Nate. 'You're wasting that licence. It must be still valid at least for a while longer. Do you remember when you received it?' When Nate shrugged, he persisted. 'Roughly?'

'It's still valid, Dad.'

'Then give Jasper a call, he'll get you in; there are plenty of traders who come and go.'

Nate supposed the workshop wasn't going to magically sort itself out. He'd have to do it eventually.

'You have a real talent,' Trevor went on. 'Show it off, make some money, let everyone else see what you can do. Jasper will have something available, I'm sure of it. And I'd be proud to see you at the Snowdrop Lane markets.'

Nowadays, he did his best not to think about what lurked behind the closed doors of his workshop: the scent of the wood shavings, the smell of varnish, the feel of the grain of wood beneath his fingers on whatever species he chose to work with. His mum was a big part of his associated memories too – converting it in the first place, showing her the pieces as he worked on them and as they became what he intended.

Without her, the workshop felt like a painful reminder of the fact that she'd gone and that he hadn't been there when she needed him the most. And so, ever since she died, he'd turned his back on it.

And no matter his dad's eagerness, would Nate actually be able to go through with it – not just having a market stall but even going into the workshop again – after such a long time?

5

'There's so much stuff in the house,' Tegan said, not for the first time since she'd arrived. They'd had lunch yesterday, played with the kids and taken them out for a long walk in the afternoon and visited the cemetery to put flowers on their mother's grave. This morning, both Tegan and Morgan had got up when Jaimie and Lily woke, which was early. So they were already stuck into the clearing out, with Lily down for a late morning nap and Jaimie back to his mat and all the cars which seemed to have made their way to most rooms in the house. Still, at least he wasn't chasing Marley any more, and so the cat could sit contentedly on the arm of the chair when he was brave enough.

'It's hard to believe, isn't it?' Morgan agreed. It wouldn't have escaped anyone's notice at the wake that the cottage was bursting at the seams and in danger of being featured on a documentary about people who hoarded things.

'Well, I think we've made a good dent in it.' Tegan looked around at the collection of boxes for a charity shop, another two bin liners of what they could get rid of.

'You've got a long drive ahead of you this afternoon.' Morgan looked at her sister, who still hadn't told her what was on her mind. But there was something, she could tell. And it was hard to probe when they were interrupted every five minutes by a hungry four-year-old or the usual demands of his younger sibling.

'I wish I could stay a bit longer.' When Jaimie's car noises got louder, Tegan frowned. 'I'd better check on him. Excuse me.'

Morgan pulled out another bag from under the spare bed, this one full of scraps of material. Maybe she'd go into the charity shop and ask them if they could think of a good use for them. You never knew, perhaps the church or the school would want the pieces for a craft group or something.

When Tegan joined her again after checking up on Jaimie as well as looking in on her daughter, who was asleep in the travel cot in Elaina's room, Morgan asked whether she was all right.

'It's an emotional time,' Tegan said without meeting her eye.

'I know that, but there's something else. Something you're not saying. I know you too well.'

She opened her mouth, presumably to deny it, but let out a sigh instead. 'You know I appreciate you coming back here to Little Woodville to be with Mum, don't you?'

'You've said so enough times, Tegan. And I know that it was easier for me to do it than you.'

'I thought you might resent me because you and Ronan haven't been able to go ahead with your own plans.'

'Did I ever say that?'

'Well, no.'

'I don't resent you at all.' Actually, Morgan had felt glad of the space, the time to think about what she really wanted. 'But right now, I know there's more for you to say; there's something you want to tell me, ask me?'

Tegan bit down on her lip. Then she looked upwards to the ceiling, either trying to stem tears threatening to flow or in search of what to say. 'Why don't we go get some more of that cheese-cake?' she suggested with a tender smile.

Morgan followed her downstairs. Her sister pulled the cheese-cake from the fridge, Morgan got two forks from the drawer and, with the dessert still in its cardboard carton, handed one to Tegan.

It was only when Morgan had a mouthful of cheesecake that her sister said, 'I feel angry.'

Morgan had used her fork to break off a piece of cheesecake but leaning against the kitchen work surface, the sink behind her, she didn't put it in her mouth. 'With me?'

Tegan pushed a piece of cheesecake into her mouth to delay speaking again. 'I shouldn't be, I know that,' she said after swallow-ing. 'I feel like a total cow for feeling anything other than grateful you came home. I mean, my life in Northumberland carried on. I wasn't here day in, day out to see Mum's decline, I wasn't working my arse off running about after her when she wouldn't tell anyone else what was going on.'

'Why do I get the feeling there's a *but* coming?'

'I wanted to be here. Henry and I would've made it work. I wanted to be in your position, doing what you were doing, but I wasn't.'

Morgan tried to work out what on earth her sister meant. 'Are you telling me you felt angry because I was here and you weren't? You were jealous?'

Tegan pulled a face, the face she pulled when she felt so awkward, it would take her a while to find the words to better express how she was feeling. Usually when Morgan saw her sister, she looked fresh-faced in a way that suggested she got a lot of time outside, the fresh air that came with life on the farm, but the dark circles beneath her sister's eyes reminded Morgan that she hadn't seen that version of Tegan in a while. This had obviously been playing on her mind.

'I wouldn't say jealous. But in the same way Mum asked you to come home and help, she asked me *not* to.'

'I'm not sure I follow.' Morgan put down her fork. 'What do you mean she asked you not to?'

'Mum and I... well, we made peace a year or so ago, you know that.' Tegan had been in communication far more than Morgan over the years, a lot of that to do with the grandkids Elaina adored. They were a lot closer than Elaina and Morgan had been and sometimes, Morgan had been jealous about it but not to the point where she'd made the extra effort to try to be a bigger part of their mother's life, at least not until she was asked to return to the village.

'She knew she was bad,' Tegan went on. 'She told me her diagnosis right before she told you. Her osteoporosis was manageable but she knew it was going to get worse and while she thought she had years, the diagnosis gave her a bit of a kick up the bum.' Her phraseology always amused Morgan, as though her sister couldn't use censored words even when she was with adults; she was so used to substituting them in front of her kids. 'She kept telling me that she needed to get to know you again, that you were in touch but she felt she didn't know the real you, that you held back.'

'I did, but you know that, Tegan.' They'd both felt unseen growing up, but it had taken Morgan a lot longer to work through her feelings and see their mother as the person she was now, after the tough years of bringing them up. Her sister had got there first; she'd always known that.

Tegan stopped eating the cheesecake and set her fork down on the other side of the carton. 'When Mum told me her diagnosis and admitted she needed help, the first thing I did was offer to look into what her options might be. But she was adamant. She wanted to call *you*. I told her you had a job, you had plans to move to Scotland with Ronan and I explained it wasn't fair of her to ask for you to give that all up.'

'I was never giving it up, Tegan.'

She shook her head. 'Put it on hold, then. It was still a big ask and I told Mum as much.'

'You did?'

'I may be bossy but I'm not so bad that I don't see you're your own person rather than just my little sister.' She cleared her throat. 'So I did what she asked. I didn't look into other options for her. She wanted you and she wanted me to stay at home, let the both of you try to sort things out, get to know one another again. She never felt that you did. The kids and I have spent a lot of time here and so it's different for me, I knew that. But Mum wanted both her daughters to know how much she loved them.'

Morgan's eyes spiked with tears and she put her fingers to the corners to stop any tears from coming. 'That's why she wanted me home so much and resisted all my suggestions, claiming she didn't want strangers in the house.' Slowly, a smile crept onto her face. 'She made a few phone calls herself when I found cleaners or home helps and made a list. I wonder now whether they were actually fully booked or whether she made that up.'

Tegan shrugged. 'I wouldn't put it past her.'

'I should feel angry, shouldn't I, that she kept me from my own life?'

'And do you?'

Morgan shook her head. 'No, I really don't. I ended up enjoying being here in a way I never thought I would. It was a hassle at first; it threw all my plans up in the air, but... well, I can't imagine how I'd feel now had we not had that time together.'

When they sat down at the kitchen table, Tegan reached her hands across to cover her sister's. 'Mum knew that if I was here then you'd take yourself off and she might lose any traction she had. She wanted you to see the way she was now, enjoy time together.'

'You know, Tegan, you thanked me for coming home to help, but I think I need to thank you for helping Mum pull the wool over my eyes.'

'Now I feel deceitful.'

'I'm kind of glad you did it, the both of you.' But then the tears came and she didn't stop them as her voice shook and she pulled her hands away to cover her mouth. 'Oh, my God, you're angry because you didn't get to spend much time with Mum and then she went and died... that was my fault... if I'd been a better daughter, you wouldn't have had to do that—'

'Enough now,' said Tegan, her own tears coming, both of them blubbing so much they each looked at one another and started to laugh at the scene they were creating.

Once they'd calmed a bit, Tegan looked Morgan in the eye. 'We both had time with her. I wasn't here but we still talked on the phone a lot and I'd seen her right before you came to the village. You have no need to apologise.'

'But you stayed away.'

'I did but it was worth it for the two of you to find your way. I see that, really. But my grief made my anger simmer beneath the surface. And because you didn't know any of it, I started to stress that you might resent me for being a part of derailing your plans because I couldn't be here.'

'Well, I don't resent you.'

'And I'm not angry with you. I suppose I'm a bit annoyed at myself; I could've just visited again anyway rather than taking her plan as gospel.'

'She was quite forceful, though.' The sisters smiled at one another. Their mother certainly was that.

Morgan's face fell. 'On some days, it was really horrible, you know. I didn't always let you know how bad when you called.'

'Oh, Morgan, I wish you had.'

'I'd worry endlessly if I had to go out and do the shopping or run errands. I worried I'd come home to find she'd fallen and broken a hip, when I'd see her peering out of the back bedroom window, I'd worry she'd go outside on her own and slip on the little steps that led over to the bench.'

'Her favourite spot,' they both said together.

'It's mine too. I sit out there and read a lot.' She'd take a cup of tea with her or a cold drink, although the last time she'd been out there she'd noticed how tired the bench was looking and the shed too. Another job to add to the list. 'I felt so alone, Tegan.' Even though her sister had been on the end of the phone and Ronan had supported her from afar when he could, calling or sending her flowers on more than one occasion, she'd taken on the burden of her mother's care and it was difficult to think of a world outside of that sometimes.

'I wish you'd called me more often so I knew what it was really like.'

'You've got a family, a farm; you're busy enough.'

'Not too busy for my sister, always remember that.'

'I'm glad you're here now.'

'Me too,' Tegan smiled.

When Jaimie came through and gave them both a peculiar look as they sniffed and Morgan blew her nose into a tissue, Tegan filled his cup with water and pulled herself together the way mothers just had to do.

When Jaimie left them alone, Tegan told her, 'Mum felt terribly guilty that Ronan went to Scotland without you.'

'She did?'

'She hoped she hadn't ruined things between you. But she also said you seemed happy and she was sure you weren't putting it on.'

'I wasn't.' And sometimes it had unnerved her, how accustomed she'd got to being here on her own. But it was what you did, wasn't it? You stepped up, you helped, and your life would still be there waiting in the wings. 'I wonder sometimes how she coped with the both of us, you know.'

'You're telling me. I might be here in Little Woodville with two kids in tow on my own, but I know that once I go home, Henry is as hands-on as he can be. I can't imagine not having that support.'

'Mum didn't do too badly, considering,' said Morgan.

'No,' Tegan smiled. 'I don't suppose she did.'

'You know, when she first called and told me about her diagnosis, I realised there had been clues each time I saw her. But it still didn't prepare me for what it would be like when I was here with her, when I could see it every day.'

Morgan never would've realised the pain her mother was in, the difficulties Elaina was beginning to have. Clutching her belongings, attempting to take as much as she could inside the cottage in one go the day Morgan arrived and the rain had teemed down from the skies, she'd almost dropped the lot as a much smaller woman than she remembered stooped in the doorway of their home. It was as though her skeleton was exhausted with the task of holding her up. She had a walking stick she leaned on and as Morgan came inside, Elaina wasted no time lowering herself into a chair, a chair that had had an extra seat cushion added to it so it wasn't too low down.

'Can I admit something to you?' Morgan asked her sister, who urged her to continue. 'It sounds terrible to say it but I'm almost relieved she had a heart attack in the end.'

Her sister shocked her when she said, 'Me too.'

'Really?'

'Really. She was in pain, she was petrified of what came next; I heard it every time we spoke.'

Her sister had summed it up well. The advancement of Elaina's osteoporosis had been something their mum was very frightened of. Morgan had seen the fear every time Elaina winced if she brushed a little too hard against the edge of the sofa, the way she began to make excuses not to move items at the market and rather had Morgan do it. The future had looked bleak to both Morgan and Elaina and more than once, Morgan had heard her mother whimpering in the bathroom. She'd knocked on the door a couple of times and asked whether she needed help, only to be greeted with an upbeat voice claiming that everything was fine, she'd be out in a minute. Dying so suddenly had stopped the agony for Elaina. It had meant she never reached the point where she couldn't do anything for herself – never mind opening a tin or lifting a basket of washing, she wouldn't have been able to bend down to fuss Marley, she might not have been able to get up from her chair in the lounge or answer the door any more, or even sit at the market stall, pretend she was fine and delight in conversation with those around her.

Jaimie came flying through from the lounge with a car in his hand. Clearly the part of the game he was playing now involved flying vehicles.

Tegan's attention went to the sound of her daughter crying from the room she'd put her down in upstairs. And life as they knew it began to carry on around them.

Once they'd all had a quick sandwich for lunch and the kids were sorted again – Jaimie happy enough watching some cartoons in the lounge, none of which Morgan recognised from their child-hood, and Lily happily playing with some building blocks in the corner of Elaina's bedroom upstairs with Tegan and Morgan – they returned to the task of trawling through their mother's things.

Morgan felt a flicker of admiration for her sister as she looked over at her niece grinning at a building block as though it had just told her a joke. Tegan had always known what she wanted out of life. When they were little girls, Tegan had told Morgan that she wanted to be married. She'd said by the time she was twenty but back then, that had seemed a lifetime away. Instead, she'd done it at the far more sensible age of twenty-seven. Tegan had always said she wanted a family too, although back then, she'd wanted six children: three girls, three boys. She'd settled at two, at least so far.

'Do you think you'll be able to have any more time away from the farm soon?' Morgan asked. 'Not just to help here; it would be good to see you. And I'll get up there again as soon as the house is all sorted.'

'I'm sure I can arrange something. The kids love seeing you, me too.'

Morgan opened up their mother's wardrobe and blew out from between her lips at the task that awaited them. 'I suppose I should start organising some valuations.' She pulled a face as she looked across at her sister. 'I told Ronan I had a couple of agents lined up.'

Tegan grimaced. 'But you haven't?'

She shook her head. 'I lied. Only a small lie and only because he's getting a little bit impatient.'

'You never said.'

'I didn't want you to think badly of him. I can't blame him. I mean, this was our plan: to go up to Scotland, he's doing what we agreed, and me...'

'You're dragging your heels.'

Morgan didn't admit it, but her silence spoke volumes.

'You know there's another option, don't you?' When Morgan looked confused, she added, 'If you decide not to leave.'

'I never said—'

'I know you didn't,' Tegan stopped her, 'but as the bossy older sister, I'm here to say that just because you made a plan, doesn't mean to say that plan can't be altered. Circumstances change, people change.'

'We agreed we'd sell. And I bet you could use the money.'

'We've managed so far without it,' Tegan shrugged. 'All I'm saying is let's sort the house out, get those valuations, but don't feel obligated to sell up.'

'Are you suggesting I stay here?'

Tegan met her gaze. 'Would that really be the worst idea in the world?'

'I'm sure Ronan would think so.'

Tegan didn't say anything for a while. 'Look, I like Ronan,' she shared after a pause. 'He's a lovely guy, responsible, has a good steady job, thinks a lot of you.'

'Come on, there's a big *but* you're going to follow that speech with.'

Tegan shrugged. 'All I'm saying is that things change. And I'm not saying it to play devil's advocate; I'm saying it because I've seen, or rather heard in your voice, a change since you came home to Little Woodville.' She pulled Lily onto her lap when her daughter got bored. Still with a building block between her fingers, the little girl sat contentedly resting her head against her mother's chest. 'At first, it was all about Mum when we talked. Then, as time went on, it became about Belle, the Bookshop Café, the pub and who you'd had a drink with, an anecdote from village life, the things you don't really talk about if you're just visiting.'

Tegan was right. Village life had crept up on her and embraced her. She hadn't asked for it; she hadn't expected it.

'Just think carefully about it, Morgan, no rush.' As if to remind her that it was a big decision, Marley trotted into the room and leapt up onto the bed beside her. 'He'll miss you.'

'I'll miss him too.' Morgan stroked him head to toe, smiling as he emitted his familiar purr. He didn't know what was coming, leaving the cottage and living his life on a farm. She hoped he'd adapt easily; she wasn't sure he was up for a big change. He'd been Elaina's cat since he was a kitten, never lived anywhere but Forget-Me-Not Cottage. Little Woodville was his stomping ground.

Morgan took a deep breath. 'I wonder how much of my hesitation and feeling at home here is to do with grief, holding on to a last part of our lives in this cottage.' She looked around at the walls like they could hear her comments.

'Maybe.' Tegan rested her chin on her daughter's head, inhaling the scent from her hair. 'But whatever the reason, it doesn't change the fact you're entitled to a little thinking time. That, and the indisputable fact that we still have a lot to do.'

'The way the cottage is at the moment would scare off any potential buyers anyway, estate agents too.'

'Then let's do the best we can with my little obstacle here,' smiled Tegan.

Morgan took charge of pulling boxes out of Elaina's wardrobe. 'It was a wonder she could fit any clothes in here.' She'd already folded those and taken four bags' worth to the charity shop as well as getting rid of anything too old that they probably wouldn't want anyway.

When she opened up the first box, she began to smile and pulled out the first of a collection of books. Enid Blyton's *First Term at Malory Towers*. 'Do you remember reading these by torchlight in this wardrobe?'

Tegan giggled. 'I'd forgotten we did that. We took all of Mum's clothes out and piled them on the bed and laid sleeping bags down as if we were on a sleepover. She brought us snacks too, I remember that.'

'Popcorn,' Morgan recalled. 'And then complained that she was finding it around her bedroom for weeks afterwards.'

'Oh, we loved those books. Would you mind if I borrowed some?'

'Of course not, we'll share them. Lily might like them when she's older.' Morgan pulled out a few more from the same series, some of the *Faraway Tree* collection, and *The Twins at St Clare's*.

As they went through boxes, Morgan started to think about the furniture, some of the more sentimental pieces. 'Mum loved this bed frame.' She ran her hand along the bed head, cast iron and perfectly in character for the cottage. 'We'll need to sort out who's having what. If either of us decide to keep anything, that is.'

'All in good time,' Tegan suggested. 'I think the sorting out is plenty for now, and the house full of furniture if we're getting valuations is much better anyway; it'll look like a home. I think as much as it would be nice to get sorted quickly, it might be better to take our time.'

'You mean in case I change my mind.'

'Busted,' smiled Tegan. 'But honestly, it's a lot to do at once and I know you're exhausted, me too. Why don't we make a list of everything and then eventually, we can think about what we want to each keep, what can be sold. I can do it before I go if you like.'

'You've got enough with the kids and the farm, it won't take me long and I'm here all the time. I'll do it gradually.'

'If you're sure.'

'I really am. And you're right: if we start getting rid of furniture now, the cottage won't look as cosy when it's valued or viewed.'

Tegan sighed as she took out another box. Lily was happily playing on her own again. Putting it onto the bed they'd covered with an old sheet, she said, 'It doesn't feel real yet: Mum not being here.'

'Sometimes it doesn't,' Morgan agreed. Although she only had to think back to the day she'd called the ambulance and the paramedics trying in vain to help Elaina to be reminded that it was very real.

They moved to the downstairs next and with Jaimie disinterested in the television and back to his cars, Lily doing her best to join in, much to his disapproval, Tegan took in the boxes piled in the corner of the lounge. 'Is that all stock for the market stall?'

'It is, and there's more too. There's a big stack of boxes beneath the stairs, and don't forget the lot in your old bedroom in the wardrobe, bits in the dining room.'

Elaina and Morgan had shopped solely online for the last couple of months, picking up job lots of bargains, items that could be cleaned up or repaired, things that some would call junk but that their mum would call treasure and vintage. Amazing how an alternative description could make you look at an item in a totally different light. Her last delivery before the heart attack had been a pair of moss-green, lotus flower, glass candle holders. When Morgan had opened the box – even that was too much for Elaina sometimes, with the constant worry about fractures in every part of her body – Elaina had burst out laughing at the sight of her daughter's face lined with distaste. But Morgan had taken those candle holders to the market stall that day and when she came home, gave her mother the news that the pair had sold for twenty pounds! Morgan had set them out and not even put a price on them before a customer approached her, gasped in delight and immediately held out a twenty-pound note. Morgan was going to price them at three pounds each or a fiver for the pair. *Told you, I've got an eye*, Elaina had said when her daughter gave her the news. And Morgan had to admit she clearly did.

'I'm sometimes tempted to put it as a job lot on eBay.' Morgan echoed Ronan's original suggestion that she'd totally ignored, although on some days now saw the value in. 'But Mum would hate that. She bought these things thinking others would get pleasure out of them; it feels right to sell them at the market.'

'It's a big ask for you to do it,' said Tegan.

'I'd been helping her anyway; a few more pushes to clear the stock and that'll be all it should need.' She'd give Jasper the market manager a call soon. She hadn't been up to a day at the markets after Elaina died, then she'd gone away after the funeral, then she'd had to catch up with her own job as well as get things sorted out, and she'd had another trip to Scotland, but perhaps it was time now.

'She was proud of her market stall,' Tegan smiled. 'The kids used to love visiting her there. She'd always have tales of who had bought what, the items she'd found, the little treasures she had to pass on to others.'

A knock at the door grabbed Morgan's attention. And when she opened it to Jasper, she had to laugh.

'Not the reaction I usually get,' he told her.

'I'm only laughing because we were just talking about the markets. It's as though we conjured you up.'

'I had lunch at the pub with my husband, thought I'd check in on you. I promised your mother I would if ever she wasn't around.' He cleared his throat.

'Why don't you come in,' she suggested, 'have a cup of tea.'

'I appreciate the offer, but I can't stop for long.'

Elaina had run the vintage stall at the Snowdrop Lane markets for around eight years. Most of the regular stallholders had come to Elaina's funeral and it warmed Morgan to know that while her mother had lived alone for a long time, she hadn't been without friends and acquaintances. Jasper, in particular, had been a very good friend to her mother. Apart from Morgan and Tegan, Jasper was the only person in whom Elaina had confided the entire truth about her disease. He had to know when she was at the markets and Morgan doing so much at the stall or attending as a replacement when Elaina couldn't make it because the pain was too much. And he was a stickler for health and safety too, Elaina hadn't wanted to upset him or put him in an awkward position.

'I appreciate you checking up on me, Jasper. Thank you. And Tegan is here, we're sorting through things.'

'That's good to hear. And... no pressure, but I wondered whether you'd want to come back to the markets at some point.'

She smiled. 'Actually, I would. Is next Saturday too soon?'

'Absolutely no trouble at all,' he said buoyantly, as though she'd just made his day. 'I have filled the stall every week, it hasn't been an issue, but now it's yours again. I'll have to do some rejigging, but I'll see you next Saturday. Great stuff. I'm glad you're carrying it on; I know it won't be for good, that it's probably until all of Elaina's stock is sold. But having you there for a while will be better than not having you there at all.'

'Thank you, Jasper. Mum would hate it if I didn't sell all the things she chose so carefully.'

'She had a definite passion.'

'She did.' She confided, 'I'll admit it has gone through my mind to go for an easier option.'

'But it wouldn't be right,' Jasper said before she could.

And who knew, perhaps the action of going to the markets and running the stall herself would be a nice way to say a proper goodbye to her mother, a way to honour her memory.

'You know, your mother was always happy, always smiling, I didn't know anything was up until she told me.' He spoke as though he felt he should've been able to do more.

Always happy, always smiling. Morgan gulped. True, the Elaina at the markets was a jolly character but it hadn't always been that way. When the girls were little, she'd been so busy with practicalities and keeping herself and her girls afloat with a roof over their heads and food on the table that Morgan had sometimes envied other girls her age whose mothers had more time for them, who took them to the movies, out clothes shopping and became more like best friends. Morgan felt selfish now that she hadn't seen how hard it was for Elaina as a single mum, that her sister had realised it before she had. But she'd be forever grateful Elaina had asked her to come home in the end. Because it had worked. And as the months rolled on, Morgan's relationship with her mother had come on in leaps and bounds. Morgan let her heart open once again and stopped letting the tougher years growing up interfere with the way things were now. And in the weeks before she died, aside from her disease, Elaina had become a pleasure to be with, a mum she loved spending time with and could talk with and laugh with.

'You were always very supportive,' she assured Jasper as he hovered on the doorstep to the cottage, 'and Mum appreciated it. We both did.'

'She's at peace now.' The leaves on the bush beside him in the front garden fluttered in the wind, flaunting the fact that they'd made their way onto the branches after another winter. 'We should take comfort in that.'

'I guess she went in her own way in the end.'

'She was never one to wait around for things to happen.' Jasper jangled his car keys. 'I'd better go, leave you to it.'

'It's good to see you, Jasper.'

'And I'll see you again next Saturday.'

'You're sure it's not too short notice for you? I don't want to make it difficult if stalls are already allocated,' she said as he turned to head back down the path.

'Don't be daft, pet.' He had a vocabulary similar to Elaina's, which comforted her. 'Happy to do a bit of shuffling around – folks are used to it at the market.'

'See you bright and early Saturday,' Morgan called after him as he went on his way.

When she went back inside, Tegan was supervising the kids having cheesecake and she left them in Morgan's capable hands while she went to put away the travel cot and collect together all the paraphernalia you hauled around with you when you had kids. She put some of it in the car before she came back inside and into the kitchen, where Morgan was filling the kids' sippy cups with water.

'We should make a move,' Tegan said. 'I wish I could stay longer, I really do, but I want to get home before dark.'

'I don't blame you. Come on, guys.' Morgan rallied to get the kids organised. Jaimie had to put all his cars away, the last items to deal with and the mat was to be rolled up. Her sister took Lily to the toilet and told Jaimie he had to go because of the long car ride.

Morgan suggested a bag of goodies for the kids to take in the car. 'Got to get rid of the French fancies somehow,' she grinned, putting a couple in with some of the leftovers from yesterday. 'Yellow for Jaimie, pink for Lily.' She knew the kids' favourite colours.

'Thanks, Morgan.' Tegan put the containers with her bags by the front door and pulled her sister into a tight hug. 'I'm going to miss you.'

'I'll miss you too. But we'll see each other soon.'

'And we'll talk even sooner,' Tegan added as Jaimie did his best to reach up and open the door himself. Adult goodbyes obviously weren't interesting enough for him. 'And think about what I said. About the cottage, what you want to do. It's your life too and things can change. If they don't, then I'll visit you in Scotland, but just make sure that whatever you decide, it's the right thing for you.'

She didn't know how to respond so she just hugged Tegan one more time.

'Time to go, guys.' Tegan lifted Lily onto her hip and picked up a couple of big bags. Morgan took the remaining bags, although Jaimie insisted he take his box of cars.

Out at the car kerbside, Morgan helped Jaimie do up his seat-belt in the back seat after he'd finally accepted that his cars, bar one, had to go in the boot, and her sister got Lily organised. Soon they'd be back in their own home, back on the farm, a life in the country with long walks, sheep baaing blissfully in the distance, the squelch of mud underfoot as you traipsed over the fields and climbed a stile.

Morgan waved her sister, niece and nephew off and stood outside Forget-Me-Not Cottage until their car had gone to the end of the street, its indicator blinking. The car turned left to head downwards towards the high street but soon came into view again as it travelled back along the main road in the village, having gone around the block, the necessary and familiar route if your car was parked facing in that direction. The street was too narrow to do a three-point turn in. And the kids had always liked it because they knew they'd go past the village green and could wave another goodbye to their grandma, who always stood outside to watch them go. Morgan wasn't going to break the special tradition and so she would do it too. She could just about make out a little hand at the open back window and waved enthusiastically until her family went out of sight.

And then they were gone. And Morgan was alone again. When her phone buzzed with a text from Ronan, she sat down on the front step to read it, letting the colour of the forget-me-nots, the sounds of kids playing on the village green, the ambience of the entire village seep in.

When she replied to his text, she told him they'd made good progress today and yesterday, the market stall was lined up for her ready to get rid of stock. And she hoped that would buy her some time. She needed him to be patient for a while longer. Long enough to decide what she really wanted.

Could she really say goodbye to all of this? Was it really that simple?

6

As far as places to live went, Llandudno in North Wales had a lot to offer. It was coastal, there were some great walks and fantastic scenery and Nate had a reasonable social life on top of his growing business. But it couldn't hide the fact it was a decent drive away from Little Woodville in the Cotswolds. And every time he came back from seeing his dad, he liked the distance less and less.

'There you go, Mrs Featherton.' Nate came down the stairs in the woman's chalet bungalow. It was his second call here in as many weeks. Last time it had been a basic change to the washer on the tap. Today, it was a leaky seal around the bathtub. And he was starting to wonder whether she simply wanted to see and talk to someone because neither had been an emergency and they'd happened in quick succession. Perhaps she'd held back on mentioning the seal so it would mean a second visit.

The fact that she'd cut two whopping great slices of fruitcake – for him! – and was pouring tea for the both of them backed up his assumption. 'You shouldn't have.' But he set his toolbox down inside the doorway where neither of them would trip over it.

'I made it fresh before you arrived. I don't have anyone else to feed and I don't think I should be eating it all myself.' Her white hair was carelessly pinned back with a few grips, more to keep wisps away from her face than to hold it in a style.

Nate discreetly checked his watch. Bud would be here in five minutes. He'd already sent a blanket email out to all of his clients giving them the dates he'd be away for, and with him about to be gone for a month, he wouldn't have felt right to not recommend someone in his absence. That was where Bud came in. When Bud had had six weeks travelling around Asia eighteen months ago, he'd done the same and recommended Nate and now it was payback time. Your fear was always that the clients would prefer the new person to you and never come back, but it worked both ways so pretty much evened out.

When the doorbell went, Nate got up before Mrs Featherton could. 'That'll be Bud, plumber friend of mine.' He didn't wait for her to ask why.

With Bud in the kitchen, a slight chap but with muscles that showed he was perfectly capable of dealing with the physical aspects of the job, Nate talked him up, embarrassing him by listing his credentials, his experience. 'He'll give you his card,' Nate told Mrs Featherton and when Bud obliged, added, 'Call him when I'm away.' And with a wink, he said, 'He knows how important you are to me.'

Mrs Featherton put Bud's business card beneath a crab magnet on her fridge door and, without asking, pulled out another plate, cut a big wedge of cake and set it in front of Bud. Bud merely shrugged, picked it up and tucked in.

When Mrs Featherton went to pick up the post as she heard the letterbox go, Bud said, 'I think I'm going to like coming here. You get this treatment every time?'

'I think she's lonely.' And by the way she was keeping the postman talking at the door, he knew he was right. He'd also known that Bud would understand. He went to visit his mother every day between jobs or after he was finished as she lived nearby.

'I'll be sure to keep in touch with her, don't worry.'

'You're a good bloke.' Nate shared his suspicion that Mrs Featherton might well come up with another non-emergency and call him out again soon.

'That's sad, that,' Bud concluded. 'Being so lonely you have to call a plumber. Lucky for her, we're all right. A lot of guys would try to rip her off.'

The last thing Nate wanted was for her to call out a plumber who fleeced her and either didn't do a proper job or took her for a ride by charging the earth. 'They might but did you see the size of that cake knife? I reckon she could hold her own and she'd soon pick up on it if you weren't playing by her rules.'

'You know what, I might walk past with Mum during the week – she likes to take a walk by the sea but won't go alone – maybe we can pop in here.'

Nate patted Bud's shoulder. 'That's going above and beyond. Thank you.' He liked to think that was what anyone would do but sometimes people didn't realise how much a person living on their own needed basic contact. It didn't take much other than a little effort to make someone's day.

Nate headed back to his bungalow, only a street away from the sea. He'd miss the sound of the waves while he was away in the Cotswolds, but all that English beauty was beginning to grow on him again. He'd run away from it all after his mum died; here had been a refreshing change to everything, but he could feel himself being pulled back. For four weeks, anyway. Starting tomorrow.

* * *

Nate was on the road with Branston nice and early the next morning. He'd emailed Jasper, the manager of the Snowdrop Lane markets in Little Woodville, when he was still at his dad's so he didn't chicken out. Jasper had written straight back to him and confirmed a stall for this Saturday and with any luck, it wouldn't take more than a few market sessions to get rid of everything he'd made once and for all.

As Nate pulled into the driveway at his dad's, he glanced across at the workshop that had once been the garage that sat separate to the house. He'd have to get in there soon enough and sort through what he was going to take to sell tomorrow. And the thought of the emotions it was going to dredge up filled him with unease.

He didn't sit there looking for long because Branston had already sat up, ears alert, knowing they'd arrived. And here was his dad coming out to greet them.

Nate got out of the pick-up and hugged his dad. 'Good to be here again.' And even better to know he was staying for longer this time.

They went inside and as Trevor put the kettle on, Nate took Branston out into the garden. He threw a stick for him a few times so he could run off some energy. It gave Nate a chance to stretch his legs too.

After a cup of tea each, talk of the drive and the traffic and the warmth of the first days of summer that had seen Nate take the journey with his windows down, Trevor went over to the wall beside the back door to the kitchen. He unhooked a key from the wooden plaque Nate had made his parents especially for the purpose.

And there was no doubt what this meant. It was time.

Nate opened his palm and his dad placed the key to the workshop onto it.

'Give me a minute or two.' Nate lifted his eyes to look at his dad. He needed to go out there alone first. Open the door, take it all in.

'Branston and I will be fine here. I'll throw that stick for him.' Trevor didn't hang around as he headed for the garden via the back door.

'Thanks.' Nate wasn't sure his dad even heard him.

Nate trudged out to the workshop. The key wasn't stiff at all in the lock as he'd expected, but then again, he'd last been out here in the winter months when the colder weather often caused the door to drop. He didn't have that problem now with the sun shining the way it had been doing all week.

His hand rested on the door handle and he looked at it as though it wasn't even attached to his body. When Nate's mum died, this workshop had died its own kind of death. It was ignored, closed off; it became a nonentity for Nate.

One deep breath and he pulled open the door a little too forcefully, as though it might be stuck after all this time. It wasn't; it had opened easily, just like the lock had relented. And although Nate had known this would happen, he was still almost bowled over by the smell he remembered. He wasn't even sure whether half of its power was in his mind – the scent of raw wood, of varnish, of shavings piled on the floor. All he knew was that it was powerful. And that was why he'd wanted to come in ahead of his dad: to gauge his own reactions and emotions without having to give an explanation.

It had been his mum who'd suggested Nate convert the garage into a workshop. They didn't use it often for the car, it was half-empty given they had two sheds at the foot of the garden to store tools, the lawnmower, bits and bobs. And with Nate making more and more things, there was always the concern that if he stored what he created in the garage, they wouldn't last that long. With changes in humidity, the fibres in wood were susceptible – they could swell and contract as moisture levels changed and were vulnerable in a normal garage which was open to damp and lack of insulation. Ruth had worked with Nate to decide what kind of layout he wanted; she'd been as interested as him as the workmen came and transformed it from a neglected garage to a place he could be as creative as he liked. They'd sketched out potential layouts themselves before they spoke with the professionals who did the actual designs. They included storage, electrical sockets, cupboards to keep surfaces clutter free. Everything in the garage had changed, from the floors and windows to the doors and the addition of another window at the back.

Nate noticed his dad had covered a lot of his things with old sheets, probably to protect them. He slowly pulled the sheets away, revealing items he hadn't seen in years. There was a small step stool, a couple of photo frames which had been a challenge to make because of the smaller dimensions and the thinner wood he'd used. There was a small side table, candle holders, a cutting board. And as he ran a hand over each of the items, it was as though he was standing here making them all over again. Cutting their basic shapes from raw wood that was beautiful in its natural state but ready to be worked with. He could remember the way his mum praised him every time he took her something else to show her, the way she wanted to really look at every item and think about how it was possible for her son to make something so perfect.

He looked over beneath the worktop on the side nearest the back window, at the sheet that covered the very thing he'd been working on when she died. He might have uncovered everything else, but he had no intention of doing that one. At least not yet. Maybe not ever.

A knock at the door announced his dad. 'Can I come in, son?'

'You don't need my permission.' He turned, coming back to the present moment, and reached out to Branston to ruffle his fur. He crouched down and took the dog's face between his hands. 'You are very excitable; I hope you're going to behave the next four weeks. Or you're going to trip Dad up if you're not careful.'

'I'm on my guard,' Trevor told him. 'He's not too dissimilar to you as a young boy – you could never keep still either.' Trevor took in the sight of all the wooden creations. 'I'd forgotten how beautiful all of this is. I covered it all up when you left, sneaked a look a few times to check it was all still secure and not ruined, but not for a while.'

'You did?'

'Of course.' He looked at Nate. 'Sometimes, I miss you. Oh, you're a big boy, grown up; I'm a silly old man getting sentimental. But coming out here reminds me of good times.'

Nate liked to think he'd be the same at his dad's age. 'Never apologise for caring.' But while coming out here reminded his dad of good times, it pained Nate to be in this environment, which was why he'd avoided it for so long. 'Do you feel like I abandoned you after Mum died?'

'Oh, no, Nate. You didn't do that. I was fine when you left. In a way, it was good for me to find my feet on my own. Hildy brought fresh flowers over so often, I had to ask her to cut back as I'd run out of vases. Gillian cooked for me and taught me some recipes. Jeremy was more than happy to have a pint with me whenever I felt the need. Peter and I walked their dog through the woods because I missed my walks.'

'That was part of what Mum hated when she was getting worse, you know. She hated that she couldn't walk as far or for as long any more.'

'I know. And it's why I had to give myself a stern talking to. While I've got legs, I'll do enough walking for me and for her. It's a way I honour her every day when I get out in the fresh air because I know she loved it. That and travel. You never seemed interested.'

'It wasn't that I didn't want to see places; I just got on the conveyor belt of life – job, place to live, family.' His shoulders drooped at the last word. 'I never forgave myself for not being there for Mum that day.'

'I know. And I've never been able to forgive myself for not being able to show you that it wasn't your fault.'

Father and son exchanged a look that spoke of the grief they shared; it was an understanding of how they'd grieved together, but separately too and hadn't talked about it properly until now.

'I'm glad you came here, Nate. I want you to see that turning your back on the village wasn't going to solve anything.'

'Not everything, but it helped a lot. It did, I promise. I needed to get away from the familiar, throw myself into the new.'

'I saw what losing your mother did to you and it almost broke my heart as much as her passing. But I could never get through to you. I tried, but you were closed off.'

Nate shook his head. 'This workshop was a big part of why I left. I hated it for a while. It was a distraction, a way to neglect my responsibilities.'

All at once, Trevor realised what Nate meant. 'Oh, son...'

'I couldn't bear to feel the joy of creating something or even looking at what I'd already made. I had to leave it behind for a while. And, at the time, I'd thought it was probably forever.'

'And now I'm even more sad. My boy, your talent, your love of the craft, and you walked away for such a long time.' He reached out his hand to cover Nate's. 'But you've done it, you've come back in here now and I'm glad.' His dad admired the bread box Nate had made. 'You've got quite a talent. Your mum loved the bread bin you made for us years ago.'

'The one I made when I was twelve? The one that fell apart?'

'The one you fixed,' Trevor corrected. 'Ruth said it was an

earlier work of a skilled craftsman and that she wanted to keep it always so you'd see how far you'd come.'

He'd lose himself for hours in here and forget about the rest of the world.

'I know you miss her, son. And I also know you feel guilty for not being with her when she died. It's time you let that go.'

Nate's eyes filled with tears. 'It's hard, Dad.'

'But you know I'm right.'

'I can't get it out of my head that I was in here, enjoying myself, when she needed me.'

Trevor was at his son's side. 'We can't be with each other every minute of every day. And this place...' He looked around. 'Do you know how much pleasure this workshop brought your mother? She'd watch you sometimes through the back window here, your brow creased in concentration. She'd stand back and to the side so you couldn't see her.' Trevor pointed to the window which would have a view of the inside and could keep your anonymity if you stood at the right angle outside. 'She didn't want to interrupt you and she loved to watch you when you didn't know, she said your true passion came out then when you thought you were alone.'

Trevor pulled his son, who was a good foot taller than him, into a hug. 'I love you, son.'

Nate almost cried. They rarely said those words. They both knew they felt that way but it wasn't a phrase batted around often or certainly not in a while.

'Love you too, Dad.'

'It's time you stopped blaming yourself now.' With another squeeze around his shoulders, his dad suggested, 'Why don't you pick out what you're taking to the markets tomorrow? And then, if you like, there's an event at the Bookshop Café I wouldn't mind going to. It's an author talk.'

Nate smiled. 'I'm up for that. Unless Jeremy is driving.'

'Don't worry, you're safe; we'll walk as I could do with the exercise. Unless you need an early night before the markets?'

'Don't be ridiculous; I can handle a late night and an early morning. And it'll be good to get out and about in the village.' He liked to see his dad's life, what Trevor had here, whether he was being overprotective by worrying or whether he was right to do so.

'Then that's settled. You unload your pick-up and put everything in the dining room for now so you can fit this lot – or whatever you're going to take – in. I've made a chicken and broccoli bake for our dinner.'

Nate raised his eyebrows. 'I didn't see that in the kitchen.'

'Hidden in the fridge. I made it before you even got here.'

'Thought I'd smelt something, assumed it was the soup you'd heated up for lunch. Dad, I'm impressed.'

'You haven't tasted it yet,' Trevor laughed.

They went through what he could take and piled it all together. Nate removed his plumbing gear from his truck, stacked it all neatly in the dining room and then reloaded his car with all his creations, ready for the markets. It would be an early start so all he'd have to do in the morning was drive around to Snowdrop Lane and make a start.

Before they had dinner and headed off to the Bookshop Café, Nate took Branston for a well-deserved walk, taking the long way around the village, past the church again and back along the high street. He ended up on the humpback bridge and despite the sun showing no signs of fading away yet, it was deserted. He lingered at the top, Branston looking up at him as if to ask why they weren't moving along.

'Come on then,' he said when the dog looked at him one time too many. And when he saw a stick in their path, he couldn't deny he'd been hoping he might see Morgan again. The girl with the glossy, mahogany-brown hair that flicked up teasingly at the ends and the heart-shaped face and deep, dark eyes. Branston would be pretty happy to see her too; she'd won his heart already that night in this very spot.

And with a whistle to the dog after he picked up the stick in his mouth and looked as though he expected Nate to throw it, they headed for home, hoping he'd see Morgan again soon. Because he knew what she was going through and although he didn't know her, he felt as though he wanted to be there for her if she needed someone who simply got it.

He should be so lucky. She was gorgeous. And she was taken.

7

As Morgan came downstairs in Forget-Me-Not Cottage, she welcomed the sound of the cat flap in the kitchen flipping shut and Marley trotting towards her.

She scooped him up and settled him on her lap. 'Where have you been all day? Enjoying the summer weather?' His fur, the light grey of a bird's feather, was soft beneath her fingers. She'd never really been a cat person but having him here since her mum died had stopped her feeling quite so lonely. And she'd missed him today as she juggled her freelance writing commitments after getting two commissions close together.

She switched to rubbing the cat's chin as he lapped up the attention. She wondered whether he missed Elaina too. Did he wonder whether she was ever coming back? Or had he accepted that things had changed?

'I'd better get on, Marley.' Although the purring and the dribbling suggested her needs came way down the agenda compared to his. 'I should ask Nel to come fuss over you again; you'd like that, wouldn't you?' When Morgan had taken off to Edinburgh to see Ronan, Nel, who ran the pizza place on the high street with her husband André, had come in to feed Marley. According to André, she was dropping hints left, right and centre about getting a cat of their own, but so far he'd put her off, given their dedication to the pizzeria.

Marley eventually trotted into the kitchen and over to his bowl of cat biscuits and with his crunch-crunch sounds in the background, she went to carry on with the sorting out, only stopping once to do a FaceTime call with Ronan. The boxes in the background showed she was hard at work and he told her all about the restaurant he'd been to the night before with some colleagues. He couldn't wait to take her there when she got to Edinburgh, and she'd tried to show enthusiasm, despite the huge decision weighing on her mind.

She checked the time, conscious that she needed to get a move on with sorting through the stock to take to the markets tomorrow if she was to make the author talk at the Bookshop Café tonight. Sebastian had a guest author visiting, a man who'd written a series of travel books including one about Scotland, so Morgan was definitely interested.

She cursed when she stubbed her toe on a box in the dining room. For the wake, she'd shifted a lot of the boxes around to various places but she and Tegan had done their best to get everything together in here to make it easier to work through.

Morgan twiddled the diamond solitaire on her ring finger as she thought about her fiancé. He was a good man. And a patient one, given the hundreds of miles that now separated them. But no matter how good a man Ronan was, and regardless of how many times she told herself that the unsettled feeling in her tummy was only nerves, the fear of the unknown, she knew she had an enormous decision to make and she couldn't put it off forever. She'd agreed to marry this man, she loved him, but coming here had changed her in a way she couldn't quite describe even to herself for now.

The table was barely visible, given it was covered in vintage items. In order to really sort through things, Morgan had had to unbox items ready to re-box, which seemed counterproductive, but it was the only way she could see it working. The dove-grey, extra-large sideboard was piled high with filled bags, the contents of which Morgan knew she had to progress through. The Welsh dresser that had once looked so elegant, with white crockery on display, instead had a collection of miscellaneous items for the markets that all needed going through. She took another cardboard rectangle and made it into the box it was designed for, folding it on the allotted edges, fashioning it into the container for some delicate items. Not everything was boxed up; some items were still in the original wrapping they'd been delivered in. She loaded in an ornate photograph frame, a silver embossed hand-held mirror with a matching hairbrush, a small flowery vase, all three things that might sit well on a dressing table from the 1950s.

She ploughed on with filling boxes with an array of items to get them organised. One rule she'd learnt from her mother was not to overpack. She'd done it the first time she helped at the markets, packed boxes as though she was moving house, not going to a market stall, and so they were all ridiculously heavy and took forever to pack and unpack. When she was done, she went out to her little car, loaded the boot and then folded down the back seat to fit in the surplus.

Back inside the cottage, she took a shower and got ready to go out. She'd hoped she might have time for a relax in the garden after all her hard work, perhaps a cup of tea sitting on the bench she was so used to seeing Elaina sit on, but no such luck, with all the sorting, she left the cottage straight away and headed for the Bookshop Café.

In jeans and a bottle-green summer blouse, Morgan walked across the village green, down to Little Woodville's high street and meandered along, waving to Betty and Peter, who were heading up to the pub. The village had earned its reputation of being quaint – a title it could still claim with its little humpback bridge straddling the stream flowing beneath, the village green that had already hosted family games of cricket now the days were long and the hours of sunshine plentiful, the Rose and Thatch pub with its small area out front with picnic tables in dark wood and its name depicted on a sign for all to see. Homes in the village were a mix of cottages and houses, some with thatched roofs, all with neat gardens, as if there was an unspoken agreement about standards that must be maintained.

Morgan crossed over the high street and made her way up towards the Bookshop Café, a welcome replacement for what had once been a photography studio. Cobbled streets separated residences and premises, the bank still served the community from its beautiful old building, and the dinky post office was still going with Clover at the helm. Her husband had been running it alongside her until they'd had a nasty break-up and nobody spoke about him much any more.

She came to the Bookshop Café. The window display showed off what was inside with some of the latest titles, a summer flower arrangement to match the weather outside, and the atmosphere was warm and welcoming the second you opened the front door. Somehow, it drew you inside without much effort at all. The bookshop made up most of the space. Oak shelves lined the walls, reaching not quite up to the ceiling, with front-facing books at the top to indicate what might be on the spines beneath. Three tables were spaced apart to create an aisle on either side and around them with books piled on top neatly and covers facing up.

Morgan said hello to Sebastian, who was moving the chairs

from the café into the bookish part to arrange a setting suitable for an author talk, and she went to find Belle, seeing as she was early.

'I don't suppose you're still serving, are you? I've been working so hard today, I keep running out of time and I'm starving.'

'Give me a sec,' Belle smiled, 'I'll sort you out.' She delivered a tray of hot drinks to the woman huddled on the sofa with three kids, all engrossed in brightly covered books.

Back with Morgan, she suggested soup and a roll. 'I've stopped food service but there is some soup left and it's on the house; it'll have to be taken home otherwise.'

'I'm not on the scrounge.'

Belle waved away the concern. 'You're doing me a favour; that way I don't have to decant it into a container and get it home without slopping it. Pull over a chair. Then your bum is on it when others arrive and you'll have your seat reserved.'

Morgan grabbed a chair from the very edge so she didn't mess up Sebastian's arrangement. 'How many do you have coming?'

'Twenty-five, I think, so a good turn-out. I've made some canapes and there'll be drinks. Sebastian is really looking forward to it. We haven't had many events so far, but I know he enjoys a chance to show the shop off whenever he can. He's proud of it. We both are.'

'And so you should be.' She looked across at the kids on the sofa, pointing to their books and chattering about them, eyes wide in fascination. 'I was always happy as a kid if you gave me a big book filled with pictures and words.'

'Me too. Children's books are the best.' At the back of the counter, Belle removed the lid to the big soup warmer and ladled out a generous portion into a white, porcelain, two-handled soup bowl. She set it down for Morgan at her table and nipped back to get the roll which came with a little packet of butter on the side. 'Lentil and vegetable,' she told Morgan, who was busy blowing across the liquid on her spoon. 'And this soup has a hint of spice as well as plenty of the vegetables coming from Sebastian's garden thanks to those veggie patches.'

Sebastian had some decent vegetable patches at Snowdrop Cottage. Belle liked to use the produce here if she could and it worked; the soup was comforting and homely.

As Morgan contentedly ate, people began to arrive nice and early to get a seat for the book launch. There were a few familiar faces, lots of new ones, and then, as she set down her spoon as she finished, she noticed Trevor come through the door. And he wasn't alone. His son was back.

She took her plate and bowl over to Belle behind the counter. 'Thank you. I'd have hated to have a growling stomach and put the author off his talk. Is he here yet?'

Belle pointed him out. 'Doesn't look like his picture, does he?'

Morgan laughed. 'Not at all. Where's the beard gone?'

She was stalling because Nate had turned up; not that she had anything to fear, but knowing he was so close had her feeling a little bit nervous. She had, after all, cried in front of this virtual stranger and told him her woes on top of the bridge that night, and he probably thought she was a bit of a loony.

The Bookshop Café was a recent addition to the village but as more people crammed inside the venue, Morgan had a sneaky feeling that this place was already as important to locals and visitors as the Rose and Thatch, the bakery, the church and everything else in Little Woodville.

Morgan took her chair back over to the group and sat down next to Clover, who'd just arrived, and it was as they chatted about the latest postal strikes that Clover wished weren't happening that Morgan caught Nate's eye. He was sitting at the front with Trevor and he smiled across at her, waved. She waved back, as did Clover, who said hello loud enough that it made plenty of people turn round and look at Morgan as though she'd been the one to call out.

Clover shrank in her seat a bit. 'Didn't mean to be so loud but I was surprised to see him. Oops.'

Morgan laughed softly as the author came to the front and the talk got underway. She hoped he'd brought enough copies of his book about Scotland because she was thinking she might buy one. Perhaps she'd recognise places she'd already seen; maybe it would trigger feelings of whether this change was something she could still get excited about. Her sister was right; she needed to think about this from all angles, not just because she'd said yes to marrying Ronan. But she felt guilty because he'd never hidden the fact he wanted to move back to Scotland one day. He'd always had it out in the open, but that was the problem: it had been easy for her to get on board with, especially in the early days of their relationship when everything was new and exciting.

The author had plenty of tales about his time in Scotland; he painted a wonderful picture, was eloquent with his descriptions and you could tell Sebastian and Belle were immensely proud of how the evening went, judging by their smiles as they handed around trays of canapes and drinks afterwards.

Clover was keen to queue to grab a signed copy quickly because her babysitter could only stay until 9 p.m. so she didn't have time to stay and chat long. Clover had only just reached the front of the queue when Belle pulled Morgan from the line.

'I can queue with everyone else,' she said quietly in case it got someone's back up that she was showing any kind of favouritism for a friend.

'In all my excitement, I almost forgot,' Belle gushed. Over at the counter at the front of the shop, she took out a copy of the book. 'This is already paid for; Ronan called ahead.'

'He did? I mean I told him I was coming, told him who the author was, but I didn't expect...'

'He wanted to make sure you definitely got the book.'

Morgan opened it up to find a personal dedication:

For Morgan, best wishes for a smooth relocation from the Cotswolds to Edinburgh, Ian F.

The author had obviously been briefed that she planned to move over there but rather than linger and talk to the author and ask him questions, she felt the breath inside of her struggle to get out and she let Belle serve someone else and stepped aside. Maybe the questions she needed answering weren't exactly the sort this author could answer for her.

'Dad bought a copy too,' a voice came from behind her.

'Nate.' When she turned, she had the copy clutched against her chest. 'Nice to see you again.'

'Likewise.'

And because she was flustered, she asked what he thought of the talk and let him speak to get her out of the spotlight, or at least what felt like it.

'Dad told me I have to get to the Isle of Skye some day.' Nate pushed his hands into the pockets of his jeans. He looked good in a navy top with a few buttons down the front. He was tall enough that Morgan wasn't looking right into his eyes unless she made the effort to look up. 'You been there?'

'To Skye?' She met his gaze at long last.

'Scotland.'

'A few times. Edinburgh, mainly.'

'Edinburgh, eh. Never been.' His words hinted he'd like to hear more about it, no matter how much the author had already shared. He wanted to know what Morgan thought.

'You should go,' she said when his eyes dipped to the diamond on her ring finger and then back up again. 'Definitely.'

'Maybe I will.' When Belle passed by with a tray of drinks, mostly red wine and white wine, both of them turned down the offer at the same time.

'There are soft drinks; Sebastian will be over next,' Belle assured them.

'Early start in the morning,' said Morgan for want of anything better to say. They'd been so at ease with each other on the bridge that night but now weirdly they were anything but. It was like this was the first time they'd met.

'Me too,' said Nate. 'Excuse me, I just want to make sure Dad is all right.' Heads above most people in here, he didn't seem to be able to see Trevor.

'I'm sure he's fine.'

Nate didn't look convinced but then his shoulders dropped as if he had his answer. 'He just emerged from the bathroom at the back.'

'You can let him out of your sight, you know.' But it was touching to see how much he worried.

'I know. Ridiculous, isn't it? When I was a boy, it would've been him tracking me to make sure I didn't wander off.'

'It's good that you care.' She was close enough that she could see the hint of regrowth on his jaw that wouldn't take long to become more. 'How's Branston?'

'He's good, thank you. Happy to be back. I think he likes all the fuss.'

'You could've brought him along tonight.'

But he shook his head. 'I exhausted him with walks today; he's probably glad we've left him in peace.'

When Morgan's phone pinged with a message, she looked at the display. 'I'd better get going. It was nice to see you again.' Ronan was messaging to see whether she'd got her surprise.

'You too.'

Nate went back to his dad and Morgan set off for home, texting Ronan that she'd call him in twenty minutes or so. He would've enjoyed the talk tonight because the author shared as much passion about Scotland as Ronan had himself.

As Morgan went inside Forget-Me-Not Cottage and into the kitchen for a drink of water, she was greeted by Marley mewing, his front paws and head the first to come through the cat flap before the rest of his body fell inside. She set the book and her phone on the kitchen benchtop and picked the cat up instead. 'You're good company, you know that?' she said into his fur as she held him close.

When her phone rang, she put the cat down and answered the call. 'I said I'd ring you,' she laughed.

'What can I say? I'm desperate to know what the author talk was like.'

'It was really good. And thank you, the book and the dedication are perfect.'

'I didn't want you to miss out on getting a copy.'

She doubted she would've done; it looked like the author had brought plenty and there would be enough left over to sit on the shelves in the Bookshop Café for future customers.

'Did you talk to him? Ask him all about Edinburgh?'

'No time, there were so many people there.' He'd never know that she could easily have queued up and waited her turn. 'Besides, I have you to tell me all about it and I've seen it a few times already.'

'True that. So is it a good book?'

'I've not had much of a look yet and with the markets early

tomorrow, I won't be doing much late-night reading tonight. But I'll read it as soon as I can.'

'Your mum would be really proud you're going back to the markets.'

The softness in his voice was comforting. 'I like to think she would be too.'

She listened to him tell her all about his day – the other reason he was calling was to tell her that work was going even better than expected; the company were really pleased with him. He sounded genuinely excited about his job, which was a good thing, and he was even more buoyant about the houses that were starting to come on the market.

'We'll find something soon,' he said, 'I just know it.'

'I'm sure it won't be long,' she agreed before they finished up the call so she could get to bed.

But sleep didn't come straight away. She looked at the book about Scotland resting on her bedside table, waiting for her. And she wondered, were her dreams beginning to pull in a different direction to Ronan's?

She glanced over at the cat, who had been on her bed before she had even done her teeth. 'I don't know, Marley. What do you think? Am I being a scaredy cat?' He barely shifted at the sound of her words, merely stretched out his paws in front of him, claws displayed before he curled his paws back beneath him as though he hadn't been disturbed at all.

8

Morgan hadn't really talked to her mum much about her love life. They'd never had that sort of relationship, at least not when Morgan was a teenager or a young adult. They'd talked about Ronan a bit more since Morgan came to live at Forget-Me-Not Cottage again, but back then, Morgan hadn't had any doubts. She'd been swept along into helping her mother, being here for her, Ronan had gone off to start his job and they'd got into their own routine. The times Ronan had called and Elaina had said hello in the background had been short and sweet and all her mum had told her was that he seemed nice and it was obvious he thought the world of her youngest daughter.

But if her mum was here now, Morgan wouldn't be able to help blurting out her doubts. 'Probably a good job it's just me and you, Marley,' she told the cat after she sorted him out with food and fixed herself a bowl of cereal, nice and generous in preparation for a day at the markets. 'I can tell you about Ronan, talk about Nate, and know it won't go any further.' Because last night, she'd enjoyed seeing Nate a bit too much for a woman who was engaged to someone else. And she hadn't only left the Bookshop Café to answer Ronan's message but to step away from a man she barely knew but to who she felt an instant connection. Nate was a man she'd met on the top of a small bridge in an unassuming British village and who'd been down to earth from the moment they started to talk. Ronan, on the other hand, had been someone she met in a cocktail bar and who'd immediately set up a date at a top restaurant with all the frills, the menu she barely understood, the quiet wait staff dotted around a room. Ronan was a man who liked to impress with a flourish; Nate, on the other hand, gave her the impression he'd be as happy at a back street café or out on a long walk with a girl he'd started dating than anything more frivolous.

She finished up her breakfast, and despite a slight trepidation about running the market stall without her mum, she also felt excited. What would her mum say if she could see her today, heading out to her loaded-up car and making the short journey to Snowdrop Lane markets? And if Morgan worked hard and kept doing so over the next few weeks at the stall, she could get through all this stock in no time. And at least she didn't have to make up stories any more to explain her mother's absence or her need to sit down at the back of the stall for extended periods of time. Elaina had kept the truth about her diagnosis from most because she didn't want everyone feeling sorry for her or making assumptions about what she couldn't do. She wanted to decide that between herself and Morgan. And so, when she needed to sit, they told people she'd hurt her ankle from dancing around the lounge at home or that she'd stumbled over a tree root in the woods. When Morgan had come here alone, they'd pretended Elaina was at home with a cold or a headache. What Elaina had wanted more than anything was as much normality as she could grab a hold of, to keep her life a happy existence for as long as she could.

Morgan reached the carpark on Snowdrop Lane, found a space and began to unload. It was a beautiful morning, cool enough for setting up the stall, the sun there in the background with its soft, steady warmth. She wasn't the first here, not by a long shot; in fact, she couldn't ever remember being the earliest trader when her mum was alive either. Several other stallholders were already unloading. She waved across to Mindy, who ran the cards, wrapping paper and ribbons stall, who called her hello with her arms cradling a big box. She exchanged a quick greeting with Kevin, who worked the sweets and treats stall, as he emerged from the entrance, presumably to come back for a second load. And with the first box of her mother's stock in her arms, Morgan headed towards the markets' entrance.

The field was nice and flat and not muddy given the sunshine and lack of rain, so there was no need for wellies unless they got a sudden downpour; Morgan's trainers would be suitable all day. She and her mum had been caught out on occasion coming here in trainers or shoes that were fine at the beginning of the day, but come closing time, they'd slipped and slid their way back to the car.

The Snowdrop Lane markets weren't huge, but they were popular and attracted both locals and visitors from further afield. Local businesses appreciated market day too because they tended to get a boost in turnover. As well as weekend trade being slightly better anyway, visitors to the markets either parked in the village or at least stopped off on their way through, had something to eat, used the post office, went to the pub or the bakery. She'd heard André and Nel say their sales at the pizzeria went up on Saturdays, Audrey and Gus from the bed and breakfast had, several times, hosted guests who'd come here for the pub fayre and the markets, and Morgan knew from Sebastian and Belle that the Bookshop Café got a lift come market day.

Morgan headed to the biggest stall and the first one visitors came to upon entering the markets. On the right-hand side, it had excellent visibility. Her mother hadn't started at this stall but rather a much smaller one towards the back, but Jasper had soon seen she had so much stock, it was time to move her.

She'd only just set the first box down when, right on cue, Pedro, who ran the craft stall, came over. 'I've finished my unloading,' he bellowed – a little bit louder than was necessary, with heavy emphasis on the jolly. 'I'll keep an eye out for you while you get everything brought across from your car. Or I can do the carrying for you?'

'Thanks, Pedro. Much appreciated. But I'll do the carrying myself – nothing's heavy but plenty is breakable.'

He sucked air in through his teeth. 'Then no way do I want the responsibility. The missus says I'm clumsy at the best of times.'

Gratefully she told him, 'I'll be as quick as I can.'

'Take your time. The missus will have me doing the bulk of the work setting up our stall if I get back too soon. This way I get a rest; I did the lugging of the supplies so her turn now.' He had a coffee in hand and seemed quite happy to do his bit.

'Love it, bit of equality,' she grinned before she headed back to the car for the next load.

After a few runs to and from the car, she finally had the last box in her arms and was headed back to stall number one, ready for the day ahead. As she approached, she looked at the large canopy over the stall in case it rained and remembered she'd have to hang up the sign – *Everything Vintage* – the way all the stallholders labelled their stalls. Jasper had made it a prerequisite of having a stall here – permanent traders and temporary alike. He said it made the markets feel like more of a village and a place where customers could mill and easily see what was on offer.

Morgan, ready to dump the last box and deal with the sign, got to the stall but there was a man with his back to her already standing behind one of the tables. Pedro must've been called away by his wife who wanted his help and roped someone else in to keep a look out. She was about to thank whoever it was and put the last of her boxes on the side where he was standing – she'd thought she'd put all of the boxes there, arrange the closest table display first before doing the second table where he was – when the man lifted a wooden item from a box that wasn't hers and set it down on the second table.

'What are you doing?' Her question was out before recognition dawned. 'Nate?' She looked at the beautifully crafted wooden box he'd set down. An attractive piece, it had a latticed top, but rather than taking the time to admire it, she was puzzled.

'Morgan, hey.' He looked pleased to see her, much like he'd looked yesterday. She half expected to see Branston trot out from somewhere, he looked so at home. 'Good to see you again.'

'Likewise.' Her brow creased, however, as she stood in the gap between the two tables that allowed whoever was working the stall to get to the back. 'What's going on?'

'I'm not sure I follow.'

'This is kind of my stall,' she said awkwardly. 'Well, not kind of,' she stumbled, 'it is my market stall.'

'I think you must be confused. This is my stall today...' But he stopped before he set down the wooden tea caddy he'd unloaded. 'Wait... this is stall number one, isn't it?'

'Yes, it's number one.' Why did he have to look attractive, even in a confrontation? She was perfectly capable of standing up for herself but something about him made her want to be nice. Perhaps it was because he'd been so kind to her when they first met.

'Then my booking is correct,' he said, pulling a face suggesting he felt bad that she was the one who'd obviously made the mistake.

She looked around. 'Let me find Jasper; he'll sort this out.' And she'd feel less terrible if Jasper was the one to tell him to pack up all his things again and relocate.

Eyes as dark brown as his hair danced as he flashed her a smile that she wished wasn't quite so powerful. 'Good idea.'

She tried not to watch the tendons flex in his forearms as he lifted out another item – this time a set of chunky wooden chopping boards with rope handles. And unlike Morgan, who gave a little shiver at the breeze that licked through the markets at this early hour, he didn't seem to feel a chill at all in a maroon t-shirt he wore with faded Levi's.

'I can't see him but I'm sure he'll be along in a minute,' she said after standing on tiptoes with no success at locating the market manager. He was usually pretty easy to find, buzzing around constantly, making sure all his stallholders were happy.

Nate hooked a thumb over his shoulder in the direction of the car park. 'I'll go back and get some more of my things while I wait.'

'Sure.' But what was the point if he was just going to have to move? She didn't voice her concern; instead, she asked anyone who came past where Jasper was. He'd sort this out quick enough. Pitch number one was to be hers for as long as she needed it. It had been Elaina's for years, week in, week out. Every Saturday.

Nate had only just returned when Jasper came racing over. He looked panic-stricken. But before he could say anything, Nate was doing the firm handshake. And Jasper looked pretty taken with the newcomer; he was Jasper's type, as tall as his husband, who might not appreciate this interlude, and with a presence and a body that could likely fetch a princely sum if he tried to sell it at the market instead of anything else.

Morgan shook away that thought. 'I was explaining to Nate here that this is my stall; for some reason he thinks it's his.'

'For the next four weeks,' Nate put in.

Jasper took a deep breath. 'I messed up, big time.' A hand on his brow, he grumbled, 'I meant to cancel you.'

'Me?' they asked at the same time.

'This stall has always been Elaina's,' Jasper, flustered, told Nate.

'And now I'm here instead,' Morgan explained.

'I booked and prepaid last week.' Nate didn't seem any more than slightly rattled and she doubted he was going to back down easily.

Morgan had banked on this being smooth sailing this morning and after a few weeks, she'd be all done, the house would be clear, she'd be ready to get her head around what came next. And now this was happening.

Jasper, on checking his phone, swore and then swiftly apologised for his language. 'I can only say how very sorry I am again.' He was looking at Nate. 'When Morgan said she wanted to trade today, I immediately said yes... I tried to cancel you but the email is still sitting in my outbox; it never went.' If it was possible on this mild early morning, he was starting to sweat. 'Oh, this is entirely my fault.' He pushed his glasses up his nose after they slipped down again. 'Nate, is there any way you'd consider leaving the market for today and coming back next week when I'll have a smaller stall available?' He pointed out the stall it was most likely to be.

'I have rather a lot to sell,' Nate explained. 'And I need to do it in a timeframe, kind of why I booked today.' A muscle in his jaw twitched. 'The other stall is tiny and I'd rather sell everything quickly; I'm not in the village for long.'

'The other stall is better than nothing,' Morgan suggested, hoping she was helping. She really didn't want to give up her plot, not just for the practicalities but because this specific market stall came with an emotional attachment. It had been Elaina's stall for a long time and being relocated to a different pitch wouldn't feel like she was honouring her mother in the same way at all.

'Is there any way you'd take it next week?' Nate asked her without any assumption lacing his words. He was good at this: arguing his case but not sounding like he was being anything other than gracious. He had, after all, paid.

And while she wanted to be equally courteous, she didn't want to give up the stall either. And she couldn't imagine telling Ronan it might take twice as long for her to clear the stock because she had a limit to how much she could sell each week. 'I have a lot of stock too and while some items are smaller, they're breakable. That stall really is better suited to sweets or confectionary rather than anything else.'

'Which puts us in a bit of a spot.' Nate didn't take his eyes from hers.

She only looked away when she heard Jasper muttering beneath his breath at the complications that were down to him. She watched the colour drain from the market manager's cheeks as his two traders found themselves at an impasse.

'I really don't have time on my side,' said Nate, eyes back on her when she looked around again. And then he looked over at Jasper. 'Don't you have a cancellation policy from both sides? So I'm obliged not to cancel so many days before and you're supposed to do the same?'

'That's right, I do.' Jasper's hands shook and he dropped his phone, bending to retrieve it.

Elaina would hate this. She loved Jasper; she'd been to his wedding when his own parents refused to witness him marrying a man, and upsetting him would be the last thing she'd want. She'd be wrapping her arms around him, telling him they could sort something out.

Morgan went over to the table Nate had been unloading onto. 'What are you selling exactly?'

'Hand-crafted wooden items, some large, others small. I've still got a bit more to unload yet.' And then it was his turn to curse. 'I left a woman in bright yellow dungarees looking after my car because the boot is wide open. I need to...'

Morgan dismissed his worries with a wave of her hand. 'That'll be Hildy. She won't leave her post.' Knowing Hildy, she'd bend over backwards for a good-looking guy like Nate. 'Look, the way I see it, we can either keep bickering or we can agree to share. I'm selling vintage items, I'm not direct competition, not food alongside furniture or anything else that might hideously clash.'

Jasper had his hands together as though offering up a silent prayer either to whatever god he believed in or perhaps to Elaina as if she was watching over them at this very moment.

'That could work,' Nate agreed. 'Would you share for a few weeks, say four? That's how long I'm here for.'

'Sure,' she found herself saying. Although aside from the sharing of the stall, her mind was more on the fact that he was hanging around for a while.

'One side each?' he smiled in a way she felt was near impossible to resist even if you disagreed with him.

Jasper put a hand on Nate's shoulder and one on Morgan's. 'Thank goodness. I was beginning to have visions of this story making the papers, Morgan. I thought you might take to your keyboard and write about it.'

'Jasper, I'd never do that to you.'

He squeezed her shoulder. 'Well, you kids just saved my arse.'

'Jasper, you're the boss,' Morgan pointed out. But she was glad she could make it easier for him, she couldn't bear to see him hurting. 'We've only saved you from yourself.'

'Let me give you a hand, Nate.' Jasper went off to help him

unload and at least it gave Morgan some time alone to think about how to position the items she'd brought with her to the best of her ability with half the space. She wouldn't be able to fit so much on, but she'd have to make do and move items in from boxes at the back as others sold.

Nate returned time and time again with items, some beautifully crafted, although he ended up with the same issue as her in that he didn't have much space to play with. 'Jasper says you're at the stall for the foreseeable.'

'I need to sell everything, then I'm done,' she told him.

'Sounds a familiar scenario.' He turned his attentions to his things and cramming as much as he could into the reduced space he now had. He put a wooden trivet with a beautiful grain pattern on display along with a wooden tidy box for household items. She wondered where he got all his stock from.

A petite, smartly dressed, blonde-haired lady came over to introduce herself. 'I thought I'd say a few hellos,' she beamed. 'I'm Sadie. I'm new here; I have the cookie stall at the far end that way.' She pointed in the appropriate direction. She was dressed a lot smarter than Morgan was – most stallholders chose outfits for comfort and staying cool now it was summer – but this woman could've been mistaken for an office worker.

'Good to meet you. I'm Morgan and this, as you can see...' She pointed to the sign waiting on the table to be put up. '...is Everything Vintage.'

'I'll have to come back for a better look later.'

Nate introduced himself too and let Sadie know what he was selling today.

'Stop by, both of you,' Sadie instructed before she waved goodbye, calling back, 'I've got plenty of tasters.'

When Erica from the toy stall walked past and introduced herself to Nate, Morgan wondered how many others would be stopping by her stall today to check out the new talent – probably a few.

'Want me to put that up?' Nate indicated the sign when it was just the two of them again.

'Oh, it's fine, I've done it before.' She brought over the chair that sat in the corner, climbed up and stood on the table as she hooked the sign over the rail at the top. 'There.' But with a wobble, she almost lost her footing.

His hand had wrapped around hers before she could fall. 'You all right?' When she nodded, he kept hold of her hand as she climbed back down to ground level.

'Thank you.'

'Jasper might have suggested I did it on purpose if you were put out of the game with a fall,' he laughed as she tried to ignore the butterflies inside of her at the feel of his touch, even though he'd taken his hand away now. 'He'd think I'd made it happen to get the stall all to myself.'

'Well, I appreciate you not letting it happen.'

'You're welcome.'

The stall was cramped with two selling their own wares and more than once, Morgan bashed her shin against some wooden item or another that was in her way as she passed from front to back of the stall to help customers and get as much sold as possible. Nate, in turn, had to step over one of her boxes and Jasper reminded them both again of health and safety so they did the best they could to clear a gap for them both to work in.

Despite being initially disappointed at not having more space, it was nice to have the company on the stall and when Trevor stopped by with Branston, Morgan didn't hesitate to wrap her arms around the dog, pleased to see him. She and Ronan had never talked about pets but after having Marley at the cottage and meeting Branston, already she saw pets in her future.

Both Nate and Morgan were exceedingly busy on the stall, although more than once she turned around and looked at the chair she'd moved back into the corner and onto which she'd put the same tatty cushion that had always been there. She'd made it as a needlework project at school using what had once been a shiny gold material but was now a bland beige. She'd been embarrassed, thought it terrible and would've preferred to have binned it when she brought it home, but Elaina had insisted she did nothing of the sort. When Elaina hadn't been up to standing on market days, she'd sat on the chair in the corner, the cushion behind her, even though it offered very little support given how flat it was. And turning now, not seeing her mother there, was emotional for Morgan. It had her catch her breath more than once. And if she closed her eyes, she could see her mum in her position, calling over advice about an item, pricing or talking with a customer, getting as involved as she possibly could.

'You okay there?' Nate asked.

She hadn't realised she'd actually closed her eyes. They sprung open. 'Sorry, miles away.'

'I'll say.'

Jasper checked on them, yet again, as though they were two kids in a playground and could come to blows at any minute. Bless him. The last time he'd come over, he'd brought them an Americano each from the food and beverage stall and lingered until he was reassured that they were actually fine. Sadie brought over cookies and Hildy arrived with a little bunch of peonies she insisted Morgan put into the glass vase with a heart pattern on the front that she had for sale. 'Customers will get more of an idea how to use it then,' she said, and at Morgan's look that questioned what else they would think it might be for, she'd laughed and said, 'You know what I mean,' chuckling all the way back to her own stall.

Morgan's phone rang on the approach to lunchtime and she'd

already ignored it three times, so this time she took the call. It was Ronan.

'Checking up to see if you're okay. You've not been answering.'

She huddled at the back of the stall and sat down in her mother's chair, which Jasper would've positioned here for Morgan first thing this morning when the market stalls were set up. 'It's been really busy here.' The rearranging to fit both her and Nate in had taken up time too. And hadn't they only spoken last night?

'Sorry, not the best time to call, is it?' It was rhetorical.

And she felt bad. He only wanted to talk to his fiancée. 'It's fine, I have a break in customer flow at this exact moment, as it happens.'

'Great.' He couldn't keep the excitement out of his voice when he said, 'I've seen a house I like.'

Her spirits didn't lift the way they should, but then again, she had a lot going on. 'What's it like?' She hoped he wasn't going to rush into anything before she had a chance to get up there and look properly too.

'It's exactly what we're looking for. A four-bed Victorian semi in a great area, a short walk from Edinburgh's historic old town. You'll love it, Morgan – period features, a traditional fireplace.' It was exactly what they'd discussed. When it was merely a pipedream. 'Well, should I book us both in to see it? Could you get here during the week?'

'I'm not sure. I've got a lot of work on after being away, then there's the cottage to sort. I'll see what I can do.' She'd only just got back to the village. 'Why don't you check it out and let me know first? If it gets your seal of approval, then that's a good sign and I can look at it when I'm next there.' And it would buy her some time to do what she needed to. She sometimes thought Ronan didn't really realise how much she had to do here. The cottage was getting sorted quickly but it was a lot of work, she had this stall, she had her own work to do. And on top of that, she was having doubts that seemed to be increasing by the day.

'I'll give the estate agent a call.' His enthusiasm suggested he was hoping she'd agree to fly up there tomorrow if he liked it. He never had been one to hang around and wait for things to happen. 'Oh, and I found an amazing cheese and wine bar that you'll love.'

'Sounds perfect.' She looked across at Nate, who was smiling as he handed a customer some change. She adjusted the cushion behind her in the chair, unable to get comfortable. But who was she kidding? It was a terrible cushion, but it made her smile to know her mum had kept it simply because it was Morgan who'd made it.

'Give me a minute, Ronan, I have a customer.' She put her phone on the table at the back while she sold the vase along with its content of peonies, and once the transaction was complete, she went back to her call, at the same time rummaging in a box for a replacement item. With so much to sell and very little space, she wanted to make the most of the day's trading.

When Nate accidentally knocked into her as she stood up and she narrowly missed being bashed in the head by the wooden stool he'd lifted up, she jolted and dropped her phone.

'Jasper would not be pleased if he'd seen that,' Nate leaned in to say to her.

She was laughing as she got back to her call and had to give Ronan a recap on the confusion at the markets this morning. 'Poor Jasper, he was tying himself in knots at his mistake,' she explained as Nate chatted with the customer who'd decided against the stool and was haggling over the price of a towel ladder.

Ronan had only met Jasper at the funeral but even he'd seen how close Jasper had been to Elaina. 'Surely Jasper has a loyalty and you shouldn't have to change your plans for the newcomer.' And Ronan never coped well when it came to other men in her life if he didn't know who they were; it was an insecurity he'd had from the day they got together.

'He'd taken payment,' she said as quietly as possible. 'Anyway, it hasn't totally derailed me; I'm still here.'

'I hope it goes well, get you finished up there as soon as possible. I know the markets weren't your favourite thing when you were staying with your mum.'

He was right. She hadn't liked it at the start; it had simply been what she had to do. But over time, the markets had become a real bonding experience. She'd loved the way Elaina had time to chat to anyone who came over, customers or other stallholders, how she loved nothing more than helping others when they had a dilemma, whether it was about what to cook for dinner that evening or how to deal with a family crisis. Elaina would multitask, carry on selling, talking at the same time. She buzzed on it here and the feeling had been infectious.

Morgan had to excuse herself to Ronan once again, this time for a customer who bought the love-heart silver trinket box that she remembered her mum getting through the post and cleaning up till the discolouration was removed and it shone brilliantly. She'd had the inside lined with plush, deep-pink velvet and when she'd sold the piece, Morgan picked up her phone again. She didn't have to tell him this really was a bad time because he sounded annoyed when he said the exact same thing. And when he told her he would be out tonight with work colleagues and not back until late, it was like she'd been given a reprieve. She was already feeling tiredness creeping up on her and she wanted nothing more than to go home after this, get into her pyjamas and watch movies for the evening.

Right after she hung up, Jasper appeared again, this time with a tuna focaccia for her and one for Nate. He apologised once again for his 'monumental cock-up' – his exact words.

Morgan spoke to him as Nate served his customer. 'Jasper, you've said sorry, we've sorted the stall to fit us both in, you've given us coffee and now lunch. It's time to stop.'

'I'm looking out for you, the way your mum would want.'

'And she'd want me to tell you exactly what I just told you.'

He gave her a hug. 'You're a good lass.'

Morgan sat in the chair to eat her focaccia while she had no customers and as she finished, she moved the cushion from the chair so she could get rid of all the crumbs she'd managed to drop. She set the cushion on the table and turned around to brush the chair clean.

Nate tucked into his own lunch as soon as he got a break. 'Thank you for being accommodating today,' he said between mouthfuls, aware that any second now, he might have to stop eating.

'It all worked out in the end,' she shrugged.

'Jasper seems a good guy.'

'He is. The best. He and Mum were good friends. And he always wants to do the right thing for everyone.'

After another bite, he asked, 'So you work for a newspaper?'

She realised it had been Jasper's earlier comment about her writing a story that would make him ask. 'Used to. I'm a freelance writer these days. I write mostly for magazines.'

'Nice gig.'

'It's not bad.' And two could play at the inquisition game. 'What made you come to the markets on this visit to see your dad?'

'I applied for a trader licence a while back and never used it. Dad wanted me to come here.'

'That's because he's entrenched in goings-on in Little Woodville.'

'Are you implying he'd never want to leave?' He put the rest of his focaccia into his mouth.

'I'm sorry if that sounded rude. I didn't mean it that way.'

'Don't mind me.' He shook his head after he'd swallowed his mouthful. 'I'm tired and a bit touchy. It wasn't rude.'

'Are you still worried about Trevor?'

'You can read me like a book.'

The word book had her feel that tingle inside of her as it reminded her of the event last night. They were frequently in much closer proximity today, but with plenty to do for each of them, there hadn't been the awkwardness of when she'd stood in front of him last night.

'How long are you staying?' she wondered. He'd said earlier that the stall was to be his for four weeks.

'A month. I've got a couple of jobs to do for Dad at Oak Cottage and there's some sorting out to be done before I head back to Wales, back to my own place and my business.'

'What do you do?'

'I'm a plumber.'

'And business is going well?'

'Very well. And steady.'

'Are you hoping Trevor will go back to Wales with you?' She puffed out her cheeks. 'Sorry, I'm probing you with questions and it's none of my business.'

His eyes lit up. 'You're taking an interest; I like that.' But then, on a sigh, he showed this wasn't easy for him. 'I just want to do what's right for Dad.'

Peter, who ran the bakery with his wife, came over to welcome Nate and his conversation with Morgan stalled. 'Betty is busy today but said to make sure you feel welcome, Nate. And you too, Morgan. You both look like you're having fun.'

'Not sure about that,' laughed Morgan. 'But we're working hard.'

'Does Betty still make the best pasties in the Cotswolds?' Nate asked Peter.

Peter's hearty laugh had them both smiling. 'I will tell her you said that and you pop in when you can, two on the house for yourself and your dad.'

'Not going to say no to that.' Nate excused himself to give his attention to a customer.

Peter moved to Morgan's side of the stall. 'Betty would love these.' He'd picked up one of the set of four tumblers with gold tipping and floral motifs. 'Maybe I'll surprise her.'

'Is it her birthday?'

'Not for a long time yet but your mum always said the best gifts are the ones you don't expect.'

'Mum did used to say that.' Morgan gulped back her emotion. She remembered the saying well but hearing that Elaina had shared it with others had a certain pull on her heart that took her by surprise.

Morgan hadn't appreciated it as a teen but coming back to Little Woodville after all this time had made her look at the village with fresh eyes. The way people exchanged greetings in the street or were willing to stop and have a conversation, how they asked after your loved ones, how without you realising, they had an eye on you and cared about your well-being. The wake had drummed it into her even more how much her mum was deep-rooted in the community here and Morgan had seen how happy it had made Elaina.

When Peter went on his way, Morgan said to Nate, 'So you remember Betty and her bakery then.'

'What can I say?' He patted what she suspected was a pretty taut stomach if the rest of his physique was anything to go by. 'I remember the bakery and its owner; obviously my head saw that as very important.'

'Obviously,' she laughed. 'So tell me, where does all this wood stuff come from?' He really did have quite the collection.

'Wood stuff?'

She grimaced. 'Sorry, that sounds terrible, bit like you asking where I get all my *old stuff*. Which, believe me, some people do ask.'

'I make it.'

She pointed to a small wooden box with a smooth finish and a lid on top. She imagined it might hold surplus coins or bits and bobs like the button box her nan once had. 'You made this?'

'That, everything else.'

'What, even the towel ladder you sold, the table, the boxes?'

He nodded.

'It's all so beautiful.'

'You seem surprised.'

'I am.' Pleasantly so. 'You're very talented. When did you make it all? Did you bring it with you from Wales?'

'I made it all a very long time ago. I haven't done much wood-working lately but I had filled my workshop, which was once Dad's garage, with all of my projects – it was time I cleared it out.'

'Ah, that's what Trevor meant by workshop. I heard him say it once,' she explained. 'I thought he meant a bench at the back of a garage, you know, the way some men have an area where they do projects. But it sounds like it's a lot more than that.'

When a man came over to talk to Nate, she moved back to her side of the stall to find her bottle of water. She was sure it was beneath the table at the back, out of the way.

Nate must have finished with his customer because after a minute or two, she could hear him asking what she was doing.

She pulled out from where she'd crawled almost under the table. 'I thought I had more water somewhere. But I've run out.'

'Go get another. I'll watch your side of the stall while you go.'

'You don't mind? I won't be long.' She was gasping but she didn't want to lose sales. When her mum was here with her, they'd always had one of them here if the other needed to nip off for food or refreshments.

'If you get customers, do you want me to take money and sell or ask them to come back?'

'If you could sell for the ticket prices underneath then that would be really great. Are you sure?'

'Yep, you go, I won't sell for less than ticket price.'

'Can I get you anything?'

'If you could bring me a can of something cold back, I'll reimburse you.'

'Anything?'

'Yep, just as long as it's cold and fizzy,' he smiled. And she had to look away because her own insides were fizzing enough already.

She set off and couldn't help exchanging a few hellos along the way – to Mindy, who was putting more cards on display rack at the front of her stall, to Zadie and Gareth on the second-hand book stall, and Ross, who sold all things gardening from spades and pitch forks to fertiliser and kneeling mats. In some ways, the market traders were like one big family and she knew that was what Elaina had really enjoyed. The first time Morgan had seen her mother here, she had realised Elaina was a different woman to the one she'd kept and built up in her mind over time. And now she wondered whether perhaps that was why she'd really brought her daughter to the markets. Perhaps she'd been more capable than she'd let on in the earlier stages but she'd wanted Morgan to live the part of her life she hadn't shared with her youngest daughter up until then.

As she waited in line at the food and beverages stall to get a Coke and a bottle of water, she checked her phone at the sound of an email alert and, sure enough, Ronan had sent through the listing for the house. She had to admit that it looked gorgeous, but she pushed her phone back into the pocket of her jeans and freed up her hands to take the drinks.

By the time she wandered back, she could see people congregating at both sides of the stall so she hurried over, set down the drinks at the back quickly, and saw to her customers.

Nate waited for the lull on her side. 'Cheers.' He flipped the ring pull and promptly glugged at least half of it in one go before pulling some cash from his back pocket.

'Honestly, no need to reimburse; you can return the favour another time.' She turned to pick up her water for a big necessary gulp and that was when she saw it. Her mother's chair. Still there, still in the corner position. But there was no cushion. The hideous, faded-gold creation of hers from years gone by was no longer in its rightful place.

She turned to get it from the table where she'd thrown it earlier. But it wasn't there either.

'The cushion?' she asked, looking beneath the table in case it had fallen.

'Cushion?' Nate frowned, setting down his can on the back table and coming closer.

'Yes, it was on the chair, then the table. Old, faded gold.'

'Oh, sold that.' He did a mini bow. 'You're welcome, never thought anyone would want it, let alone pay a fiver for it.'

She felt a cold flush go right through her and her lip quivered. 'But it didn't have a tag.'

'There was one underneath.' He went to rearrange some of his items that had been rifled through and left a bit untidy. He hadn't noticed her reaction, at least not until the silence lasted so long, he looked across at her. 'Morgan? I thought you'd be pleased.'

She stared at him but the sheen in her eyes from the gathering tears made it hard to see properly. 'I... I...'

She didn't say another word. She ran from the stall and out to the car park where she jumped into her car to hide from the rest of the world.

She'd thought it would be easy to come here, straightforward to sell off her mother's stock.

But grief had had other ideas.

9

The morning after the markets, Nate's alarm went off early and he was up and out in no time, taking Branston with him for the ride to the timber merchants. Locals and anyone who'd come from further afield had been impressed with his work, he'd sold plenty and made a decent amount of cash in the process and, believe it or not, he already had his first commission. Now he had to hope he could still remember how to handle wood and make what he wanted. And he also wished he could stop thinking so much about Morgan and the way she'd run off yesterday. He'd thought she'd be pleased about the cushion, the near-impossible sale in his opinion, given the state of it. He'd almost chased after her and might have done if they didn't both have a lot of stock on display and there for wandering hands.

As Nate drove, he switched from thinking about Morgan to the gentleman who'd approached him and asked whether he had any chessboards for sale. Nate had assumed he'd tell him that no, he didn't, and the man would be on his way, but instead he'd admired several of the other items and bemoaned the fact that a handmade chessboard would've made the perfect gift. Apparently, he'd been looking and hadn't found what he wanted and didn't want to try online because he didn't trust it. He worried that he might end up with a flimsy board that had no quality. In that moment, Nate found his mouth getting away with him and offering to make one for the following week. 'No commitment necessary from you,' he'd told the guy as he questioned his own sanity. He hadn't made anything for so long, he wasn't sure he was even capable any more. 'If you're not happy with it, I'm sure I'll sell it on the stall,' he'd finished, doing his best to sound as though this stall was a regular thing for him and that this commission was no big deal. It also gave him a bit of a safety net because if he couldn't pull this off, the man wouldn't lose out by paying for something which a kid in a woodwork class could've made.

After the man left, Nate began to feel his passion bubbling up inside of him, not to boiling point, but a gentle simmer. He'd made a chessboard years ago for Gus, who ran the local bed and breakfast, and according to Trevor it was still going strong, used by guests as well as the owners. Nate remembered then that he'd used instructions online and so when he had a quiet moment at the stall, he'd used his phone to search for a reminder of how he might have tackled it. He found what he was looking for and began to wonder if doing the chessboard was something he'd leapt on because it would make him have to try. He *had* to make something, he *had* to give it a go.

It was one thing stepping into the workshop for the first time in forever and his dad assuring him it was time to let go of the guilt, but it was something else to actually be in there for a length of time, using his hands to craft something new and remember how his mum had loved to see him work and what he could create. It was something special they'd always shared, at times making him feel like a little boy all over again wanting a parent's approval, and he wondered how he'd deal with the emotions that were sure to return every time he went into the workshop. But now he'd made a promise to someone, a commitment, and he knew he had to see it through.

Making the chessboard also came with the added bonus that it kept him busy so he could let Trevor live his life rather than going on about the long-term and what might happen. His dad was happy doing it that way, so perhaps Nate needed to get his head around doing the same. Nate still remembered talking to his mum about getting her some better help when she started to worsen. What he'd meant when he made the suggestion was that they could see whether someone could come to the house to help out – he had his job, his dad was finding it all a lot to cope with. Nate had thought even someone to come in and clean or cook meals might go some way to helping. But he hadn't had a chance to explain any of that because his mum had dissolved into floods of tears, thinking he wanted to put her in a home and forget about her. And that really wasn't the case. He wanted her at the house he'd grown up in and that she'd been happy in for years, he'd never once wanted anything else, but she'd shut the subject down and he'd tried for a while to address it with his dad but Trevor only claimed that he loved his wife, it was his job to look after her and they didn't want any strangers in their home. And so that had been that.

Nate was reminded of the talk with his mum every time he tried to talk to his dad because he didn't want to get it wrong. He hated the thought that his own hang-ups and worries might push Trevor away; he wanted his dad to be more of a part of his life, not less. They'd talked the whole time Nate worked last night, fixing those cupboards in the utility room and then replacing the shower unit with the new one they'd ordered. The simplicity of the tasks and conversation had made Nate appreciate his dad's company all the more. And it had reassured Nate that actually his dad was still sprightly enough, he had a lot of friends and social engagements, he had a life here.

At the timber merchants, Nate collected supplies of wood, nails, varnish for this latest project and in his head as he walked up and down the wide aisles had been the gentleman's face, lit up in delight at having a custom-made chessboard if Nate could pull this off.

As he drove home, his thoughts switched to Morgan. Sharing the market stall had been unexpected and although she still had an aura of sadness he'd sometimes caught in her expression when she was miles away at the stall or when someone mentioned her mother in passing, she'd been good company and easy to talk to. It pained him when he thought about how her face had paled, how her big, brown eyes lost all their vibrancy when he told her what he'd done with the cushion. She'd said the prices were beneath the items and when he'd seen the tag under the cushion, he'd thought he was doing the right thing by proceeding with the sale. But apparently not. The tag must have belonged to a different item and he hadn't realised. He'd apologised to her profusely when she came back to the stall but she'd kept her head in the game for the rest of the session and although she chatted with customers and other stallholders, the friendly banter between them was swapped for politeness and stilted conversation until the day's trading came to a close.

Home from the timber merchants, Nate had a mug of tea with his dad and then opened up his workshop. Branston trotted past his legs and over to the basket Nate had brought here from home – one of a few he had to leave in various places to make it easier on him and the dog.

It was a lovely day with a fresh breeze: perfect working weather. He opened up the blind that covered the rear window and despite it being summer, he switched on the lights to illuminate the bench,

ready for him to work. As he stood at the workbench ready to
make a start, he looked around him and rather than fearing what
was inside here, the way he had ever since he moved away to
Wales, he felt a sense of calm wash over him. What was the worst
that could happen? He'd make a rubbish board and the man at the
markets would take one look and walk away? It wouldn't be the
end of the world. He thought about the time he'd tried to make a
tray and the plans he'd gone through again and again until his
mum urged him to make a start. *So you do it wrong*, she'd said. *So
what?* She'd given him permission to fail, not a word he liked to
associate himself with these days, but that was what any craft was
about: experimenting, feeling your way, taking a chance that you
could start with raw materials, whatever they might be, and turn
them into something beautiful.

'Right, Branston, you're gonna have to shift.' Unfortunately
Nate had put the dog's basket in front of the metal cupboard he
needed to get to now.

When the dog moved, he dragged the basket out of the way
before opening up the cupboard and pulling out some leftover
rosewood. A naturally pale straw colour, he recognised it as what
he'd used to make a side table which had been the first item he
sold at the markets. Making the table had marked his elevation
from hobbyist to craftsman, he supposed. It wasn't a bad way of
looking at things when, up until recently, he hadn't caught sight of
any of his handiwork, let alone come in here or shared it with
other people.

He glanced over at the covered item, the only one left beneath
a sheet. He didn't need to peel the material off to know exactly
what it looked like – made from rosewood also, it was a blanket
box for his mum. He'd been making it as a surprise. And he'd
never got to give it to her. He felt his anxiety rise but tried to
remember the way his dad had looked at him when they were in

here, the softness in his voice as he told his son he needed to let go of the guilt.

Nate crouched down to give Branston another fuss. He deserved it; he was a good dog and a loyal companion. And here he was at his side again, pretty content in his position, with a shaft of sunlight coming in through the open door and giving him an extra lick of warmth.

Nate lined up all the wood he needed on one of the work-benches and ran his hand along the good-quality, ebonised wood he'd bought at the timber merchants. It would be perfect for the darker squares of the chessboard and he'd also be able to use it for the border. He moved over to the second workbench, aligned end to end with the other in the centre, allowing plenty of space on both sides for manoeuvre, and switched on the power to the saw. He picked up the first strip of wood and felt a flutter of nerves, anticipation that unsettled him for a moment because it wasn't like he was scared of using a saw, or cutting wood the wrong way – if he did that, he'd start again, no problem, and the wood would be repurposed. He'd learnt that in the past, several times over. Maybe it wasn't so much a flutter of nerves but a sign of excitement at doing what he loved again.

Slowly, Nate got into a rhythm. With each piece of wood flat on the workbench before he cut it, he passed each one through the saw fixed on top to cut it into narrower lengths. Each time one was complete, he piled it onto the other workbench. The sound of the saw cutting the wood took him back in time as did using the miter saw to cut each length into pieces of approximately sixteen inches each, allowing a bit of leeway for when they'd be fixed together and ready to cut into strips.

The way he worked had him smiling. Back in his school days, he'd have attempted this all by hand, his arm aching using a manual saw. He'd done that when he started out making things at home too and when he'd worked any place he could find – on the patio in his rental, in a shed that was freezing cold and damp, out in the sunshine when the weather had allowed. By the time he'd moved back to Oak Cottage, realising his mum's condition was progressing and she was getting worse, Nate had a good job and therefore the funds to pay for the garage-to-workshop conversion as well as adding labour-saving devices that had seen both his speed and skills improve with time and practice.

Nate laid out the sections of wood, alternating the light and dark shades. He turned each piece onto its side, spread wood glue along the edges, flipped them back over and pushed them all together. Then he clamped the boards and checked the time. They'd need a good thirty minutes to an hour to dry properly.

When Branston's ears pricked up, Nate knew someone must be coming. And sure enough, his dad was heading out this way with two mugs of tea.

'Safe to come in?' came Trevor's voice.

'Course, Dad. Branston...' he warned in the tone that the dog knew meant he needed to listen. If the dog wasn't careful, he'd trip his dad over by getting excited.

'You'll get my attention, Branston,' Trevor said as Nate took one of the mugs of tea. He swore he drank more tea in Little Woodville in a day than he did in a week when he was living alone. 'Maybe even a walk.' The word *walk* did nothing to calm Branston who sat even taller in his basket.

'Settle,' Nate instructed the dog, who reluctantly slumped back down.

With a warming mug of tea, standing side by side with his dad, it felt like a slice of years gone by being in here.

Trevor admired the wood in the vice, drying.

Nate explained, 'Some was left over; the rest I picked up.'

His dad sat on the high stool Nate had brought over from the far wall. He'd stand. He rarely sat in here at all, the stool had always been for visitors.

'You'll need some chess pieces,' Trevor said after another mouthful of tea.

At that, he laughed. 'I think that's beyond my skill level.'

'Oh, I don't know... one day, perhaps.'

They talked a bit more about the markets, what he'd sold, what he'd brought back with him.

'They're a wonderful bunch at Snowdrop Lane markets,' Trevor agreed. 'Was colourful Hildy there?'

'Bright clothes, bubbly personality?'

'That's the one.'

'She was; she watched my car and the stock for me while I unloaded.'

'That was kind of her. You know she delivered flowers every week without fail for your mother. Hildy would always stay with her for a tea and a chat too. I'm surprised she didn't say anything to you today. But then again, maybe I shouldn't be. She's not one to blow her own trumpet.'

'Don't think she needs to with those loud clothes.'

Trevor chuckled and took in the space at the edges of the work-shop which were no longer piled quite so high. 'Looks like you made a small dent in what was in here.'

'Could've done better with more stall space but it worked out all right in the end.' Apart from when he'd upset Morgan, that was. 'Jasper has added me to the website as a temporary trader so folks visiting from far and wide can see what's on offer.'

'You know, as a lad, you would've sat at the end of the driveway and done a garage sale.'

'At thirty-eight years old, I suspect I'm a bit past all that. Although I did make a bit of cash the year I sold the wooden coasters I'd made.'

'I wonder if they're still in circulation.'

'Dear God, I hope not. They were plain and boring. I think I sold ten and made a fiver at fifty pence each. Perhaps people felt sorry for me.'

'What will you do when all of this is gone?' Trevor looked around at the stock Nate still had: the small table, the wooden blocks, the key box, a couple of well-sculpted feature shelves in the corner, a tidy box.

'I haven't thought that far ahead. But I know I had to clear this place out, not fair to leave it all here.'

'You know this place is yours whenever you need, don't you?' Trevor shrugged. 'It's good you're back in here but I'd hate to see you rush out again. It's not like I need the extra storage space either; what I do like is knowing you're using it again.'

'Thanks, Dad.' When Branston got out of his basket to stretch his legs, his tummy heading all the way to the floor as he did so, Nate mouthed the word *walk* to his dad.

'I'll change my shoes.'

Nate and Trevor were soon out of the house with Branston, who had likely done his stretch as a massive hint that he'd been patient long enough.

'Let me know if I'm walking too fast, Dad,' said Nate as they made their way past the field on Snowdrop Lane where the markets had been held – nothing but green space now – and on to Snowdrop Woods.

'Don't be daft. You used to keep up with me, remember.'

'When I was about three foot tall,' Nate laughed as they reached the gate to the woods. Being reminded of childhood memories always made him feel warm inside.

Branston, off the lead, sniffed his way into the thicket off the path in the woods that in the rain would likely be impassable in this section unless you had a good pair of wellington boots.

'Do you think he'll be back?' his dad pondered.

'Maybe,' Nate joked, although they hadn't walked much further before the dog came bounding up behind them.

They tramped along a path, reminiscing about the walks they'd come on when Nate was a kid: him, his dad, his mum. 'There were a few times when your mum and I thought we'd have to send out a search party for you,' said Trevor. 'You'd take off much like Branston and we wouldn't see you for ages. It was probably only a minute or two that you were out of our sight but believe me when I say that for a parent, that time feels like forever.'

'I love these woods. I mean the garden was great, I never wanted for more outside space. But in these woods, I'd run free, discover pockets I never knew were there. I don't think I've even discovered it all yet.'

His dad reached another fork in the path. 'This way, let me show you something you might have forgotten.' He led the way down a much thinner section.

Nate had no problem with exploring. He didn't do this in Wales that often. He liked to walk, especially in the winter, all bundled up when the weather tried to make it impossible, but with work it was difficult.

A contented and fond expression appeared on Trevor's face as they reached the narrowest part of the path and found themselves stepping out from between the trees on either side to the vast expanse laid out in front of them. The land was bursting with beautiful buttercups dazzling in the sunshine. 'Your mother loved this. We'd come here every day, until she couldn't.'

Nate smiled, remembering. 'She talked about it often.' He turned and threw a stick back down the path for Branston to chase after. The last thing he wanted was for the dog to squeeze beneath the wooden post and rail fence and disturb the buttercups, their delicate heads vulnerable. 'She loved the woods and the change of season.'

'We both did. She particularly adored the snowdrops around Little Woodville, of course.'

'And the daffodils,' said Nate before his dad could.

Trevor embraced the memory. 'Didn't matter what variety, she loved flowers.'

With the buttercups in view to one side of them, they meandered along until they reached the end of the fence and the natural woodland path took them back up towards the way they'd come. Nate had got lost plenty of times in here as a kid but he'd never been scared. It had been another part of the adventure and he'd always known he'd find his way home in the end.

Branston fell into step and they decided to head into the village for a bite to eat. They had a choice of the Italian restaurant, although that was a bit fancy for a quick lunch, the pizzeria, the café or a pub lunch, but his dad insisted on going to the Bookshop Café.

'We have Branston, remember.'

'They're dog friendly,' he told Nate as they made their way there.

'Do you hear that, Branston? Dog friendly but you'll need to be on your best behaviour.'

It was nice walking through the village and the more he did it, the more Nate remembered. He could recall going to midnight mass at the church with his parents one Christmas, dipping his toes in the stream on hot summer days, having ice-cream as they'd sat together on the village green watching the world go by. The memories had always been there, of course, but it was as though they were buried deeply under everything, every year that had passed, and were only accessible gradually over time.

When they reached the Bookshop Café, Belle opened the door

to them and immediately announced their dog-friendly status when she saw Branston. 'All we ask is that people with dogs are seated on the farthest side from the counter and obviously the dog and the owner need to behave.'

'I appreciate the warm welcome. And he's been in many a café with me, don't worry; he knows the score, so do I.'

'There's a bowl of water I've set down by the side entrance at the back,' she said as they led the way through. Sebastian gave them a nod as he served a customer buying a whole stack of books.

Branston was more than happy to find the water and once he'd had a drink, settled down next to their table. Belle had opened the side window so plenty of fresh air could circulate and with the summer day holding the promise of lasting sunshine, they ordered cold sandwiches and big glasses of freshly squeezed orange juice.

It wasn't long before his dad grabbed Sebastian's attention as he came past and asked him whether he had any good recommendations for a thriller that didn't have too gruesome an ending. Nate wondered whether there even was such a thing.

'I'll grab a few options for you,' said Sebastian, 'but I'll leave them at the counter, I've got to make a call and I need to do it before I get another customer.'

'Trouble?' Trevor asked.

'Leaky toilet at the cottage. And do you think I can get a plumber? They're like gold dust. I thought I'd secured one but when I said I had a second toilet, they bumped me to Monday. And I like to have the downstairs toilet operational for the next dinner gathering. Much easier than making guests traipse upstairs.'

'You could ask me.' Nate popped another piece of tuna and salad sandwich into his mouth.

Sebastian puffed out his cheeks. 'Didn't think of that. And now it looks as though I knew full well what you did for a living and I was hinting.'

'No worries. I can head home and grab my tools and go over to Snowdrop Cottage once I've eaten this, if you like.'

'Lifesaver. Thank you. Belle can mind this place. I'll find those books for you, Trevor.'

When Belle came to take their plates, she said, 'We've had a plumber under our noses all along. Might have saved an hour's worth of phoning around earlier if we'd been clever enough to work it out.'

Trevor sat back in his chair. 'I'll stay here, choose a book from whatever Sebastian selects and I'll take Branston home. He's had a good walk.'

'Cheers, Dad.' The dog was tired enough that he wouldn't mind being on his lead and he was unlikely to be too much for Trevor. Sometimes, if Branston had been cooped up for whatever reason, he could tug at the lead, be fractious until you let him run it off, but right now he looked as though he was ready for a sleep on the rug in his dad's sitting room.

Nate ducked back to the house and got in his pick-up to drive to Snowdrop Cottage because it meant he had all his tools at hand.

After a quick inspection of the downstairs toilet, he emerged into the kitchen. 'Good news is the problem is simple,' he told Sebastian. 'One of the seals has deteriorated – wear and tear, nothing more sinister than that.'

'You can fix it?'

'I've got some sanitary-grade silicone in my pick-up, so I'll use that for now while we wait for the part I'll put on order. Should keep it from leaking any more and in a couple of days, I'll come and replace the part properly.'

'Cheers, Nate.' Standing in the kitchen next to the Aga, Sebastian took out his wallet.

'No charge.'

'You can't work for free.'

'It took me seconds to see what it was, it'll take another few minutes to apply the silicone, not long to come put in the new seal.'

'Still—' But Nate's shake of the head said he wouldn't hear of it. 'Then you come to the next dinner here. I insist.'

'Dad always likes heading to your place to eat. I think he enjoys having somewhere else to be and seeing people as much as he appreciates being fed.'

'You're both welcome. So you'll come, on Sunday?'

'I'd like that.'

'I'd offer you a cup of tea but I have to get back to the Bookshop Café.' He picked up a brown paper bag from the benchtop. 'Take these instead.'

Nate peered into the bag. 'You're giving me leeks?'

'Fresh from the garden, bumper crop. You won't take my money, gotta do something.' Sebastian picked up his keys.

'I appreciate it. I'll use them for dinner tonight.'

'Must be nice for Trevor to have you around for a while.'

'It's good to be here. And it's good to see Dad doing so well and know he has so many people around him. I mean, he always told me he did, but you know what it's like; you need to see it with your own eyes.'

'He's got plenty of people in his corner, no need to worry about him.' He made a face. 'Morgan mentioned to me that you were a bit concerned.'

'I try not to be too overbearing.' Not only was he glad that Morgan was clearly looking out for Trevor; Sebastian's comment also suggested she thought of him perhaps as much as he thought about her. 'Where's Morgan's fiancé?' He had to ask the question. And at least Sebastian seemed to think it was normal for Nate to enquire, given they shared the stall.

'He took a job in Scotland. I think she plans to join him.'

Nate nodded. 'Makes sense.'

Sebastian locked the door to Snowdrop Cottage behind them before Nate climbed into his pick-up and drove the short journey back to Oak Cottage. His dad was walking down the driveway as he pulled in and Branston bounded up to Nate when he climbed out of the pick-up. It always tickled him that the dog showed his appreciation of his master every single time, no matter whether they'd been together only an hour before.

'I don't know about you, Branston,' said Trevor, 'but I want to spend the rest of the day in the lounge in my favourite chair.'

'Don't tempt him,' said Nate following his dad in through the front door. 'He'll try and climb into it with you if you're not careful.'

'He's got a basket, haven't you, boy?' From the cloth bag he'd had over his arm, Trevor took out the pile of books he'd bought and sorted through which one he'd make a start on.

'Thought you were buying *one*?' Nate grinned.

'Couldn't help myself. I'm glad they opened the Bookshop Café; it's much nicer than ordering online. Browsing is one of the best parts of choosing a new book and Sebastian's recommendations are even better.'

'You settle down and enjoy a read for a bit. I'll deal with dinner.'

'Call me if you need help.' Trevor headed for the lounge without argument, Branston obediently following at his heels, while Nate went to make a start on the beef stew. And now they'd have fresh leeks on the side courtesy of Sebastian; he'd do those in some butter and show them off, given they were homegrown.

Once the stew was in the oven, Nate took his dad a cup of tea. He found Trevor sitting in the tatty chair that looked ten years older than the rest of the furniture, engrossed in his choice of book, Branston curled up in the basket right at his feet. Both of them perfectly content.

Back in the kitchen, Nate checked the temperature on the oven was low enough and headed for the workshop to carry on with the chessboard. The glue was dry on the different shaded wood pieces and he found a low-grit sander sheet from one of the drawers beneath the workbench and fixed it onto the electric sander, another power tool he'd added to his collection over time. The electric sander easily coped with the task of smoothing over the newly adjoined wood until it was flat and even. Once that was done, he used a gauge on the table to cut off the rough edges of the board, the leeway he'd allowed previously. He used the same gauge and a stop so that he could crosscut the board into strips and after he laid out each strip, he flipped every other one so that the overall pattern became that of a chessboard. Once the pieces were glued and clamped again, he went back inside the cottage. Trevor hadn't moved and Branston had only shifted so that he was sitting on Trevor's feet.

As Nate peeled some potatoes, his dad came through to the kitchen, brandishing a magazine. 'I forgot to give this to you – picked it up in the village.' He set the magazine down on the kitchen table and as he returned to the lounge, Branston, who'd trotted in here after him, followed. Traitor.

Nate picked up the magazine. It was a woodworking one, the same magazine as he'd had for years when he lived here but not picked up since. Flipping through the pages, he saw some items could only ever be attempted in his wildest dreams. There was a feature on a course for beginners to get them started making things out of wood, other plans for simpler items he knew he could do without need for much more than a sketch pad and a pencil. There was a feature on decorative knife carving that had him whistle at the sight of a wooden troll on top of a fence that someone had fashioned with a blade. Some people had talent. And his dad still believed in his, the way his mum always had. It was just that she'd been around more to tell him. His dad had always been busy with everything else, and Nate felt a moment of sadness that sometimes, he hadn't realised that not only had his mum needed company and comfort; his dad might well have needed the same. He'd been living with his wife and his son, some would've assumed that of course he wasn't lonely, far from it. Sometimes, it was as though the daily routine had threatened to swallow Trevor whole and Nate knew it must've been hard for his dad to have any normality outside of that, any escape. But he seemed to have found it now with the folks in Little Woodville and it was good to see.

While they waited for dinner, Nate got back to his own project and wondered whether it would pass the rigorous standards of the magazine's editors. He inspected the chessboard. This was what he had always loved the most – the ability to see a creation he'd envisaged in his mind long before his hands and his tools came together to do the work and then what it looked like at various stages. He cut a piece of plywood to the size of his chessboard and fixed the board onto it using glue. He flipped it up, secured the pieces with clamps and, using his nail gun, put brad nails at intervals around the board to hold it all together. He wondered what the man who'd made the request would think of the finished product.

He rummaged through some of the wood he had stored in cupboards, mostly offcuts but some of decent size and length, and he searched on the shelves on the walls to see what else might be of use. When he was in the kitchen before, he'd noticed the herbs his dad was trying to grow on the windowsill. Currently in plastic pots that did the job, they'd look better lined up in a planter box, and so that's what he would make. It was the perfect gift for the upcoming Father's Day. And so in between finishing the chessboard – cutting edges, fixing them onto the board, rounding the wood, smoothing and clamping – he got started on the planter box which he'd make out of a grainy wood to go with the traditional kitchen, finished in oak.

Every now and then, Nate glanced over at the sheet that covered the unfinished blanket box. A gift he'd never got to give to his mum. He knew he had to peel the sheet away eventually, but would he ever be able to finish the piece? And what would he do with it if he did?

10

The following Saturday, Morgan was at the Little Woodville markets before Nate and she was glad to have time to shunt back and forth to get things from the car before she'd have to face him. She'd embarrassed herself last week and she knew it. Since then, she hadn't bumped into him in the village and for that she was thankful. She'd seen him in the street one day with Trevor and Branston, but she'd ducked into the bakery and ended up buying another loaf of bread she didn't actually need as Betty leapt straight in to serve her. The last thing she was going to admit was that she was hiding from someone.

Morgan got all her boxes to her stall with Hildy's help this time. Morgan swore nobody ever got to these markets before Hildy did, nor did they ever look as bright and bubbly as the florist stall operator's bright-pink, woolly jumper over inky leggings and brown boots with fur bursting from the tops. Pedro watched her stall and everything on it while she ran to get a herbal tea, as well as a bottle of water, plus a large tea for him. The warmer days were upon them and she'd been caught out enough times not having enough fluids at her disposal. She didn't intend to let that happen again.

She'd put on a loose-weave cardigan over a plain t-shirt and jeans but took it off, despite it not even being mid-morning. This was one of those summer days where you really didn't need another layer.

Moments after she relieved Pedro and he went back to his own stall, Nate arrived with a brief nod and a hello.

'Good morning, Nate. Lovely day.' She opted to go with ignoring the events of last week. It seemed the easiest thing to do, rather than talk about the grief that sneaked up on her and took her by surprise when she least expected.

The same thing had happened to Morgan a few times since Elaina's death. She'd been caught out in the street, at the convenience store and even at the bakery the day she saw the French twist on display in the window. It had reminded her of her mum recalling the stage she and Tegan went through when they were learning French at school and were obsessed with practising at home in case they should want to go to Paris one day and see Notre Dame and the Eiffel Tower. The girls had wanted French plaits in their hair and Elaina had done her best, but it was time consuming and a lot when you had to do it for two girls day in, day out. In the end, she'd told her daughters that it would be better if they learnt to do them on each other. The novelty had soon worn off. But remembering the conversation, the way Elaina had told the story of her two little girls demanding fancy hairstyles when they had to get to school on time, came hurtling back to Morgan the day she saw the French twist resting in its basket in the window of the bakery. And she'd reacted much the same way as she had at the markets last week when the cushion had suddenly gone.

Morgan watched Nate set down the first two boxes he'd brought over in one go with smaller items inside, presumably. He had big hands, the sort you expected were used to manual labour, and she tried to imagine his fingers crafting, using a firm touch when it was needed, lighter when the task called for it. 'I'll watch everything while you go back and forth,' she suggested.

'Appreciate it,' he said to her without fixing his gaze on her for more than a few seconds before he was off again. It seemed he wasn't going with the *nothing happened* approach, which made her wonder whether he was worried he'd break her if he upset her again.

Nate had soon gone to and fro to his half of the stall and although he wasn't yet sorted out, he was at least in situ.

'Nate...' She paused when Madeleine, who had a stall with baked goods and locally renowned crumble squares, stopped by with bottles of water from Jasper and a reminder to stay hydrated.

'Don't tell me...' smiled Morgan, glad to have extras, 'he said, and I quote, "I don't want anyone passing out on my watch".'

'Got it in one.' Madeleine's laughter ricocheted off the stalls around them. She wasn't known for being particularly quiet. 'You're doing well.'

Morgan was puzzled. 'I haven't started trading yet.'

'I mean to be here, at your mother's stall, now she's gone.'

'Oh... well, you know, it's what she would've wanted.'

What followed was a recollection of the funeral, the wake afterwards, a memory or two of Elaina until Nate interrupted her full flow, asking Morgan to help him shift a coffee table. Madeleine moved away to deliver water to the rest of the stalls.

Morgan took one end of the table but lifted it up before he even gave her the count. 'It's not exactly heavy. Where are your muscles?' She blushed when she realised they were on display, with the t-shirt sleeves hugging them quite nicely.

'Thought you could use rescuing,' he said without looking at her for longer than was necessary; either he was awkward or was sparing her feeling of unease.

'Oh... you mean from Madeleine.'

He was writing on a bright orange star shape with black marker pen to dictate the price, which he put beneath a set of three wooden photo frames already lined up on his table. 'It did my head in, all the condolences over and over again after my mum died. I never handled it as well as you did just then. I left the village; that's how I coped in the aftermath.'

She was shocked at his sensitivity and insight, as well as him sharing something so personal. 'Well, I suppose I'd already upped and left the village, so I didn't want to be too predictable.'

'She looked like she was in for the long haul.' He tilted his head in the direction Madeleine had disappeared.

'She would've stayed for a good twenty minutes more, I reckon. She wasn't here last week; I should've expected it.' He caught her gaze then. 'Mostly I'm fine to talk about Mum but sometimes... well, sometimes it catches me off-guard.'

'What was it you were going to say to me before she came over?'

'It was about the cushion...'

'I was afraid of that,' he smiled kindly. 'I'm really sorry I sold it. I honestly had no idea the cushion had sentimental value. I thought it was for sale and so I went ahead when a customer showed an interest.'

'I can't believe they paid a fiver for it.' She waited until he looked up from the coffee table he'd moved on his own with ease to the top of the table at the back where he could point it out to customers who might be looking for a bigger item. 'It was awful,' she said.

'Wait, you didn't even like it?'

'No! It was dreadful... can you believe I made it?' When he pulled a face, she added, 'When I was at school. Mum insisted she keep it, but I'd have far rather she'd thrown it out.'

'It was her job to make you feel good about it. She was being a good mum.'

'Yeah, she really was.' She paused. 'When I saw it was gone, it just threw me, and I'm sorry I reacted that way, made you feel so terrible.'

'Don't be; I get it.' The way he was looking at her, she knew he really did. And unless you'd been through a similar loss yourself, it was hard to understand how well-meaning remarks or actions could absolutely floor you.

'If Mum had been here last week when you made the sale, she'd have thrown her arms around you and congratulated you on being salesman of the year. Because much as she said she didn't want to part with it, she knew it was old and well past its use-by date.'

'It sounds like I missed out on meeting her.'

Morgan simply smiled and soon enough, trading got underway with a steady flow of customers throughout the morning. When there was a lull, Morgan grabbed both of them a cup of tea and settled in her chair to read the book about Scotland. She'd brought it with her for the quiet moments, so she could honestly tell Ronan that yes, she was reading it, enjoying it and more importantly, learning all about the place they'd agreed to make their future. But she'd no sooner opened it than a customer appeared and she was up again. *Always the way*, her mother would've said, not minding one bit.

When she'd finished serving, Nate had just said goodbye to a customer who, between him and his wife, took the coffee table. Morgan looked across at him. 'Everything all right?' He was frowning.

He told her about the chessboard he'd made for the gentleman who came to the markets last week. 'He's not going to show, is he?'

'You made a chessboard, as in from scratch? I knew you made things, but I thought that was past tense.'

'I thought so too. But I'm back in the workshop.' He sounded proud of it too.

'So where is it?' She looked around the stall, but there was nothing that looked remotely like it could be used in a game of chess.

'I couldn't lay it out in case it was snapped up.'

'Good point. But show me, please.'

'You really want to see it?'

'Of course.' She pointed to the black bin liner lurking beneath the table at the back on his side. 'Is it in there?'

He nodded.

'Be careful, Jasper could take it away as rubbish; he likes a clean market place, has high standards.'

'I'll try to remember that.'

'May I?' she asked before taking out the beautifully crafted piece that had last been touched and formed by Nate with the same attention and care that obviously came naturally to him. 'You're really talented. What will you do if the guy doesn't come back for it?'

'Put it on the stall next week, I guess.'

Morgan sensed if the man didn't turn up, he might be a bit more peeved than he was letting on. 'Well, if he doesn't show, it's his loss.'

They took turns to man the stall while the other grabbed lunch, eating on the move as so often happened when you were a market trader, and Morgan snatched some time to read her book when she could.

'I hear you're heading up to Scotland.' Nate nodded to the book in her hands after he thanked a customer who had only browsed rather than bought anything.

'Ronan, my fiancé, is already there. Working.'

'It's an exciting step for you.'

'Yeah.' Although the longing for a new adventure and enthusiasm for their long thought-out plan had dampened down over the months she'd been here. She'd been hoping the book and its content would reignite the flame of excitement.

'So you're leaving Little Woodville again. Off to see the big wide world.'

She closed the book. 'I never thought I'd settle here; it was never a factor, never in the mix. At least, not until I came back. I don't remember it being hard to leave the first time.'

'It's hard now?'

'Harder, yes.' She was reluctant to say any more. 'What about you, how did you end up working in Wales?'

'When Mum died, I was keen to get away from everything: the memories, the familiarity. A job opportunity came up in Wales and I just went for it. I felt bad leaving Dad, but I think he was better when I wasn't here moping around. He kind of found his feet.'

'He's pretty self-sufficient.'

'I'm beginning to see that for myself,' he smiled, leaning against the table at the very back. 'After Mum died, I didn't just head to Wales; I ran, couldn't go quick enough.'

'I understand the need to leave.'

'I suppose some people run and others immerse themselves in the familiar when they come up against a wall of crap.'

She burst out laughing. 'Wall of crap? I like the description.'

'I'm better with wood than with words.'

She looked at the beautifully hand-crafted pieces. 'I can see that.'

'Do you know what I mean, though? Some people feel safer with the familiar. I didn't. I needed something different, something else.'

'And you're settled in Wales?'

'I have a lot of work, a good client base.'

'That wasn't what I asked.'

He quirked an eyebrow. 'Hey, this talk started about you and Scotland. How is it that we're talking about me?'

'A skill I've got: flipping the attention away from me.'

'I need to take some lessons from you.'

She looked back at him. Was he flirting? Was she?

'When's the big move?'

'I'm not sure.'

'Tell me to mind my own business, but...' He eyed the paperback on her seat, closed with a leather bookmark inserted at the last place she'd reached. 'Every time I looked over, it was as though you were reading a boring essay rather than an exciting promise of your future.'

He'd been watching her?

'It's just the thought of all the practicalities,' she fibbed, deflecting his spot-on observation that her interest wasn't quite where it should be.

But he wasn't buying it. 'No different to moving over here, really. Are you selling Forget-Me-Not Cottage?'

She leaned out of the stall, pretending to look around for any customers lurking nearby.

'What are you doing?'

'I'm looking for Madeleine. I'm sure her questions and anecdotes weren't as bad as this.'

He rubbed a hand across the back of his neck. 'I apologise. I'll keep quiet.'

'No need, I'm kidding. But Scotland feels a bit of a way off yet. There's a lot to do here with clearing out Mum's things and getting the cottage valued.' And the problem was, she didn't merely need time for the practicalities; she needed time to think, to make a firm decision about whether she even wanted to say goodbye to Little Woodville for good.

'But Scotland is the dream?'

'It has been for a while,' she said.

'But...' He focused on her now his customer had moved away. 'Come on, I can tell there's more.'

'It sounds silly.'

'Try me. It might not if you say it out loud.'

She hesitated, but not for long. Something about Nate, perhaps that he didn't know her all that well, made her want to share. 'I feel guilty. If I'd moved to Scotland when I planned, if I hadn't come here to be with Mum, it might have been different, but now I feel guilty for getting excited about a new start away from here, as though I don't value the things Mum loved, what she wanted.'

'Grief and death bring out different emotions and reactions in each of us. You need to feel your own way. Give it time and don't be too hard on yourself.'

His understanding was unexpected and yet at the same time, she could hardly imagine him saying anything different.

'Did you and your mum get on well?' he asked.

'Not when I was a teenager, when I had that anger and resentment it's easy to harbour. Mum played her part, but she was a single parent; she had it tough. We kind of lost our way but since I'd come back to the village, we'd begun to get on really well. We had a laugh, she was good company.'

'Time to treasure, right?'

'It really was.'

'This may seem an odd – or even insensitive – question, but was there any part of you that was tempted to go to Scotland and carry on with your plans rather than coming back here?'

She shook her head. 'I didn't see it as a choice when Mum called me. My sister has a family, works on a farm; it couldn't be her. And Mum had nobody else. I don't think I could've lived with myself if I'd turned my back.'

'I felt the same way with my mum. She didn't ask me to come home, neither did Dad, but I could see they needed the extra help as her Parkinson's progressed.'

'And I'll bet you were glad you did it.'

He smiled at her, holding her gaze for longer than she'd anticipated, his eyes darting between her eyes and her lips.

She wanted to tell him the rest. 'I feel guilty in a different way.' And now she couldn't look at him when she said, 'I feel bad because I'm relieved.'

'Relieved you don't have to be there for your mum any more?'

She swiped a tear from her cheek. It had arrived unbidden.

He pulled a tissue from his pocket and handed it to her. 'It's clean,' he said as though she didn't already know that.

At least that made her smile. 'Sorry, I don't know where that came from.'

'Don't apologise.' He looked around to make sure they were alone and then quietly told her, 'I know what it's like to feel guilty for many reasons, not least of all the relief I felt too.'

'When your mum died?' They were side by side now, sitting on the table at the back, their forearms touching every now and then. And she knew it wasn't the breeze that made her shiver.

'Watching Mum suffer and deteriorate was the worst thing I've ever had to do in my life.' He clasped his hands together on top of his thighs. 'When she died, I felt glad it was over for her, but I know that I was relieved for me and for Dad too. It's impossible to imagine until you're in that situation but seeing someone you love and who has been there your whole life suffer is often worse than when they die.'

She turned and looked at him, taking in his open admission. And she was still staring when a man cleared his throat at the front of the stall and broke the moment. And when Morgan saw Nate stand a little taller as if on alert before he turned to pull out the chessboard from the bag at the back, she felt a little thrill. This was the moment he got to show what he'd created and see his customer's reaction. And it was a wonderful one; the man was delighted.

As the man walked away after money was exchanged for the beautifully crafted chessboard, Nate and Morgan stood side by side and only when he was out of sight did they turn to face one another, beaming.

'One satisfied customer,' Nate concluded.

'I'll say.' She'd heard the man praising the workmanship, the finish, how much pleasure he'd get to give the board as a gift.

Hands in the back pockets of his jeans, Nate looked down at the ground before his gaze came up to meet hers again. 'Morgan, I... well, I was wondering, are you going to the dinner gathering at Snowdrop Cottage tomorrow?'

'Yes, you?'

Neither of them had the chance to carry on the conversation before a woman came charging over to the stall. And she didn't look happy. In fact, she looked furious. 'Are you the owner here?' She addressed Morgan, who stood at the stall beneath the vintage sign hanging above.

'I run the stall, yes.' She had her best welcoming expression in place to head off whatever confrontation was coming her way.

The woman yanked something from a carrier bag that looked as though it had done the rounds and could no longer claim to be a *bag for life*.

'I have a complaint. This cushion is ridiculous. It doesn't feel like a cushion. My sister bought it last week, it was a gift for me because gold is my favourite colour. It isn't even gold! And look, the seam at the back isn't even sewn straight. My sister didn't get a receipt but I'm telling you, it's a disgrace to sell something so inferior, something so—'

Morgan didn't hesitate. She pulled a five-pound note from the money belt strapped around her waist. 'Here, full refund, no questions asked.'

The woman seemed disappointed she didn't get to argue a bit. 'Well, I should think so too. You shouldn't sell below par items, you know.' And with that, she snatched the fiver and off she went.

And she'd only been gone a second when Morgan turned to Nate, took one look at him and they both burst out laughing.

11

Branston followed Nate into the workshop. The beauty of the long summer evenings was that when a working day ended, your time wasn't over. If you had things to do, it was always easy to carry on with the light, the energy it generated for everyone. And no matter that he was depleting stock to clear the place out; making one or two extra items wasn't going to make much difference in the grand scheme of things. He'd give them away to friends if he had to. Although, rather than feeling rushed in the way he had at the start, thinking he had to get his dad organised and maybe even on the move, he'd begun to move at a more sedate pace already and go with the flow. And that included with this place.

Branston settled in his basket. He'd been out with Trevor today while Nate was at the markets and it sounded as though they'd had a nice long walk around the outskirts of Little Woodville. Jeremy had gone with them and they'd bumped into Peter walking his dog. All three men had sat on the village green, Betty had brought each of them a bowl of fresh strawberries and cream, and they'd done their best to quell Branston's urge to chase the ball being used in a game of cricket close by.

Today, Nate was making a start on a key organiser. He'd seen one in the woodworking magazine and as it didn't take much wood or much time, it was perfect. He'd finish the item with the English chestnut wood stain he'd ordered a couple of days ago.

He started with a block of wood and once it was cut to size, he measured and drew a line about three quarters of the way up. He cut into the line to make an angled groove into which the keys could slot, avoiding the need for any additional hooks. Once it was sanded, he found the rotary tool in one of the drawers beneath the workbench and hoped it still worked. He'd kept the battery separate and luckily the tool leapt into action as though he'd never been away.

He took out a stencil from the pile he'd kept for this purpose, found the style he wanted, and in no time at all, pencilled in the lettering. With the rotary tool, he made indentations over the top of the pencil marks. He made them even deeper in the wood and smoothed out each of the edges and what was left was all ready to varnish. Feeling pretty pleased with himself, he plucked the bottle of stain from the shelf and coated the key organiser before he headed inside. His dad had insisted he cook, freeing up Nate's time for the workshop, and so tonight, it was Spanish omelette. Nate was only glad his dad really had moved on from tins of cold sweetcorn and tuna with a bit of bread slapped on the side.

He heard a crash as he was almost at the back door and broke into a run. 'Dad!' The frying pan was on the kitchen floor, its contents spattered everywhere.

Trevor had already stepped over the debris and to the sink, where he switched the cold tap on and put his hand and wrist beneath.

'What happened?' Nate was at his side.

'Now don't fuss. I dropped the pan, that's all.'

'Keep it under there,' Nate instructed. Branston had followed him, but give the dog his due, he was hanging back before helping himself to what was on the floor.

'I'm not stupid,' Trevor muttered and Nate turned his attention to rescuing the pan and cleaning up the mess. The last thing he wanted was for his dad to slip on it, making the injuries worse.

'Branston,' Nate said in the voice that Branston knew meant to go for it now he'd made sure there was nothing other than food-stuff on the tiles. The dog cleaned the floor in no time at all.

When Nate had made sure his dad had held his hand and wrist under the water for long enough, he urged him to let him take a look. 'It's a big burn.'

'I knocked the frying pan and then reached out to catch it with my other hand.'

Nate winced. 'I'm going to run you to the hospital.'

'Don't be ridiculous. It's a minor injury; they'll laugh me out of the place.'

'I'd rather take you to be sure. The last thing we want is for it to get infected. Come on.'

The hospital wasn't that far away and although his dad bemoaned the fact they were going at all, it wasn't much of a wait and Nate was reassured by the outcome – it was classed as minor. The nurse had assessed Trevor, asked him what happened, and applied a dressing suitable for burns.

'A lot of fuss over nothing,' Trevor told Branston when they came back through the front door less than a couple of hours later.

'It wasn't nothing, Dad. And having that dressing will stop it rubbing on the bedclothes tonight; it'll stop it hurting if it touches anything.'

'I suppose he's right, Branston, much as I hate to say it.'

'Remember, no getting it wet for forty-eight hours.' Nate took over in the kitchen while his dad sat at the table, and the first thing he did was to make Trevor a cup of tea.

He checked the fridge and there were still plenty of eggs, so with a washed pan, he cracked the eggs and tried to put what had happened into perspective. It was a minor injury, an accident Nate might have easily had himself. It did not mean Trevor wasn't capable of living on his own, but it had made Nate start to think again about what it would be like if they left it too long before they thought about his dad's future plans. His mum had had both him and his dad around, but Trevor was on his own now.

As the omelette sizzled in the pan, Nate was glad to see Trevor had already put all three herb pots into the planter box Nate had made on the kitchen windowsill. 'They look good, Dad.'

'Much better than the plastic pots on their own. Thanks, son.'

'You deserved the upgrade.' He'd set his Father's Day card beside the television in the lounge, so he could see it when he watched his programmes, he'd told Nate.

Nate served up the omelette, added the salad from the fridge that his dad had already made and they sat down to what was by now a very late Saturday night dinner.

Part way through his half of the big, puffy omelette, Nate broached the subject. He wanted to give his dad options, something to think about when he was ready. 'There's a bungalow up for sale near me.'

'You going to buy it?'

'I already have a place, Dad.'

'So as an investment property then? Or do it up and sell to make a profit?'

'I don't mean for me, Dad.'

Trevor didn't look up from his omelette. 'I know you don't; I'm not daft. You want me to leave here, live near you in Wales.'

'I want you to do what's right for you. It's just something to think about, that's all. But I can see the life you have here, so I'm not going to push you into anything.'

'Your mother always loved Wales.'

'She did.'

'I'm glad you're happy there, son.'

'But it's not for you?' he guessed. He chewed another mouthful. 'You won't even consider it? I'd like to have you near me.'

Trevor ate his omelette thoughtfully. 'I'm not trying to be difficult. I hear about children of elderly parents completely altering their lives to care for whoever is left—'

'Dad, no need to put it that way.'

'It might be a little crass, but it's the truth. If your mother was here, you wouldn't worry about us both as we'd have each other. Am I lonely? Sometimes. But I'd be feeling even more lonely in Wales.'

'But you'd have me. You'd have the sea, you love the sea.'

'At this stage, it's a no. I want to be here in this house surrounded by my things, my memories.'

Nate finished the last of his omelette. He may as well say everything he needed to. He was running out of time and didn't want to leave Little Woodville without any idea of what they'd do long-term. 'I'm worried, Dad. I stopped worrying for a while because I can see how many friends you have here. But the burn today scared me. I know it could've happened to anyone, but it didn't; it happened to you. My dad. And if I wasn't here...'

'Then I'd have done exactly what I did: put it under the cold tap and probably called you to have you nag me to get a taxi to the hospital. And you'd have made sure I went too. You would've called the nurses, charmed your way into getting information.'

'I'm not that bad. And my charm hardly worked on that nurse who seemed to think I'd been pushing you around. The way she talked to you, checking your answers added up, not wanting to really look at me.'

'Well, whatever she was up to, you're not mistreating me and I'm managing fine.'

'Dad—'

'Nate, I know you want to plan for the future, know what's what, but for now, let's keep things as they are. Would that be all right with you?'

'Of course.' He hesitated. 'But I should confess, I've made enquiries.'

'Enquiries?' He put his cutlery together and let Nate take the plates away and over to the sink.

Nate turned around and rested against the sink, arms crossed as he looked at his dad. 'I've been looking into options for warden-assisted places, somewhere you'd have other people, help in an emergency.' He leapt in with, 'They're only enquiries, Dad. And I made them before I came here and realised you're doing so well.' He'd made enquiries around here and back in Wales, but nothing had come of anything; most had wait lists which is likely what made Nate panic that bit more. What if they needed something quickly and couldn't get a foot in the door anywhere?

'You jumped the gun a bit.'

'I know. I just wanted to know what options you'll have.'

'Put the brakes on, son.'

Nate nodded.

'Promise me,' his dad added.

Somewhat reluctantly, he assured him that he would try. 'I won't make any more calls until we need to.' Because the expression on his dad's face was enough to tell him that this man was actually worried now Nate had made his confession, worried that his son, no matter what he said, was going to try to ship him off somewhere away from everything he loved. And that wasn't Nate's intention at all. 'I'm really sorry, I've upset you.'

'I know you mean well. But you said yourself, you've seen what I have in this village.'

Nate smiled. 'I have. I was even telling Morgan the very same thing.'

Trevor raised an eyebrow. 'Morgan?'

Nate began to laugh. 'Don't get any ideas; she's engaged.'

It was Trevor's turn to be amused. 'You two looked very comfortable at the stall together. Reminded me of Sebastian and Belle working at the Bookshop Café.'

'I'm warning you, Dad, don't go getting any ideas.'

'Would I do that?' he asked innocently. 'Now, I've had a terrible shock. Why don't you fix us both a glass of Pimm's and lemonade?' He pointed to the pantry cupboard. 'There's a bottle of Pimm's at the very back, should be a couple of cans of lemonade too. And we'll take a glass outside, drink it beside the oak tree.'

'Mum's favourite spot.'

Ruth could be found on many a summer's evening sipping Pimm's and lemonade in a deck chair beneath the shade of the tree and it felt fitting to go and do the same in the place where his mother's ashes were scattered.

Nate needed this reminder tonight. The reminder not to try to be there for every eventuality, to enjoy the moment, reflect on the past and embrace life as it was right now.

He owed his dad that much.

Later on when he was content that his dad was fine in his favourite chair watching *Mastermind*, Nate took Branston for a walk. He was surprised to see Morgan coming out of the bakery as he passed by on the familiar route.

'They're open late.' He gave Betty a wave as she turned the sign on the other side of the glass door from *Open* to *Closed*.

'Keep walking,' Morgan said through her teeth as she waved at

Betty too. 'She's watching us.' Morgan had a paper bag tucked under her arm.

Nate turned to see the owner of the bakery was indeed watching them walk away. 'She's obviously keen for some local gossip. Maybe I should kiss you now, give her something to talk about.' He'd meant it as a joke, but as soon as he'd said it, he realised he meant it and perhaps Morgan even knew that. He tried to keep that rock of an engagement ring firmly in his mind to act as a reminder she was taken.

When they reached the village green, neither of them addressing the kiss comment, Nate picked up a stick from the ground and threw it for Branston.

'What did you do to your hand?' Morgan asked.

He turned his hand over and, sure enough, along the edge was a nice brown streak. 'Didn't notice that. I stained a key organiser I made but didn't think to check my hands afterwards. I ended up at the hospital with Dad.'

'What happened?'

He hadn't meant to sound so dramatic. 'He's fine, sorry, should've led with that.' He detailed what had gone on. 'It's minor, should fully heal in a week or so.'

'Thank goodness. I remember every time Mum hurt herself, it didn't matter whether it was minor or not; it was another reminder of why I was there with her.' She looked over the village green and up to Forget-Me-Not Cottage. 'Didn't matter either that minor accidents could happen to any of us at any age.' When she looked back at him, she asked, 'So no plans to haul him back to Wales yet then?' This time, she bent down to pick up the stick, ready to throw it for Branston and despite the loaf tucked safely beneath one arm, even managed to give the dog a stroke along his glossy brown coat before she did so.

'Dad doesn't want that.'

And more importantly, he was beginning to realise that perhaps it was going to have to be him who made a move. Already, he'd been wondering whether he should get his place in Wales valued so he'd know what his options were.

But was there anything left for him here other than his dad?

'I'm glad,' she said and before he could question *glad about what?* she added, 'that Trevor is hanging around.'

'You might be off soon yourself.'

'Good point. But...' She broke off.

'Were you going to say you'd be back to visit?'

She threw the stick again when Branston brought it to her. 'I was. I suppose because the village has always been here, Mum was always here, so letting go completely is bound to feel odd. It's a place I've come to know better. But if I'm miles away and Mum is no longer around, it's unlikely...'

He let the quiet embrace them both as Branston refused to stop with the game and dropped the stick at their feet once more. They were standing close enough that either of them were an option to participate.

Nate picked up the stick and did the honours this time. 'If Dad wasn't around, I'm not sure I'd get back here, but I suppose Little Woodville has always been there in the background for me too. It's always been available. It's only when there's the possibility that something might not be that we really start to think about it.'

'I guess you're right.'

'Would your sister ever head back this way?'

She shook her head. 'Tegan and Henry took over his family's pig farm and while it's hard work and stressful, I know Tegan loves it. It's not a massive farm – about fourteen acres.'

He whistled. 'Big enough.'

'It sounds it but apparently that's classed as a smallholding. I can't remember how many pigs they have and I don't like to think about what happens to Wilbur and his mates and how they make their living, so I don't ask too many questions.'

Nate laughed because he could imagine she wouldn't like it if she knew.

'They have fresh fruit and vegetables, more than I realised until she talked about it recently, and they open up for picking when the seasons allow. I think that was the way it worked when Henry's parents ran the show too. The kids have all that countryside and freedom. Tegan has really found her home up there.'

'Do you ever wonder whether you've found yours here?'

'Maybe,' she said, taking him by surprise. He'd expected her to answer with a quick *no*.

'Wow, so that makes Scotland...'

'Complicated.'

This time, when Branston dropped the stick at their feet, his tongue was hanging out in a way that suggested he was spent and was continuing for their benefit. 'Come on, let's walk this lady home.'

'There's no need,' Morgan told him with a laugh. 'You do know my cottage is right over there, don't you? And it's still light.' They both spotted Jeremy walking from the direction of the Rose and Thatch towards his conspicuous, ruby-red vehicle parked on the road near Morgan's place and gave him a wave.

'My dad always says to walk a lady home.' Nate rubbed Branston's head.

'You're your father's son.'

'I'll take that as a compliment,' he said as they began to make their way towards Forget-Me-Not Cottage, Branston between them.

They stopped at the top of the green. 'I can take it from here, Nate, honestly. But thank you.'

'My pleasure. Good to see—' But he said nothing more before he ran from where they were standing, out in the road in front of

Jeremy's car, which came to a grinding halt. Thank goodness. He'd been preparing himself for impact.

Marley innocently trotted from near his ankles over to Morgan on the green as though he hadn't just almost been run over.

Morgan had dropped the loaf of bread she'd bought and instead scooped the cat up in her arms. He heard her ask the cat whether he was all right. Nate didn't miss her say, 'That was close. Don't you die on me, you hear. I can't take another loss. I can't.'

A distraught Jeremy was out of the car and at Nate's side. 'I didn't see him.'

Nate put his hands on the old man's shoulders, anchoring him. 'I know you didn't, nobody would have, he just walked out, oblivious. I don't think he looked both ways.' But his joke fell flat. The man was shaken, badly.

Jeremy looked just about close to tears as he said to Morgan, 'Love, I'm so sorry, I didn't see him.'

'He's fine, Jeremy.' Her voice shook ever so slightly. 'Thank you, Nate.' He got the impression she would've burst into tears had Jeremy not been so cut up about what just happened.

'Honestly, Jeremy, look at him,' she urged as Jeremy kept apologising over and over. The cat was purring in her arms and Jeremy reached out a shaky hand to fuss the feline. It had probably been more traumatic for Jeremy than Marley.

'Come inside the cottage, Jeremy, please,' Morgan insisted. 'Let me make you a cup of tea with sugar.'

'I've just had three cups at the pub.'

'Then another won't make much difference, will it?'

Nate loved the way she shifted the attention from herself over to someone who needed it more.

'I don't want to put you to any trouble.' Jeremy could barely look Morgan in the eye.

'You're not. Now park up again and come inside. I'll throw in a few biscuits, too.'

When Jeremy went over to move his car from the middle of the road to one side, Nate checked whether Morgan really was all right.

'I am, thanks to you. But that was bloody close.'

Nate smiled at her curse. 'Very bloody close. But I don't think we can blame Jeremy's driving. Marley really did just walk out as though he was strolling across a garden rather than a road.' He hadn't meant to but as he stroked Marley, still in her arms, his hand lightly brushed her collarbone and he was sure she felt the same bolt of electricity.

'Any ideas how I can train a cat to be road savvy?' she asked, looking up at him for answers.

'Not a clue, but I'll let you know if I ever do.' He bent down, picked up the loaf and handed it to her.

She looked over to see Jeremy at the gate to Forget-Me-Not Cottage. 'I'd better go.'

'I'll see you tomorrow at Snowdrop Cottage.'

'You can come in too if you like?'

He was tempted, more than a tiny bit. 'I won't, but thanks for the offer. I'll let you calm Jeremy down; I don't think he needs too much of an audience.'

'Thanks again, Nate. For saving the day.'

'It was my pleasure.' And with Branston trotting at his heels, Nate set off for Oak Cottage.

He was glad he'd bumped into Morgan tonight. And he'd meant it earlier when he said about kissing her, even though they'd both swept the remark aside as though it had been nothing more than a joke. He was ashamed for feeling that way when she was very much attached to someone else. Then again, he felt sure she felt the same connection as he did. The way she looked at him sometimes at the markets, or at the Bookshop Café, even on the bridge that first night and again just now, told him that maybe her doubts about Scotland weren't just about moving away from the village.

He was beginning to wonder how much her doubts had to do with him.

12

After Jeremy had had a couple of sweet biscuits and enough tea that Morgan was confident he was over the shock, she made sure Marley was inside and walked him out to his car.

Back inside Forget-Me-Not Cottage, she leaned against the closed front door. Marley's little stunt tonight had been a shock but the bigger surprise was how she was feeling right now.

Had she been a fool not to see this coming?

Even at the market stall, there'd been signs – prolonged eye contact, her watching Nate for longer than she should and vice versa, shared jokes that had bonded them in ways she hadn't foreseen. And then, the way he'd jumped in front of a car to save her cat had been a true testament to his character.

Tonight, she'd realised that what she'd seen as a friendship was already so much more.

What was she doing? She had a fiancé who was miles away, who was loyal, who was waiting for her and eager to start their future together. A man she thought she loved.

Glancing at her engagement ring, she was catapulted back to the moment Ronan had got down on one knee in a fancy wine bar to ask her to be his wife. There'd been a round of applause from onlookers when she'd said yes. The night had been full of dizzying excitement it had taken days to come down from. They'd eagerly talked about what they envisaged for their wedding day – the castle venue Ronan knew of in Scotland, the guests they'd invite, a honeymoon in Vienna, perhaps. Ronan had told her he'd wear a kilt exactly like his father and his grandfather had done at their own weddings and they laughed when she said she wouldn't share any details of her dream wedding dress because it would be bad luck.

Ronan. The man who wanted her for life. And the man who knew nothing about her doubts.

This was all so unfair. She couldn't do this.

Marley trotted towards her along the hallway and weaved in and out of her ankles. She went into the kitchen and poured some water into his little bowl before making herself a hot chocolate. It might be summer, but she wasn't in the mood to sit in the garden on the bench and she knew she wouldn't be able to concentrate on reading anything. She wanted the comfort of a hot drink and she added the milk she'd warmed in the microwave to a couple of squares of dark chocolate in a mug.

Curled up in the armchair in the living room, cradling her hot chocolate, Morgan gazed out of the window. She could hear excited chatter as a lady with two children walked past. She watched a man head in the opposite direction, most likely on his way to the Rose and Thatch. And then her mind was back to Nate's suggestion earlier that he kiss her to give Betty something to talk about. It had been a joke, but the way she'd reacted inside definitely wasn't. It had been easier to focus on Branston and throwing a stick for him as they talked rather than on Nate himself. Effortlessly sexy Nate in the jeans and t-shirt he wore so well, the man who was genuine and honest and shared his feelings, a quality she found endearing.

By the time she'd finished her hot chocolate, Marley had curled up and gone to sleep on the arm of the sofa. But Morgan knew she wouldn't be able to rest. Not after tonight, not after she realised what was happening between her and Nate. She needed to speak to Ronan. And she had a feeling that as soon as she heard his voice, she'd know what to say.

It took her a change into her favourite lilac summer pyjamas, a glass of water, cleaning her teeth – all the ways she could think of to put the call off – before she finally picked up her phone and tapped to do FaceTime.

She was greeted with his usual happy grin, although he looked sweaty, as though he'd been out running.

'I've been at the gym,' he said.

'This late?'

'Got to fit it into my day somehow.'

'Work keeping you busy?' The small talk made her impatient but it was natural the way they fell into it.

'Very.'

Morgan, heart thumping in her chest, propped her phone against her knees as she sat up in bed and leaned against the headboard.

'You look worried,' Ronan noticed. 'What's wrong?'

She didn't know how to disagree with his claim. 'I'm not sure I know where to start.'

'Hang on a sec.' There was a crackling noise as he moved around and then reappeared, this time sitting beside an open window, a towel around his neck. 'Sorry, had to sort myself out and get some water. It was a long session.'

'Maybe I should call back at a better time.'

'No.' He said it so suddenly, it took her by surprise. 'You look serious, Morgan. Whatever it is, you look like you need to get it off your chest tonight.'

She wasn't sure how to respond and desperately tried to think how to begin when Ronan suddenly suggested that he did.

'You're not coming, are you?' He said it with such clarity.

She was about to launch into an explanation, reasons, anything she could grapple with but after a breath, shook her head. She hadn't known it for definite until tonight and until she saw him, heard his voice. 'No, I'm not.' She gulped. 'I'm sorry.'

He let realisation settle and when she apologised again, he told her, 'Don't be sorry.'

'But it's me who's changed our plans, not you. Aren't you angry?'

He wiped the towel across his face then dropped it down again. 'I'm disappointed rather than being angry.'

'You've been waiting so long; you've been really patient.' And she hated hurting him.

'It was getting harder to wait,' he admitted. 'I knew something between us shifted a while ago. Since I came here. Without you.'

She felt terrible. Totally to blame.

'We agreed you should go.'

'We did.' He managed a small smile from across the miles. 'I'm not blaming you and I'm not blaming myself, I think it just... happened. We both started out wanting the same but life has a way of unfolding. Things change.'

Did he think she'd changed? She had, but it felt unnecessary to dissect who had changed in what way, all the little things and the bigger decisions that had led to this moment. And that was before she even processed the way she felt about Nate. She wasn't going to share that with Ronan, it would be hurtful and unnecessary and he didn't deserve that.

What she did wonder was why he'd persisted on the Scotland

dream when he thought that something had changed. 'Why didn't you tell me how you felt? I had no idea you were thinking anything other than that our future was still in Scotland, that I'd join you eventually.'

He deliberated for a moment. 'I asked you to marry me; I couldn't give up that easily, so I suppose it was my way of fighting for you. I gave you the space you needed to stay in Little Woodville with your mum, and after she died, I wanted you to realise that this, this fresh start was your dream too. But over time, it began to dawn on me that it might not be what you want.'

'How did you know? Even I didn't know.' Her voice trailed off.

'I didn't know necessarily; it was more a feeling that crept up on me.'

She pinched the top of her nose as tears began to form.

'Don't cry, Morgan. I think it's for the best that we realise it now rather than after we're married. And in a strange way, things worked out for the best – your mum got you, you got to be with her right up until the end and that's something to treasure.' When she sniffed, he confessed, 'I almost didn't come to Scotland, even though we both agreed I should.'

'Because of me?'

'Of course because of you.' The realisation comforted her more than she'd thought it would. Because no matter that they hadn't lasted long-term; it cemented the fact that what they'd had had been strong and very real once upon a time. 'But I went not just for the job but because I knew if I was still around, you'd likely be seeing me often and it would mean you might not have that time with your mum, the way you both needed to.'

The tension she'd been holding onto at the start of the call finally give way, although she swiped at another tear that fell. 'You're a good man, Ronan.' She blew out from between her cheeks at the new horizons opening up for the both of them. 'Coming here changed me, you know.'

'I noticed.' He spoke with fondness. 'And it's a good thing.'

'I'm not so sure. I knew what I wanted before.'

He nodded, understanding. 'Just remember the media company were very interested in you before you said you were staying behind. They were disappointed when you said you couldn't make the move.'

When Morgan made the decision to return to Little Woodville, she'd emailed the company and explained what was happening in the event they were to offer her the job. She hadn't thought she'd hear anything from them but they replied and said they understood and that should she ever be in a position to make the move, she should let them know and they could arrange a further interview.

'Don't disregard it, Morgan.' Ronan could read her doubts in her silence. 'And from what I remember, they had other offices around the country, so you never know. Don't take the job change off the table completely. It's something to think about – a great opportunity for you. And if you have to come to Edinburgh for the interview, then you're always welcome to stay with me any time you need to.'

'Quit being so nice. We're ending our relationship and you're still looking out for me.'

He smiled. 'It's a hard habit to break.'

And yet she knew he'd be just fine. They both would. This was for the best.

Nate walked to Snowdrop Cottage with his dad. Although he'd passed it enough times and come here to fix the downstairs toilet, today he realised how its frontage and presence could very well be a part of a magazine. It was picture-postcard perfect, depicting the quintessential English village with its thatched roof, ivy creeping up the front walls, the white plaque on the periwinkle-blue gate displaying its name.

Nate closed the little gate positioned between boxed hedges behind them and remembered just in time to duck beneath the pointed roof of the porch that wasn't the highest when Sebastian welcomed them inside.

In seconds, Trevor became the celebrity of the moment.

'I heard you'd had a bit of a battle with a frying pan,' Sebastian started.

Trevor turned to Nate. 'Word travels fast.'

'Hey, I only told Morgan... I bumped into her last night.' He ignored the raised eyebrows he got from his dad.

'It's my fault,' Belle informed them as she came down the stairs. 'I saw Morgan this morning when I went to get some more milk, she told me. I told Sebastian. How are you?' She looked at Trevor's covered wrist, on display given he had a short-sleeved, beige, checked shirt on and it was too warm for another layer.

'I'm still in one piece,' Trevor reminded them. 'They went over the top at the hospital; it's only a burn and they did so many checks, I thought we'd never get home again.'

'A check-over is good,' said Belle. 'And it sounds as though they were being thorough, doing their job.'

'Well, I could've done without all the fuss. Although I was amused by the looks Nate kept getting.'

Nate explained, 'One nurse was definitely suspicious, as though I'd pushed Dad or done something equally untoward.'

Trevor began to chuckle.

Nate handed Sebastian the bottle of wine he'd brought. 'I wasn't sure whether this was what you did but Dad said it was fine.'

Sebastian wasn't going to argue. 'Wine is always welcome and it's great to have you both here.'

'It was nice to be invited.' Already, he could hear that they were either last to arrive or close to being the final ones. 'And something smells really good.'

'It's summer,' Belle declared. 'Sebastian has been at the barbecue today so we've got everything from sticky chicken wings and drumsticks to lamb burgers and vegetable kebabs.'

'My appetite just went up another notch,' Nate laughed as they went through to the kitchen and the gathering. The windows were flung open to the sunny day and the smell of barbecue intensified. At intervals along the table were salads, riots of colour, large platters with vegetable sticks fanned around the edges of bowls containing creamy dips.

Sebastian went outside to get the last of the meat which he was transferring to oven dishes to serve inside – Belle whispered discreetly that some preferred a sit-down meal and didn't want to attempt to eat as they went, as so often happened at a barbecue. Belle took over introductions in the kitchen or rather reminders because Nate had met everyone here at some point over the years, albeit some of them only briefly. But the prompts now were welcome; he'd hate to offend anyone.

Nate caught Morgan's eye. Did she look pleased to see him? He thought so. Unless he was imagining it to console himself that she was out of reach. As he said his hellos to people and received several compliments about what he'd been selling at the markets, he surreptitiously took in her appearance. She'd stood up to reach some of the cutlery Belle had passed over and between them, they were setting places with knives, forks and spoons. As she got to where he was, her body skimmed past his in the narrow space. She'd chosen a pair of pale jeans and a shirt in a lighter blue shade, both of which suited her in a way that had him looking for a distraction, any distraction.

Gillian came over from her place at the table to talk to him once he'd accepted a glass of wine Sebastian poured for him. She extended her hand. 'I'm Gillian, Belle's gran. It's good to see you again. Well, you might not remember me, of course.'

'I remember you well,' he assured her. 'I used to Trick or Treat at Halloween as a young lad and I remember everyone knew you as being very generous and a good stop to save until last.'

She bellowed with laughter, mischievous hazel eyes the same colour as her granddaughter Belle's. Belle was watching Gillian and clearly embracing her return to the cottage that had once been hers. It had to be weird, though, Nate thought, that the cottage now belonged to Sebastian rather than Belle, and perhaps he'd get the full story about all of that if he hung around long enough. He'd got snippets here and there already.

Gillian's lively personality was matched with a hand gesture as she clapped her palms together. 'I loved to make goodies in time for Halloween. I'd make monster eyeball cupcakes, yogurt-dipped strawberry ghosts, spider pizzas. Belle was always so proud when we handed them out to anyone who knocked on the door.'

'I really was,' Belle chimed. 'They were unique treats.'

'I'm not even going to ask what spider pizza is,' Sebastian laughed.

'Some of the kids were dubious,' Gillian admitted. 'It's such a pity now that we don't get Trick or Treaters up at the home I'm in.' She cupped a hand at the side of her mouth and whispered, 'I'm on day release.'

'Gran, you're not a prisoner,' Belle scolded good-naturedly as she brought over a big jug of iced water and set it down on the table.

'You're right, I'm not. It's a wonderful place. If it wasn't, I'd be turning up on your doorstep and moving back in, Sebastian.'

'Fine by me,' he called across as he came back inside with a big oven tray filled with something that upped the aroma in the room.

Sebastian brought in more barbecue food and transferred it into a dish from the oven. Nate looked across at his dad, his hands thrown up in the air as he demonstrated to Betty how his burn had come about, the way the pan had gone flying and its contents launched across the floor. He was holding his wrist with his other hand as though it still hurt – Nate knew it didn't unless his dad hadn't been truthful this morning. He suspected that now it was a prop in his story.

Gillian carried on the talk of Halloween. 'It sounds as though Sebastian still gets a few callers – trouble is, he's not home as much as I always was.'

'He's got a business to look after,' Nate agreed. 'And I have to say the Bookshop Café is a great addition to the village.'

'I'm thrilled for him,' said Gillian and with a twinkle in her eye, added, 'For them both.'

And as she smiled, he recalled something else about her. 'You made Mum a carrot cake once, for her birthday.'

'I did indeed.' She seemed happy that he'd conjured up such a detail. 'You're a good lad, remembering that.'

How could he forget? It had been her last birthday, she was in a bad way, and in the depths of despair when Nate had answered a knock at the door to find Gillian proffering a tin which contained his mother's favourite. She hadn't imposed, she'd let him get back to his mum, but he'd never forgotten the unexpected gesture.

'How long are you staying with us?' she asked, picking up on the sensitivity the memory had evoked for him.

'Four weeks in all.'

'Well, make the most of these dinners whenever they're on. I don't always come along but I'm pleased I saw you today.'

'I'm pleased I saw you too.'

'You can't stay longer?'

'Unfortunately not.'

'But the markets, they're going so well. Word has it you've made some beautiful items. Your mum would've been really proud to see you sharing them with everyone.'

'Gran,' Belle chided. 'Give the guy a break.' And then to him, as Gillian dismissed the remark and set off in the direction of the downstairs toilet he'd come back and fixed properly when the part arrived, she said, 'She'll talk your socks off if you're not careful.'

'Heard that,' Gillian called back.

Belle rolled her eyes. 'Still sharp as a tack.'

Sebastian and Belle between them brought the barbecue food over to the table accompanied by warnings not to touch the dishes they'd set on mats because they were piping hot.

The remaining seat at the table wasn't next to his dad but Trevor dismissed Belle's concern that he'd want to sit with Nate. 'He's old enough and ugly enough to look after himself.'

'Cheers, Dad,' Nate laughed.

He didn't miss Betty nudging Morgan and telling her in a voice that carried pretty much all around the room, 'He's the opposite of ugly. *And* he can fix a toilet.'

'Yes, and after all, that is what every woman wants in a man,' Belle said with a roll of her eyes.

The only chair left was next to Morgan and he wondered whether this had been orchestrated without either of them noticing. Whatever, he didn't mind. He could be sitting next to anyone, but her company was something he wanted more of even if it wasn't going anywhere. Although the way she looked at him suggested perhaps she hoped it was and that made him feel helpless. He couldn't make a move on another man's girl; he wouldn't. And that left them as just friends.

White wine was poured for whoever wanted it and talk soon went to the markets. Nate and Morgan recounted the story of the woman returning the tatty cushion and demanding a refund, prompting Nate to ask what she'd done with it.

'I put it in a bag of things that I'll keep.' She shrugged. 'It was special to Mum so it wouldn't feel right to get rid of it. And now I can think of that woman demanding her money back too so it's a cushion with a story.'

'A cushion with a story... I like that,' he approved.

'Thanks again, Nate. For what you did for Marley.'

'Saving him from an untimely death, you mean?' At least that made her laugh and lessened any tension between them. Perhaps it was his imagination, but she definitely wasn't as relaxed with him as she'd been on the green last night. 'Where is Jeremy, by the way?'

'I've no idea. I hope he's not still upset. He took a while to calm down after it happened.' She took the opportunity to go and ask

Belle whether Jeremy was coming and was assured that he was; he was just late.

Sure enough, less than two minutes later, Jeremy came bustling inside to the gathering, smiling and greeting everyone with a tentative wave over to Morgan as chatter continued and plates were filled with good food.

As they ate, there were plenty of compliments to the chef as always and Nate realised this was a true glimpse of the village not many would ever choose to leave. His dad was fine; he had all these people around him, they were all pretty wonderful and it had him wondering whether this could be something in his future as well as his dad's.

'Nate...' It was Morgan, offering a salad bowl in his direction.

'Sorry, miles away.' He used the tongs to add salad to his plate and passed it on.

'Is it nice to be back in the village again and come here to one of these dinners?' Morgan began to eat while she waited for her answer.

No matter how great the crowd was, he wished it was only the two of them. 'Actually, it's pretty wonderful to be back.' He might as well be honest. 'And these dinners, they're something else.'

Talk around the table turned to some of the dinners from years gone by: both those Sebastian had hosted and those Gillian had taken charge of herself. And once they'd finished eating, Sebastian urged everyone to go outside and enjoy the garden.

'It's a great space out there,' Nate complimented.

Sebastian nodded his agreement as he put the plug in the kitchen sink, turned on the taps and added washing-up liquid.

Beyond the window was a greenhouse, an impressive set of vegetable patches and plenty of lawn space. The barbecue was still out waiting to be cleaned and several deckchairs had been set out in anticipation of a relaxing afternoon in the British sunshine.

'Let me help.' Nate plucked a tea towel from its hook.

Sebastian delivered a stack of plates to the benchtop beside the sink as suds began to form in the water in the sink. 'Won't say no to that.'

There were plenty of offers to help as guests filed outside but Belle, also heading this way with a pile of dishes, claimed too many people trying to help out would be a nightmare. 'The kitchen isn't big enough if everyone stands up,' she insisted, waving everyone away, but she accepted Morgan's offer to wipe down the table.

The dishwasher was already on and Belle insisted she took over the washing up while Sebastian went out to retrieve the barbecue tools ready for cleaning.

'I'd forgotten about those,' he said before he pecked Belle on the cheek, as though leaving a room without doing so was near impossible.

Morgan came over to the sink to wet her cloth more than once as Belle washed and Nate dried and Nate didn't mind her squeezing past him to do so, nor when he had to reach down some dessert plates for her to take over to the table, ready to serve whatever treat Betty had brought along to enjoy later. If anyone could fit it in, that was.

'Do you use much of the garden produce at the Bookshop Café?' Nate asked Belle as he plucked another knife from the drainer.

'I try to use as much as I can.' She pulled a plate from the suds and slotted it into the drainer. 'Soups are dependent on season, sandwiches are versatile but even then depending on what we've grown I might add in spring onions or chives or radishes. I'm always thinking about what to do next as the seasons turn and we pick something different.'

'You've not moved in here yet, then?' He stopped, plate mid-air as he dried. 'Sorry, was that a bit forward? It's just that you and Sebastian... well, it's like you both live here.'

'I don't think we'll leave it too much longer.' She recapped how they'd met, how quickly they'd become a couple, how they wanted to enjoy one another before living together.

Nate understood. He wished he'd done the same in past relationships: taken a step back to really know what was what before he leapt in and things ended badly. And he should know better than to ask questions. The night before he'd left Wales, he'd been to the pub with a few mates, a bit of a *farewell, see you in a month* type thing. They'd tried to set him up with the barmaid, who was great, a good laugh, friendly enough, but he'd left feeling glad he was away for a while. He didn't get others' incessant need to have him paired off.

'Well, it's good to see the business thriving.' He took the next plate. Belle was handing them straight to him to make it easier.

'It certainly is. Where's Branston today? I thought you'd bring him; he was so well behaved at the café.'

'We took him for a long walk this morning in the woods; he'll be happy sleeping. It'd be too much excitement for him here, although he'd lap up the attention.'

'Well, he's always welcome. Next time, maybe.'

'Appreciate it.'

'You are, too.'

He laughed. 'Thanks for clarifying.'

'You seem to be enjoying being back.' She managed to look at him as she waited for him to finish drying the plate he had and take the last one.

'I am, more than I thought I would if I'm completely honest.' When he realised he was looking at Morgan again as she finished putting the plates and some spoons in their relevant places on the table, he finished the last piece he was drying and hung up the tea towel.

When Jeremy came inside and asked for another couple of glasses, Morgan asked, 'What's that they're all drinking out there?'

'It's Pimm's,' said Jeremy. 'How's Marley?'

'He's absolutely fine; please don't worry about him. I'll have to teach him road safety,' Morgan assured him. 'Now let's get those glasses for you.' She took them from Belle, who'd found them from the appropriate cupboard, and handed them to Jeremy, who carried them between his fingers.

'Pimm's isn't my usual tipple, but Trevor says I have to try some; it's proper British to enjoy Pimm's in the sunshine.'

'Sounds like Dad,' Nate smiled.

'I had a sneaky suspicion I'd want to enjoy myself with a glass or two of something so I left the car at home.' Trevor winked before he headed back outside.

Nate leaned close to Morgan and spoke under his breath. 'Thank God for that.'

Once they finished the clearing up, Nate and Morgan headed outside and helped themselves to Pimm's.

'I haven't felt this relaxed in a long time.' Morgan had pulled sunglasses down from the top of her head.

It was quite a gathering, helped by the sunshine, of course. Although Nate doubted the winter meals held inside lacked any atmosphere, not with this lot, anyway. 'I must admit I wasn't entirely convinced I should come.' He wouldn't tell her that his attendance had a lot to do with her presence and how increasingly difficult it was to be near her and not tell her how he felt. 'I'm glad I did, though.' As birds twittered all around them and the smell of barbecue and freshly cut grass hung in the air, he confessed, 'We've been here less than a couple of hours and it kind of feels like a big family gathering.'

'That's what Mum loved the most. It was just her, me and Tegan, no large family gatherings. Dinner was more on the practical side for us – eat and clear up and no time to linger. Mum worked a couple of jobs and was usually pretty tired by the end of the day. But she raved about these occasions; she couldn't wait to bring me to one.'

Betty had taken charge of the dessert by the looks of things because already she and Belle were going back and forth inside and emerging with plates of pavlova, the light meringue filled with strawberries and cream, and delivering them to those who wanted it.

'I said I was full up,' said Nate, his fork breaking off the first piece, 'but I wouldn't say no to this.'

Betty was adding in the explanation to everyone that dessert was now rather than waiting any longer because Gillian would need to head home soon, seeing as she was tired.

Sebastian was right behind Nate and told them both, 'She has a card game with Bruce, another of the residents. And word has it your dad was interested too.'

He'd intended it to be a secret shared but Betty overheard, the news went to Peter and before they knew it, everyone had heard.

'I'll be back for another dinner soon,' Gillian promised as she fielded complaints that she was leaving.

'Betty never disappoints,' Nate declared as he finished his pavlova and scraped the very last of the cream from the plate. 'I know I've said it before, but that woman can bake.'

'Good job!' Peter laughed. 'Given we own a bakery and all.'

Talk turned to Nate's profession until someone pointed out that while they were eating, they shouldn't be discussing toilets.

'Well, what about the markets?' Peter suggested. 'Let's talk more about those instead.'

'It's been good to see him back in the workshop.' Trevor

proudly told everyone about the chessboard Nate had made, the planter box for his windowsill. 'Get your orders in quick.'

'Don't suppose I get a say, do I?' Nate wondered.

Trevor continued to extoll the virtues of Nate's woodworking skills – he seemed to be recounting everything from teenage projects to the things Nate had made and left inside the workshop for far too long.

The crowd were impressed and Nate was embarrassed. But Morgan gave him a nudge. 'Take the compliment; you deserve it.'

When it was time for Gillian to leave, she followed Belle inside at the same time as Nate took in a big stack of dirty plates ready for washing.

He watched Gillian pick up a bag from the side of the room. 'Here, let me take that; it looks heavy.' And it was when he lifted it up.

'You're a good man. Good husband material,' Gillian trilled, earning a reprimand from Belle, who handed Nate her car keys for him to put the bag inside before dashing up the stairs to use the bathroom before she drove her gran home. Nate and Gillian had gone from the kitchen to the front door.

'I apologise,' said Gillian, 'but I have to be direct at my age. No time to pussyfoot around.'

'Seriously, what's in here?' Nate asked as Gillian pulled open the front door.

'It's the fruit cake Betty gave for me to share with everyone – as dense as it is large. There are a fair few of us. I'm hoping your dad comes along at some point.'

'I'm sure he will.'

'Especially if there's cake,' she grinned with mischief. 'But this one will likely be mostly demolished by the end of tonight. Knowing some of the others, they'll be having big slices *and* coming back for more.' She winked. 'Secretly, I'm hoping to feed them all up enough that it puts them off their card game. With any luck, there'll be a bit of money on it tonight.'

'You really like living there, don't you?'

She looked around the cottage but she didn't need to think about it. 'This was once home, still is in many ways, so I'm lucky to have both. But yes, I've found my place. I love the social side but I also love that I can come back here often. Not everyone there has the choice. I've made some good friends; you can never have too many, you know.' But then her look changed. 'You're not really asking about my welfare, are you... you're thinking about Trevor.'

He looked down at the floor like a boy scolded. 'I apologise. And I said to Dad I'd leave it for now, see how things go.'

Softly, she told him, 'It shows you care. You were always a kind boy. Too kind to be single.'

'I'll ignore that,' he laughed.

'I would. I interfere too much sometimes. But try to remember everyone is different, that's my advice. Me, I've loved it where I've ended up. This cottage was too much for me, Sebastian is the perfect owner, Belle would've been too if he hadn't bought it and she had. But some people, well, leaving their home would break them; it's something unimaginable for them.'

. 'Mum was that way.'

'I know she was. I suspect a lot of that was to do with her age, she wasn't as old as I am, but it was also a lot to do with feeling safe and secure. Some people never feel that way anywhere other than their own home.' She stepped towards him then and put a papery hand on his arm. 'Your mum wanted to stay right where she was, close to you, close to your dad. And she did.'

'Just one more thing, Gillian.'

'Anything, ask away.'

'Can we go out to the car now? I think my arms are about to break with this bag.'

And with that, she burst out laughing as Belle came to join them.

Nate waved them both off and stayed out the front of the cottage, leaning against the wall covered with ivy. The summer sunshine warmed his skin and he closed his eyes to embrace the village life he had once been a permanent part of.

'I wondered where you got to,' came a voice a few minutes later as Morgan came out of Snowdrop Cottage and closed the front door behind her.

'Just taking a minute. I think the mix of barbecue, wine, Pimm's and pavlova might have been a bit brave.'

She agreed. 'Not sure my waistline could withstand one of these every week.'

Her waistline, and the rest of her for that matter, looked pretty fine to him.

She'd leaned against the cottage next to him and when he looked, she'd closed her eyes the same way he had until he was interrupted. He hoped she'd stay that way too; it gave him a chance to take in her features – the face that if he used his fingers to draw would outline a heart, skin he wondered what it would feel to touch if he ever got close enough to kiss her. He did his best not to stare at the way her shirt caressed her collar bones and the top button threatened to come undone.

He looked away when she came to again as though she'd remembered where she was. 'Your dad thinks you came out here to coax Gillian into trying to get him a spot in the home she's in.'

Nate smiled. 'I wouldn't go that far. But I did ask her about it.' He shrugged, hands still in his pockets, one foot lifted against the wall behind him. 'I wanted to know, that's all. He knows I'm going to try to be more like he is and let things unfold. Hard, though.'

She looked across at him and smiled. 'I know. All you want is for your loved ones to be happy. It's what I wanted for Mum.'

'You were selfless to put your plans on hold.' It said a lot about her as a person. 'Not everyone would've done it.' He hadn't intended to change much about his own life until he'd come back here for an extended period and now... well, things were beginning to look a little different.

She suddenly stepped away from the wall and swished a hand across her neck. 'Is there something on me?' She lifted silky dark hair he longed to run his fingers through so he could inspect her neck. 'Please tell me there isn't. Quick, tell me.'

He moved closer, his fingers at the back of her collar. 'Nothing there. I think it was just the ivy.' But his fingers didn't move away instantly and he felt her shiver beneath his touch.

She turned and looked up at him. 'Just the ivy,' she repeated on a sigh.

He reached out and hooked her hair behind her ear on the side where the breeze was pushing it across her face. 'It might have been your hair.'

'Maybe.'

The way she was looking at him, it would be so easy to dip his head and kiss her. Do what he'd wanted to do for such a long time. 'I can't do this, Morgan.' And with a step back he moved away. 'I'm sorry.'

'No...' Flustered, she said, 'I'm sorry.' She headed for the front door.

'Morgan, I—'

'Honestly, Nate, it doesn't matter. Let's go join the others.'

And reluctantly, he did just that. He couldn't make a move on another man's girl but part of him wished he'd lowered his standards and kissed her anyway.

Because now all he could do was wonder what it would be like. And wondering felt like a form of torture.

14

Morgan flung open the windows at Forget-Me-Not Cottage. In her summer pyjamas – yellow and white daisy shorts and top this time – she stood at the window in the lounge, looking out over the village green. It was another beautiful day, the sun shining, a light breeze making the forget-me-nots in the garden flutter their morning greeting. A group of youngsters were playing frisbee already and the high street looked as though it had already recommenced Monday business following a lazy weekend, with cars parking up and people milling about.

Moving away from the open windows and the fresh breeze any house owner welcomed in the summer when their home had been closed up all night, it was time to get her head around work and away from Nate. But it wasn't easy.

After she and Ronan had talked and she'd had a long cry, Morgan had decided that for now, she'd keep the news of the break-up to herself. And so she'd said nothing at the dinner at Snowdrop Cottage and she'd kept her engagement ring on so that nobody would suspect a thing. She needed time to process, time on her own. She wanted to get her head straight before she leapt into anything.

The great thing about freelancing was that you could fit it around your own schedule. It was all too easy to put off the workload with other distractions but when she had bills to pay and a house to look after until formalities were finalised, she was good at multitasking and focusing when she needed to. With her laptop resting on her knees as she settled herself on the sofa, she began to read her research notes. She'd got enough of them now to pull together a decent article using quotes from interviewees and information she'd gathered to write an article about mood boosting and immunity. She wondered if there were any cure-alls for emotional distress, a break-up and also falling fast for someone too soon after you'd broken off your engagement. But she doubted it.

An hour into her work, the phone ringing grabbed her attention away. As predicted, it was Tegan. Nobody else called the landline. 'How's life on the farm?'

'Fine,' said Tegan, but there was a little giggle too.

'What's so funny?'

'I'm not at the farm.'

And then she heard it, a giggle not only down the phone in one ear but on the other side of her. And there was her sister, standing at the open front window. 'Well, are you going to let me in?' Tegan asked unnecessarily into the phone.

Morgan leapt up, and when she opened the front door, the sisters flung their arms around one another. Morgan savoured the moment.

They talked in such a rush that they each had to multitask – talk and listen, listen and talk, words clashing over one another until finally, with a cup of peppermint tea each, they sat at the kitchen table, sharing the Eccles cakes Tegan had picked up from the bakery before she came here. Tegan's husband had managed to get the in-laws to come in and help on the farm and with the kids to give Tegan time to come here and be with her sister, do some more of the sorting out, and have a good forty-eight hours, just the two of them.

'That's really kind of them; thank them from me,' said Morgan.

'They're wonderful and I wouldn't have suggested it. Henry did.'

'Then thank him as well.'

Tegan noticed the laptop lying idle on the sofa. 'I've interrupted your work. I'm sorry; I should've asked when the best time was.'

'No way, don't apologise. I'll take my sister visiting when she can; I know it's not easy. And I'm ahead of the game as it is.' And already she knew that her concentration today would be difficult to achieve with her head full of Nate.

'You got plenty of work on?'

'Enough. I'm writing this piece and then I've had an acceptance for a short story for a magazine. I've written it but it's at first draft stage – needs a few more rounds before I'll let anyone else take a look.'

'You're good at what you do. My sister, the writer.'

Morgan smiled. 'Remember the job I was interviewing for in Edinburgh?'

'The one you turned down because you came back here?'

'I got in touch with the company, let them know I might still be interested in the position but in a different location.'

'And...?'

'And nothing. They didn't reply.' She shrugged. 'But it was worth a try. They likely only wanted to fill a job in Edinburgh, but I thought I might as well ask. I was really looking forward to the security of a permanent position.'

'Hang on a minute, back up a second...' Tegan seemed to have caught up on what she was saying. 'Why are you talking about offices other than in Scotland?'

She took a deep breath. And then over a second Eccles cake each and a mug of tea, she told her sister everything. She told her about the way she felt about the village, how she hadn't realised how much she was becoming attached. She explained about Ronan, how he'd known something between them had changed. And then she told her about Nate, the man who'd come to the village and who she had feelings for.

'Wait, not Nate Greene?'

'Yes, why, do you remember him?'

'Of course I do! "Sexy-as-hell" was what we used to call him. My friend Cindy had the hots for him big time. I think he said hello to her once in the village and she almost passed out.'

Her sister might be laughing but Morgan could almost believe it given the way he'd made her feel standing outside Snowdrop Cottage.

'I had to end things with Ronan when I realised how I felt about Nate,' said Morgan.

'Of course.' But Tegan spotted Morgan's ring still on a very important finger. 'You're still wearing it.'

'I don't want to have to explain to anyone, not yet.'

'Does he know? Nate, I mean? Does he know you're no longer with Ronan?'

She shook her head. 'You're the only one I've told. I'm not ready. I don't want to leap from one man to the next.'

A smile spread across her face. 'I don't know, he was pretty hot from what I remember. Leaping onto him might not be a bad thing.'

'Tegan, behave yourself.' And more seriously, she added, 'He might not even feel that way. And he's leaving the village. This is just a visit.'

'Ah, don't even give that much thought. Look at you, intent on leaving and now you want to stay.' Tegan put a hand against her forehead. 'This means you want to keep the cottage rather than sell it.'

'Do you mind?'

'Mind?' She flung her arms around her sister. 'I think it's amazing. This cottage suits you as much as it suited Mum. Wait, was it my big sister talk the last time I was here that convinced you?'

Morgan shoved her sister on the arm. 'Nice try, claiming it as your handiwork. But thanks for the advice. I did need to think about it; you were right.' She looked around the room: the reminders of Elaina that were still there, memories of childhood, the promise of a future as she made it her home. 'We'll need to make it official, make sure it's all fair between us.'

'All in good time,' smiled Tegan as Marley jumped up onto Morgan's lap to join in the conversation. 'I'm thinking Marley will be staying here with you,' she laughed. 'Lucky you, Marley. Jaimie would've been a bit much as you get older. He's a ball of energy. Permanently.'

Marley seemed pretty content with the arrangement and purred as Morgan tickled him beneath his chin.

'Will you be okay financially?' Tegan asked.

'I should be. The sale of my flat helps.'

'Good, I'm glad.' She reached over to fuss Marley too.

'Right,' said Tegan, getting up from the sofa. 'We still need to sort this place out, no matter whether you're staying or not. And I'm all yours for forty-eight hours, so why don't you get back to work and I'll get on with some sorting out. How does that sound?'

'That sounds like a terrible idea,' Morgan laughed. 'Let's do it together.'

'I'd really like that. Start at the top in the loft and work our way down.'

Morgan stopped off at her bedroom to at least pull on some day clothes: a pair of shorts and a t-shirt. Tegan was happy to be the one on the ladder and everything she passed down they put on Elaina's bed, which was still covered over.

'We'll have to decide what we can bin, then what each of us might want to keep,' said Morgan.

'Agreed. How did you even fit all of your things into this house with all of Mum's stuff here already?'

'I've never hoarded much and because we intended to move; we sold off items of furniture before I got rid of the flat.' She shrugged.

'I think things worked out for the best, didn't they?'

'In a funny way, they really did.'

'Nate... Nate Greene,' her sister repeated, looking at Morgan for more gossip. Although Morgan was giving her nothing.

'Focus, Tegan.'

'Okay, I'll grill you about him later.' She sat on the other side of the box that Morgan had placed on top of the bed.

It took them an hour and a half to go through a few boxes but they filled three bin liners with items neither of them wanted and that held no sentimental value: there was a box filled with old maps, another one filled with old bedding that Morgan knew they couldn't even try to sell and wondered why her mother hadn't got rid of it, and a few boxes contained the girls' things they'd never taken with them.

'What's this one?' Morgan opened up another box they'd dumped on the bed for their attention. It looked like it was filled with old magazines and she drew one out to flip through.

'Intriguing.' Tegan brushed dust from her fingertips and peered over Morgan's shoulder. 'Recycling?'

Morgan was about to say yes when she picked up another magazine to confirm but saw a familiar title on the front. With her

heart in her mouth, she flipped to the index and then the appropriate page. And there before her was an article she'd written more
than a decade ago. She put the magazine on the bed and
rummaged through the rest. Sure enough, magazine after magazine had a feature written by Morgan Reese. There were even
pages removed from newspapers that dated back some ten years –
one about a motorcycle group who'd taken it upon themselves to
brave the snow and deliver Christmas presents to the hospital, one
on a local restaurateur who'd returned from Vienna and opened
up his own restaurant – Morgan could still remember the exquisite
food she'd had during their face-to-face interview – and another
that tugged at her heartstrings as she remembered researching it
and putting it together. It was about a foster carer who, because of
a long-term health condition, could no longer do the job she loved.
Morgan could remember feeling absolutely spent after the interview that had all but broken her heart.

It wasn't long before Tegan took the magazine from her sister's
hand and saw what had her so discombobulated. 'I remember you
telling me about this one.'

'You do?'

'Of course. It broke my heart too. That woman with all that love
to give.' She gulped. 'You never knew Mum had these?'

'I had no idea. She never really said much about my writing.
Well, apart from telling me I should get my head out of the clouds,
get a real job, train in something.'

'She was proud of you, Morgan.'

'Sometimes I doubted it. But I see now...' She gulped. 'She
really was,' she said, eyes misting over.

'You know, I think she probably encouraged you to do something with stability because of what happened to her. When Dad
left, she fought to make ends meet; she didn't want that to happen
to either of us.'

'I wish she'd told us that rather than making us feel as though she didn't approve of our choices – well, mine at least.'

'Easy for me,' Tegan smiled. 'I got an office job before we took on the farm and was never the creative type, so she didn't nag me.'

'I just wish she'd moaned about how bad it was so we'd know how hard things were for her, why she was always so busy, why we felt she didn't have the time for us.'

'Me too. It took me a while to understand her.'

'Not as long as it took me.'

Tegan put a hand on her arm. 'Don't feel bad, not any more. I think having a family was what did it for me. It got me here more often; it made me see things from Mum's point of view. And you came when she really needed you. At the end, she knew how much she meant to you and vice versa.'

Morgan sniffed. 'You're such an older sister with your wisdom.'

'I have my uses.'

Without saying much else, they ploughed on, finishing what had come from the loft before starting on Elaina's bedroom. Clothes were bagged up to drop at a charity shop, a lot was thrown out including old make-up and toiletries that would never be used again. They sorted the drawers up here and then moved to the dining room cupboards.

'Photographs *always* slow the process down,' Tegan claimed when they came to a box of albums as well as a few loose in the box.

'Let's have a few minutes of enjoyment,' Morgan urged. 'I could use a rest.'

The reminisced over photographs of them as little girls, of them as a family of four, some of their memories tinged with sadness, others with the happiness they'd once felt as a family unit.

'I remember this day,' said Morgan, holding up a photo of both girls with their dad. He had the bowls set out in the garden with his daughters. 'I wonder why we were never good enough for him, Tegan.'

'I don't know. All I know is that if Henry left me high and dry with two kids, I'd find him… and well, let's just say there'd be damage to his manhood.'

'Do you ever think about trying to work things out with him?'

'With our dad? No, not really. He's had years to reach out and try to be a parent to us, Morgan. And he hasn't. I've made peace with that. Why, do you want to have him in your life? It's fine if you do.'

'I don't think so. I'm not sure I could get past the fact he just walked away and never showed much interest.'

'I'm not even sure why you told him Mum had died.'

Morgan shrugged. 'Neither am I. I suppose a part of me wondered if he'd send a big emotional tribute, be there for us. But I'm almost glad that he wasn't. He wasn't a part of our lives, a part of Mum's in the end. It's best he just sent a card and that was that.'

Morgan carried on wading through photographs and pulled out a picture taken in the back garden of their family home before their parents had split and the girls had moved with their mother to Forget-Me-Not Cottage. Taken in their teens, both girls were sitting on the bench at the back of the narrow but very long garden with a rose bush behind. 'I remember having the picture taken because the thorns from the rose bush got tangled in my hair.'

Tegan laughed. 'I remember too! I had to untangle you and it took forever!'

'Mum was threatening to have to cut my hair off. I was so distressed.'

'She never would have. She loved your hair, said it was thick and luxurious and hoped you never cut it short.'

'She said that?' Morgan gulped at the personal nature of the comment her mum never seemed to make, not to her ears, anyway.

'She did.' Tegan paused. 'She said it to you often enough.'

' 'I don't remember.'

'I think somewhere along the way, you got frustrated with Mum. And I know she was to blame for a lot of things, but you became blinkered, when she tried to make things right, you didn't always see it.'

She opened her mouth to argue but she couldn't. Tegan was right. Over the time she'd spent with Elaina, she'd slowly been able to see for herself that that was exactly what she'd done. Her mum wasn't a perfect person, but neither was she. Was anyone?

'I think part of me might have blamed Mum for Dad leaving,' Morgan admitted. Tegan looked at her. 'I know that isn't fair and I know it isn't true. But I think that's what I did for a while because it felt less painful than admitting he'd just left because he didn't love us any more.'

'Henry never could fathom how any man could do it.'

'Hmm...' Morgan agreed. 'Henry is a good man.'

Tegan grinned. 'So is Nate.'

'Stop that.' Moran wagged a warning finger at her sister.

'Do you remember the winter before Dad walked out?' Tegan asked, joking aside now as another memory came to her.

'Vaguely.'

'I do. We had no heating that year. You and I curled up in front of the open fire to read bedtime stories. Mum made a game out of it, said it was like camping where nobody had heating. She told us the heating would soon be fixed.'

'And it never was...' Morgan's voice faltered as she remembered it all too. 'Not for the rest of winter, anyway. And Mum came down with flu and couldn't work. I remember making soup from whatever I could find in the fridge.'

'And not having any bread to go with it.'

'She kept her struggles so quiet from us.' Morgan wished yet again that she hadn't. But she'd done what she thought best, protecting her girls.

They ploughed on with sorting out, remembering more about those darker days that Elaina had tried her best to keep from them.

Tegan flopped down onto the floor an hour later. 'Can we please stop now? I need food, I'm so hungry.'

'Pizza?'

'Yes, please. Extra large, extra pepperoni, extra chillies.'

'Consider it done,' said Morgan, patting her sister on the thigh before she got up to get her phone from beneath Marley. For some reason, he'd decided to keep them company and curled up on top of where she'd placed it.

'Pizza and wine,' said Tegan, eyes still shut. 'And then I want to hear more about Nate. And I'm not taking no for an answer.'

Morgan called through their order. A gossip with her sister was exactly what she needed and talking about Nate was a good place to start: Tegan was the only one to whom she'd admit quite how far and fast she was falling for him.

15

Nate came down the steep, narrow staircase at Jeremy's house. Jeremy had apologised over and over for taking advantage when he called Trevor to ask whether Nate could come out and see to a burst pipe and Nate had had trouble convincing him it really wasn't a problem.

'All fixed,' Nate, toolbox in hand, called over to Jeremy, who was outside on the driveway, the bonnet of his car propped open as he topped up the oil.

'What's the damage?' Jeremy put down the can of oil and then dropped the bonnet. He took the invoice Nate had written. 'Not as bad as I thought.'

'It was easy to deal with.' He'd massively discounted his price because it didn't feel right to charge the full whack when the man was his dad's age. Mind you, if he kept doing that, he'd soon go broke. 'I replaced both pipes under the bathroom sink – they were old and when I took them off, there was a fair bit of rust which likely weakened the walls of the pipe that burst.'

'You're a good lad. And thank you again for coming here so quickly. I took advantage of my friendship with Trevor.'

'No, you didn't. And I'm a plumber, this is what I do.' He went over to his pick-up and set the toolbox in the tray once he'd pushed back the metal cover that kept everything secure from the elements and wandering hands.

Over beside Jeremy, who was busy with his Robin Reliant, Nate ran a hand across its roof. 'This must surely be a collector's item.'

'It's almost as old as me,' Jeremy laughed.

'Not thinking of hanging up the driving gloves yet then?'

'Between you and me, I think I might have to.' With a sigh that had Nate less likely to laugh at his driving prowess – or rather lack of – and feel sympathy, he said, 'My attention span isn't the best these days. And there are so many cars on the roads.'

'Please don't tell me this is anything to do with the Marley incident.' At the look on Jeremy's face, he insisted, 'It could've happened to anyone – me, Morgan.'

'But it happened to me. Oh, I felt terrible. That girl has lost enough.'

He wasn't wrong there. 'Morgan doesn't blame you. Marley was the one in the wrong and it's hard to get through to a cat.'

Jeremy appreciated a little bit of humour. 'I think maybe my eyesight is getting worse, too.'

Now that really was something to take seriously. 'Then you should get it checked. It could invalidate your insurance. It's not something to mess around with.'

'It feels like if I give up the car, it's another piece of independence lost. And then what? What comes next? My marbles?'

Nate put a hand on his shoulder. 'You seem pretty with it to me. And giving up the car will be a wrench but there's a bus that goes plenty of places – and you'll see other people on the bus.' *Rather than on the road, leaping to get out of the way*, he didn't add. He also didn't tell him that he and Sebastian had spoken about this the day he'd been at the cottage sorting the plumbing. They'd agreed perhaps it was time someone hinted to Jeremy about giving up the car and had thought it should be Sebastian, then perhaps Trevor, who was closer in age. But now Nate had the perfect opportunity to bring it into casual conversation here.

'I didn't think of that. I could chat to people while someone else did the driving.'

'Exactly.' He knew from his dad that chatting was often what put Jeremy off his game when he was driving. Never mind his eyesight. He'd turn and look at his passenger, which Nate suspected was due to him being hard of hearing too. 'You might find the bus gives you a whole new lease of life in many ways.'

Jeremy patted the bonnet of his car. 'I'll miss the old girl if I let her go.'

'You'll save money too, remember. No maintenance costs on the car, you're at an age where you get a free bus pass, no more messing about with oil.' He indicated Jeremy's filthy hands. 'Water's back on now, safe to use. I'll leave you to it.' He sensed this was a significant, emotional decision for the man to make and sometimes those things needed thinking about alone.

'Thanks again, Nate. Can I interest you in a pint at the pub at midday to show my appreciation?'

'Bit early for me.' But he didn't want to disappoint Jeremy. 'How does four o'clock sound?'

Jeremy brightened. 'I'll see you there.'

'Leave the car at home. Dad and I will meet you and we'll all head over together.'

'Right you are.'

Back at the house, Nate said a brief hello to his dad and Branston and made for the workshop. He was glad he'd been called out by Jeremy because it stopped him thinking too hard about Morgan when he was busy. The way they'd almost kissed outside Snowdrop Cottage was difficult to ignore. And in the garden afterwards, he'd caught her watching him more than once, but she'd looked away every time. And she'd made sure not to be on her own with him, sure to stay with others as everyone chatted well into the evening.

In the workshop, Nate found the wood he needed to provide another distraction from thinking about Morgan and the fact she was with someone else. He'd been to the timber merchant in the week and picked up enough to make another side table like the one he'd already sold. It was versatile for the home, which was probably why they were popular – light and easy to move around, could be casual or formal furniture. And it wouldn't take forever to make. He was confident it would sell easily enough and if not, well, he'd take it back to Wales with him. The original idea might well have been to whittle down stock, but he was embracing this intense urge to keep on making things.

* * *

The pint with his dad and Jeremy was definitely welcome come the end of the day after he'd measured, cut, sanded and varnished. All three of them talked animatedly about Jeremy's dilemma – car versus the bus. Jeremy was obviously getting his head around the idea. Kiara, the pub landlady, joined in with the debate, as did landlord Logan, and Jeremy seemed to be enjoying himself so much that Nate left both men in the pub, declaring he needed a good long walk after working all day. He'd go along the street at the top of the green all the way to the end, then head down to the high street and walk back towards the humpback bridge. He'd offered to take Branston with him but his dad said they'd take him home with them when they left in another hour or so. The dog had waited patiently while they ate and seemed in no rush to move.

Nate couldn't help but pause as he got to Forget-Me-Not

Cottage. He hovered outside. Should he knock? Say hello to Morgan?

But the decision was taken out of his hands when he heard a scream come from inside the cottage.

He tore up the front path and was about to knock when he saw Morgan through the open window. And she spotted him. She was clearly okay, so he waved and turned to walk away, but her voice stopped him before he'd reached the end of the path.

'Did you hear me scream?' She appeared in the doorway.

'Kind of why I was coming to the door. It sounded like someone was being attacked.'

'I was. By a shelf.' Her hand was clasped against her chest as though she was still calming herself down. 'It scared me half to death. It fell down on top of me.'

'You all right?' She was rubbing the back of her head.

'Might get a bruise but it was the fright that was the worst.'

'Want me to take a look?'

'Are you a doctor now?'

He smiled wryly. 'At the shelf, not the head.'

'Oh...' She stood back. 'Sure.'

He went inside and her proximity reminded him of how close they'd been outside Sebastian's place.

The shelf was still on the sofa and he could see it had fallen from the wall behind, the one that faced the fireplace. On closer inspection, he could see the screws that had held up the brackets had worked their way loose, presumably over time. 'Not the best screws for this shelf.' And when he looked at the pot plant, the magazines, the books, a couple of photo frames and an ornament strewn on the sofa, he suggested, 'You might have overloaded it too. I'd suggest making new holes in the wall above the existing ones – the foot of the shelf bracket will hide the old hole.'

'Right...'

'I've got the tools. I can walk home, grab them and be back in ten minutes, the job will be done quick enough.'

'I can sort it.'

He quirked an eyebrow.

'All right. Please help... is that what you want to hear?'

'It'll do,' he grinned and as he passed her again, his arms brushing against hers in the hallway he leaned closer and whispered, 'I won't make you beg, don't worry.'

He headed across the village green and back to his dad's. He'd only had half a pint at the pub as he'd intended to go back in his workshop this evening, so he was fine to drive after he'd grabbed his tools and found some better screws. He kept a whole range in a special tray, so it wasn't hard. And he found a couple of better brackets too. That was the great thing about having a workshop; it meant you could collect things over time and they came in handy when you least expected.

He was back at Forget-Me-Not Cottage quicker than he'd anticipated and as he went inside, he noticed the book about Scotland beside the phone.

'Getting yourself ready for the big move?' He nodded towards it.

'Something like that.' Morgan noted the toolbox he was carrying. 'You should let me pay you for this.'

'What, for putting up a single shelf? I think I can stretch to a favour for a friend.'

The word *friend* felt nice but strange to say out loud. It was kind of what they were, he supposed. And it would have to do if it couldn't be more.

He moved the sofa out with her help so he could get to the wall and measured up using a pencil to mark where he'd drill. 'I've got some better brackets.' He showed her their size compared to the ones previously used. 'They'll take more of a load so it's less likely to fall down again.'

'Then I'll definitely pay you, for your time and the materials.'

He picked up the drill, ready to make the holes. 'Really, no need, I found them in the garage, couldn't even tell you when I bought them, let alone how much they cost.'

She scrunched up her nose. 'Should I be worried? I mean, do they go off after time?'

'Do they have a shelf life, you mean?' He winced. 'Sorry, terrible joke.'

But she was laughing and it lightened the atmosphere. 'I thought it was funny.'

When he'd made the holes and secured the brackets, Morgan handed him the shelf and once it was in place, she put the pot plant, which he'd noticed was the fake kind so no earth had poured out, back on top first.

He passed her both photo frames. 'That's a nice one.' He pointed to one with her with another little girl and a woman who he assumed was her mum.

'It was taken on a holiday in Norfolk. We had one of those beach huts right by the sand. We went to the beach every day that week.' She looked happy reflecting.

'Mum hated the beach. Too much sand, apparently.' Again, she laughed. He liked that: that he could make her happy.

'Tegan hated the sea. Too much seaweed.'

'Each to their own. Can't say I'm a fan of it myself; always feels like some creature wrapping around your legs.'

He wondered how long it would be before she showed him the door, but she offered him a cup of tea or coffee. 'Or I've got cold cans of cola in the fridge,' she offered. 'My sister stocked up as she loves fizzy.'

'Your sister's here?'

'We've been sorting through Mum's things, but she's headed out to the cinema with an old school friend. I don't think she gets much time to socialise at all, so I almost had to push her out the door.'

With a smile, he accepted the offer of the cold drink. 'Do you have a vacuum?' He indicated the mess he'd made behind the sofa.

Morgan got the vacuum, he insisted he cleaned up while she went for the drinks and once she was back, she set the cans on the coffee table.

'Sit down,' she urged, pointing to the sofa. 'That way if you did a rubbish job, the shelf falls on your head first.'

'Thanks,' he laughed, flipping open his can of cola. 'Hmm, that's good, needed that.'

On the arm of the chair next to her was a folded blanket that reminded him of one of his mum's favourites. She'd had enough of them – all sorts of colours and textures and patterns. Some of them left bits everywhere, others were itchy; she'd been quite the collector. And they were all still stored in space bags beneath the bed in the room where he slept now, waiting to be sorted and either kept or got rid of.

Sitting at the other end of the sofa, Morgan curled her legs beneath her, facing him, and tilted her chin upwards towards the shelf. 'Hasn't fallen yet.'

He looked up too and saw he was in the firing line; she was enough to one side that she wasn't. He reached out, grabbed her hand and pulled her closer. 'We're both testing it,' he insisted and he didn't miss the colour that came to her cheeks at the intimate exchange of hand on hand.

He jumped when Marley leapt up onto his lap and settled there as if he didn't want to miss out on the fun. 'Hey, you.' He stroked Marley. 'You being careful crossing roads?'

'I'm keeping a close eye on him,' said Morgan. 'He likes you.'

'I think you must be right.' He kept on stroking but told Morgan, 'Jeremy still feels bad.'

'I keep telling him it wasn't his fault.'

'So do I. But he was still going on about it earlier, although now they're all at the pub debating whether or not he should give up driving. He's in really good spirits about it all.'

She smiled. 'I thought you'd been to the pub.' Awkwardly she added, 'I could smell beer on you when you arrived.'

Her comment had him realise he'd noted the smell of her too. Whether it was perfume, shampoo or a soap she'd used, it didn't matter. Whatever it was had assaulted his senses as he checked his handiwork with the shelf one final time and she put her pot plant back on top. And the fresh scent made his way over to him again now, taunting him.

'How's your dad's wrist?' Morgan asked. Her hand was running from Marley's head to his tail and every time she did it, her fingers grazed Nate's arm and he wondered how long he could hold himself together because with every stroke, it reminded him of the way he felt about her: as more than a friend.

'It's fine... he enjoyed getting a bit of attention at the dinner but he wasn't happy I made him go to hospital.'

'You did the right thing. I'd have done the same.'

'The dinner really opened my eyes, you know. The friendships across all ages with everyone seated around that table.' They held one another's gaze for a moment. 'It floored me a bit. All those people, not family, but people who live in the one village, different circumstances but looking after each other.'

'It's really quite special, isn't it? It was one of the things Mum loved about Little Woodville. I don't remember any of this from my teenage years. But what teenager would? You've got enough going on of your own with adolescence.'

'I remember it painfully well,' he admitted. With the warm,

summery air drifting in from the outside through the open windows, he was enjoying being with Morgan a little too much.

Awkward when it felt as though they were sharing another moment like the one outside Snowdrop Cottage, he eyed the laptop on the table. 'Have you got plenty of work on?'

'It's steady at the moment, the best way.'

'Do you still enjoy it?'

'I do. I always loved the fact I could work anywhere. I wasn't fixed to one location.'

'I can see the appeal. See the world a bit that way. Have you?'

'Sure,' she claimed as though she was about to reveal she'd worked in a multitude of exotic locations. But instead she told him, 'I've worked from my flat in London and the sofa in Little Woodville. Perhaps I should contact *National Geographic*, see if they'd like me to do a piece on the writing life in far-flung destinations.'

'Might need a bit more research.'

'You think?' She grinned.

'So will you be off to Scotland soon?'

After a brief hesitation, she told him a company in Scotland had been interested in her. 'It was for a content editor position; it would've been an office job with a steady income. I had to pass up the opportunity when I came back here to be with Mum. I emailed them recently but haven't heard anything back yet.'

'Well, you never know.' It pained him to say it almost as much as it hurt every time he saw the ring on her finger or caught a glimpse of the book about Scotland.

'Yeah. Only time will tell. If my mum was still around, she'd get very impatient with me; she'd want me to push a bit harder, make something happen.' And then she spotted something on the blanket that was lying across the arm of the sofa. 'She'd also tell me off for spilling cola on her favourite blanket.' She groaned at the brown circle that had soaked into one of the paler, frayed edge pieces of the navy and caramel lambswool blanket where she'd rested her can.

Morgan went to the kitchen, came back with a cloth and wiped at the spill a few times. 'It's not coming out and unfortunately it's dry clean only, so I can't even throw it in the washing machine.' She did her best and at least the mark wasn't quite as noticeable when she'd finished. 'Mum loved her blankets.'

'Really?' Her own memory warmed him. 'Mine was the same. Mum had far too many of them, although of course she would never admit it.'

She was about to take his empty can out to the kitchen when her phone on the table began to buzz and move about the surface as if it had a mind of its own. 'Funny name,' he said noting the display.

She paled. Looked at the phone and then looked at him. 'It's the company I was telling you about. The one that was interested in me for a job. It's as though they heard us talking.'

'Answer it, don't miss your opportunity,' he urged. And as she clicked the call to answer, he mouthed that he'd see her at the markets in the morning.

Nate left the cottage and swore when he climbed into his pick-up because no matter what might be between them, even if it was only friendship, Morgan was leaving the village and that meant no matter how much he came to see his dad, he wasn't going to be seeing much more of this woman he'd grown to know and care about.

16

Nate loved the summer months with their endless evenings; he went straight into his workshop when he got back to Oak Cottage. Right now, Morgan was likely discussing a job offer that would change her life, and he needed a focus.

Nate felt a welcome catharsis going into the workshop these days. And never before had he needed his talents to be a distraction as much as he did this evening. He inspected the side table, which had had one coat of varnish and didn't need another, so it was time to start something new. This time, he was making a box to store firewood – it wasn't the right time of the year at all but out-of-season items could be impulse purchases. The idea had come to mind this morning when he'd stubbed his toe on the log basket next to the fireplace in the lounge.

Branston followed Nate back and forth as he sorted through the wood he wanted. There were some beautiful pieces he'd collected over the years, some he remembered had started their life as floorboards and were set for the skip following a local house renovation, others were pieces from the shelves he'd once had in his bedroom here until they'd been replaced with a big wardrobe for more storage. He put each piece on the worktable in turn. 'You're gonna trip me up if you're not careful, Branston.' He stopped then and crouched down to fuss the dog. 'What's with you? You've had plenty of walks today and you just walked home from the pub with Dad. Is it because I was gone for hours? Is that it? Did someone else demand my attention? You know I love you the most, right?'

And then he heard someone laughing and looked up to see Morgan hovering in the side doorway.

He stood up. 'Didn't see you there.' But he was more than pleased she'd come and by the looks of it, so was Branston, judging by the wagging tail and his approach to say hello. Mind you, the dog would be pleased to see anyone; it didn't have to be a woman who sent shivers across Nate's body and blood rushing to places he shouldn't mention.

'Evidently not,' she replied with a grin. 'All that lovey-dovey talk, who would've thought?'

'I'll deny it if you tell anyone.'

'Figured,' she answered. She fussed over Branston but then pulled something from her bag and passed it to him. 'You left this at mine.'

He patted the back pocket of his jeans, obviously found it empty and remembered taking his wallet out and putting it on the side table at Forget-Me-Not Cottage earlier so it didn't go missing. Seemed a wise idea at the time; not so much now given he'd mislaid it anyway. 'Thanks. I didn't even think about it, but I would've missed it when I tried to buy myself a coffee at the markets in the morning.' He put it on a shelf out of the way.

She was looking all around her, taking in the space. 'So this is where all the action happens?'

Her comment pleased him. 'I suppose you could say that.'

'It smells like you.' And then she caught herself. 'I mean, smells like your things, your wooden things.' She rolled her eyes more at herself than him and turned away, continuing to take in the wooden items piled at one side, the raw planks of wood leaning against a wall, the collection of pieces on the workbench. 'What are you making?'

'Thought I'd make a firewood box.'

'Don't let me stop you.'

'You don't mind me carrying on?'

'Of course not; I'd like to watch.'

And it felt right to carry on while she was here. Otherwise he might not be able to control what his hands wanted to do right now, most of which involved pulling her against him and touching her face to see whether her skin was as soft as he thought it might be.

He opened up one of the other cupboards at the side of the room. 'Pretty sure I have some rope in here for the handles.' To explain, he added, 'I bought some rope to make a swing for a mate's kid and never got around to it.'

'The wood you're using is beautiful.' She'd left Branston and gone over to the workbench to inspect the materials more closely.

Nate pulled out a length of rope that had been coiled for storage and somehow worked its way to the back of the cupboard behind a plastic, sectioned box containing nails in an assortment of sizes.

'Are you putting it on the stall tomorrow?'

'Next week, I think. The glue will need to dry properly, I'd want to make sure it's ready for sale, try loading it with logs myself to test it out, that sort of thing.'

'Sounds wise.' She met his gaze. 'You've sold a lot of your stock.'

'I've made quite a bit and next week, I'll be able to make a hefty donation to the Parkinson's charity that means a lot to Dad and me.'

'You're donating all your profits?'

He nodded. 'I can't think of a better thing to do with the cash. Well, I tried to give it to Dad but he refused to take any of it. It's hard enough to get him to take money for groceries. And so I suggested the charity.'

'That's really kind, Nate.'

He shrugged. 'It feels like a nice way to remember Mum.'

'It'll be your last week next week,' she said.

They were looking at one another until he snapped himself out of it to get started. And while he began to work, he asked, 'How did the phone call go?' He wanted to know and yet he didn't. But it was polite to ask. And they were friends.

'They still want me.'

Who wouldn't? 'That's great,' he lied. He ran a pencil along the edge of the ruler to mark out the wood he was measuring.

'I set up a time for an interview over Zoom. And the money they're offering is actually better than I thought.'

'Great.' He'd said that already. He'd have to vary it up a bit unless he wanted to sound like a total idiot.

'So why didn't you get around to making the swing?' she asked after a while.

'Mum deteriorated. It was a really tough time.' And it wasn't the only thing he'd been trying to make and had never finished.

Branston stole the limelight again by nudging in front of Morgan's legs as she stood next to Nate at the workbench.

'Sorry, Morgan. You'd think he'd got enough fuss at the pub earlier, wouldn't you?'

'He's obviously very sociable.' She crouched down to give Branston her full attention.

Was it possible to be jealous of a dog? Yeah, it was. Although he had to warn Branston to calm down again because the dog was already checking her out with his nose, putting it in places she might not be comfortable with.

Nate ran the pieces of wood he needed to cut through the saw. He concentrated the best he could with a beautiful woman in the corner of his eye. He cut the pieces to size – two longer lengths, two shorter, to make the rectangle shape he thought best for a box to store logs which would come in all sizes, as well as another piece for the base of the box – and found the right nails and glue from one of the drawers beneath the workbench.

'I love his name,' Morgan declared. 'Branston.' She said the dog's name as if to be sure of what it sounded like on her tongue. 'Like the pickle.'

'Exactly.' His stomach grumbled a little. 'And now you've made me hungry. I could go a few rounds of cheese on toast with Branston pickle.'

'That's a thing?'

'You mean you've never tried it?' When she shook her head, he suggested, 'Let me make us some – call it a thank you for the safe return of my wallet.'

'How do you know I haven't cleared all the cash out?'

'You wouldn't do that.'

'Well, I'll take you up on the offer if it means I can spend more time with Branston here.'

'Cup of tea too?' he offered. 'We'll go in the house if you like. Or I could bring it out here.' And that way, he wouldn't have to explain her presence to his dad or disturb him. Trevor was intent on watching *Midsomer Murders* tonight and deemed himself ready for a "binge watch", although knowing Dad, that meant two episodes before he headed upstairs for an early night. The older generation didn't really have the stamina for a binge watch, not the way people his age did. It was hardly good for you, just that nowadays your favourite shows were at your fingertips and who wanted to wait before they found out the ending to something that had well and truly hooked them in?

'I'm happy to eat out here.' Morgan eyed the window at the side of the garage, the golden glow cast by the sun which had started its descent. 'It's a beautiful evening.'

'It really is.' He came to her side but then realised he had to actually go to the kitchen to get the job done. 'I'll be back in a bit.'

He thought he'd have to tell Branston to wait here but it seemed Branston wouldn't have heard him anyway because at Morgan's feet, he'd already rolled over for a tummy tickle.

Nate checked in on his dad and asked him whether he needed a snack made, but he didn't. He settled on a cup of tea and Nate said he'd be out in the workshop if he was needed, although Trevor barely looked up from his programme.

He took out the bread and toasted each slice before slathering the other in pickle and covering it with cheese. Once it was melted and bubbling, he sliced it and took the gooey treats out to the workshop on a big tray along with the mugs of tea.

'You've been fed already,' Nate told the dog who, with a bit of convincing, lay in his basket and gave Morgan a chance to eat in peace.

'What do you think?' he asked when her eyes rolled heavenward at the first bite.

'How have I never tried this before? It's top-quality comfort food.'

'So you like my cooking?'

She covered her mouth as she laughed. 'I think *cooking* might be dressing it up a little.'

'Hey, don't knock it. I'm not bad in the kitchen as it happens. Sometimes it's hard to bother cooking for one but I've enjoyed making meals for me and Dad.'

She finished her mouthful, another piece poised between her

fingers. 'When Mum was alive, cooking for two was something I did without thinking. It's crazy that it doesn't take long to stop thinking that way and for one seems like too much effort when it shouldn't. You're going through the same motions, only with less food.'

As they ate, they talked about the food at the Bookshop Café, the way Sebastian and Belle seemed to be running the place with practised ease already.

'Not always a good idea to be in business with another half,' he said, 'but they seem to be making it work.'

'I once did a temping job – before I got into journalism.' She licked her fingers to get a chunk of pickle that had escaped from the piece she was eating. 'I was a typist somewhere way out in the country, middle of nowhere. I had to type up seed orders.'

'Sounds riveting.'

'It was not. And the husband-and-wife team argued *all* the time. With me there too. They yelled at each other, hurled accusations. I lasted a week before I was out of there.'

He put the empty plate out of the way and when Morgan urged him to carry on with what he was doing again and showed no desire to leave, he continued with the firewood box. He used glue and nails to assemble the piece and Morgan divided her time between watching him and making sure Branston wasn't neglected.

'What's next?' she asked when the box looked pretty much finished.

'Now it needs to dry properly. Not sure if it needs staining. The wood is pretty nice as it is but maybe a light coating to protect it.'

She leaned against the workbench, her fingers finding the coil of rope. 'What happened with the swing? You said you were going to make it but your mum deteriorated.' She looked at him then. 'I'm sorry, tell me to mind my own business if you like.'

He leaned against the workbench next to her. 'Mum was suffering more and more. Every day, movement was getting harder for her and her tremors were worsening. I stopped making the swing because I wanted to make something for her instead.' His voice caught. 'But then she died.'

'I'm sorry, I—'

When she went to step away, he put a hand on her arm and gently pulled her back next to him at the workbench. 'I don't really talk about it with anyone other than Dad.'

'Try me; I'm not a bad listener.'

He appreciated having someone here, someone who'd experienced a similar loss all too recently. 'A part of me shut down when Mum died.'

After a while, she said, 'I think a part of any kid closes off when a parent dies. A parent is a part of you – or you're a part of them at least – and then all of a sudden, you're disconnected from an existence that up until that point, had always been the way it was. It was all you'd ever known.'

He hesitated but having her at his side, being back in the workshop and finally working through the emotions he thought he'd left behind, he admitted, 'I felt guilty for a long time. It's only recently, since coming back in here that I've started to let those feelings go.'

'Why did you feel guilty?'

He had to wind back a bit to explain. 'Mum had Parkinson's. It took years to reach a point where she needed extra care and she got that living with Dad and then when I moved back in. We were fine taking care of her – I mean, we knew we might not be in the years to come, but we were taking it one step at a time. Her balance was affected – she lost her footing easily which frustrated her and the mental drain was a battle for her as much as anything else.'

'Go on,' Morgan encouraged when he faltered, disappearing into his own head for a bit.

'We'd reached a point, Dad and I, where we knew she shouldn't be left on her own for too long. She didn't want to admit it, but she had declined enough that we could see it was risky. She refused to be moved to a room downstairs; she wanted her bedroom the way it had always been. She was stubborn.' His frown deepened. 'When someone needs you so much, you'd do anything to make them happy. Dad and I said we'd carry on as we were for a while. She never wanted to talk about it: what would happen when she really couldn't manage. We helped her up and down the stairs, Dad helped her shower, going out in the garden was something to do with one of us.'

'It sounds really tough.'

'It was. But I'd do it all over again if I had to.'

'Me too.'

'Mum had this overwhelming anxiety; she'd cling onto my arm and on those days, I'd stay with her no matter whether I had a job. Some days, she wanted to stay in bed, other days in front of the television. Sometimes, I'd get her a chair and she'd come watch me in here.'

'That's nice, that she liked watching you work. Bit like Mum and me at the markets.'

'It was special, really special. She liked the smell of the wood. She'd close her eyes and listen to the tap tap of a hammer as I finished working,' he said with a smile. 'She was fascinated at how a piece of raw material could be turned into something completely different and she watched in awe as though I was the only one capable of such a feat.'

'She was proud.'

'She was.' He swallowed, hard. 'One day it was freezing cold but I desperately wanted to work on something special I was making for her. It was too cold for her to sit out here, she was better tucked up inside, so I left her and came in here on my own. I checked on her every hour. I made her lunch and took it to her. We argued over whether my scrambled eggs were better than hers or not.

'I came back out here to carry on and after another hour, went inside. She'd fallen down the stairs.' He looked down at the concrete floor, the wood shavings coating it like a fresh carpet. 'She was gone, just like that.' His hands tensed against the workbench and through gritted teeth he blurted out, 'And I wasn't there. I was supposed to be looking after her. And I was out here, enjoying myself. For a long time, the guilt almost finished me off. I thought Dad would blame me.'

'He wouldn't.'

He shook his head. 'Didn't stop me blaming myself.'

Morgan let him have the time to process, and when he opened his eyes, he realised her hand had covered his. He could feel the warmth of it, the softness of her skin. He looked heavenward to stem the tears threatening to make him look like a wimp in front of this woman who was the first person other than his dad that he'd shared his honest feelings with.

'I haven't cried in a long time,' he said.

'Remember I told you I felt guilty too?'

'For the relief,' he said, recalling their conversation about it a while ago.

She nodded, took her hand back as if she didn't deserve the comfort. 'I was glad that Mum died quickly. I hated seeing her in pain, seeing the look in her eyes at the thought of losing her independence, her dignity. She went without a long, strung-out, miserable ending. Some might think that makes me a terrible person.'

'I don't.'

'And I don't think you are either. You aren't terrible for being in here doing what you loved, because you weren't with her every second. You did your best.'

'After Mum's funeral, I was watching Dad pottering around the kitchen, devastated at our loss, and I thought how he'd got to remember his wife looking and being more or less the same woman he'd always known. She'd had her moments of distress, we could see physical changes, but they weren't as bad as they would've been if she'd carried on. She could still talk to us easily enough, she sounded like herself; we had that comfort. I feel guilty because her life was cut short, but I'm glad that's how Dad got to remember her. I'm glad he didn't see her at the bottom of the stairs like I did. Dad remembers her sitting up in bed that morning next to him, where he'd left her when he went to church and on to do the weekly shop.'

'Do you ever...'

He knew what she was about to ask. 'Wonder if I'll get Parkinson's too?' He shrugged. 'They think it's a combination of genes, environment, lifestyle.'

'Same with me; there's a chance I'm more likely to get osteoporosis with a family history, but there's a lot I can do to protect myself.'

'I'm glad.' The words came out with more feeling than he'd intended to share. But she seemed to have that effect on him. The effect of making him confess his deepest, darkest secrets. 'You know when losing Mum really hit me all over again? It was the year after it happened and I took Branston for a long walk with Dad and when we passed Snowdrop Cottage. All the snowdrops were out; it was like a blanket of white and I had this powerful image of Mum's smile. I must have been about thirteen years old and we'd been walking our old dog, Rocky, and me being a teenage boy, I'd been tearing about and trampled on the edge of the snowdrop clusters. She got so mad at me.' He shook his head smiling at the memory. 'She bent down, straightened up the little heads of the flowers the best she could and told me they were nature's gift. She told me so was I, gave me a hug and I never trod on a snow-drop again after that.'

'Glad to hear it,' she nudged him.

'Remembering the day with Mum, it was as though someone had turned up the gas on a pot of water and sent it boiling over the edge. Dad and I stood there, eyes glistening, watching the heads of the snowdrops in the breeze. Both of us silent, the world around us noisy and carrying on. I missed the snowdrops this year but next year, I'll come back for them.'

'They don't have snowdrops in Wales?'

'Course they do,' he grinned, 'but there's nowhere quite like Snowdrop Cottage to see them.'

'Sebastian should hand out tickets for people to come from far and wide.'

'Maybe he should,' he agreed. 'There's a place in Snowdrop Woods too with clusters of buttercups. Mum loved those as well. Dad and I saw them the other day but this time, it didn't floor us but rather made us remember the happier times.'

They were still standing side by side at the workbench, their arms close but not touching, their fingers only inches apart.

'The markets are helping me cope with losing Mum more than I ever thought they would.' A soft look came over her face. 'My intention was to use them to get rid of everything she'd bought and collected, to honour her in a way. I thought it was one last thing I could do for her as I suspect it's what she would've wanted. Being amongst all those people she was so friendly with has been a real gift. Like she gave me something from beyond.' She laughed at her own dramatism. 'Perhaps that's why Mum dropped little hints here and there about me having to know how the stall worked so that should I need to, I could run it by myself without any of her input. I know she thought she had a lot longer, but perhaps that was her way of asking me to do it.' She shrugged her shoulders.

'Not being able to ask questions is horrible.'

She looked him right in the eye. 'Nobody tells you that, do they? I hate that I can't ask Mum things. And it's not the big things necessarily, is it? Not long after Mum died, I got a craving for her homemade cauliflower cheese and so of course, I got all the ingredients and had a go myself. But it didn't taste the same at all. I looked up recipes online, I asked my sister if she could remember how Mum made it. It sounds silly but I was devastated that I couldn't recreate it.'

'Doesn't sound silly at all.'

'Yesterday, I was checking the food cupboard to make sure nothing had expired and right at the back, I found a sachet of cheese sauce.' She grinned. 'I'd been making the sauce from scratch and I'd totally forgotten she used a packet mix.'

He could feel his fingers almost touching hers now, as though each of them had subconsciously moved closer. 'I suppose the big question is... are you going to make cauliflower cheese using a packet mix or not?'

'I don't know. I'd rather fresh but if it tastes the same as Mum's...'

'Treat yourself.'

'I could make it for you,' she suggested. 'You know, seeing as you "cooked" for me.' She put the word cooked in air quotes.

'Hey, less dissing of the cheese and Branston on toast.' The dog's ears pricked up and his tail thwacked against his basket. 'Not you,' they both chorused with laughter.

'I'm not dissing your cooking at all. But maybe I'll make it. One day next week before the last market session for you. A going away meal. You're still planning on heading back to Wales at the same time?'

'I think so.'

'It's not definite?' Was it his imagination or did she sound as eager as he felt that that plan might change? 'Is it because you're still worrying about your dad being on his own?'

'I think that will always be a worry. A lot of that stems from Mum and the guilt but I know I have to back off. I know it's been a lot for Dad to have me stressing over what will happen when he's doing pretty well here.'

'Very well,' she agreed. 'You can go back to Wales and know that he's all right.'

He caught her gaze then. 'What if I don't want to go?'

She bit down on her bottom lip, a habit he'd noticed she did when she was nervous and thinking hard. 'But you're here for four weeks.'

'What if I'm not?' The air between them was thick, barely allowing for breath. But then it dawned on him, again, as if he needed reminding, that he had no right to suggest anything when she was with someone. She had a fiancé, a plan. 'You're right, four weeks is what I planned for. And I've got jobs lined up when I get back. I can't let people down.'

'No, I don't suppose you can.' Looking around the workshop, she asked, 'What's under the sheet over there?'

He went over and unveiled the item. 'This was what I was making for Mum.'

She came over and ran her hand across the rustic, reclaimed wood. 'It's gorgeous.'

He crouched down on his haunches the same way she was. 'It's a blanket box. I told you Mum had a lot of blankets – I thought she could perhaps store them all in this at the foot of the bed.' The summer heat coming in through the open door wasn't the only rise in temperature he could feel being this close to Morgan.

He didn't miss her swallow, the delicate movement in her neck hard to look away from.

And then she lost her balance and fell against him rather than the blanket box.

'I'm sorry,' she laughed. 'Balance never was my strong point.' She pulled a wisp of hair away from her mouth and stood up.

'You've got sawdust on your knees.' Still crouched down, he brushed them gently to get rid of the debris. And when he looked up at her, the way she watched him had to be more than friend-ship, didn't it?

But there was the engagement ring again, glinting right next to his face.

He stood up, so close and yet with more distance between them than he wanted. His chest rose on a breath. 'I've been that guy, Morgan.'

'What guy?'

'The one on the side. I didn't know at the time, but if I had, I never would've got involved. I won't do it again.' And yet he still wanted the kiss so badly, it hurt.

She looked away but only for a second, and only over at the blanket box. She didn't bother to respond to what he'd just said either, simply told him, 'You should finish it. It's too beautiful to leave or to scrap.'

'It needs hinges, a varnish.' He felt it easier to talk about the practicalities, what had to be done, than try to work out what she was thinking or deny what he was.

He moved the sheet completely out of the way and piled it in the corner by the back door. 'Do you want to help me varnish it once I've done the hinges?' He began to find everything he'd need to do the job.

When he looked over at her, she beamed a smile his way. 'I'd really like that.'

They worked together once he'd done his bit, their brushes periodically dipping into the tin of varnish and as they worked back and forth with gentle brushstrokes, he knew that no matter whether she left, he'd remember her forever as the girl who'd come into his life by chance and the one he wished he could hold onto forever.

17

Morgan drove from her cottage to the Snowdrop Lane markets, already looking forward to spending time with Nate again, no matter that she'd only seen him last night.

It saddened her that today was Nate's penultimate stint at the stall – he had quite the talent, which she'd appreciated all the more last night watching him in action. The things he made were beautiful; the way he worked was true craftmanship. Even the way he'd used the varnish was different to the way she did it. She simply applied the coating with the brush, whereas his strokes were carefully considered, his artistic hands finishing the job he'd started a long time ago. He was a man who downplayed his skill, which spoke more about the sort of person he was than anything else. And so did donating all the proceeds to charity.

When she pulled into a space on the field, slowly so the bumps not made for little cars didn't upset any of her stock in the boot, she paused for a minute. Hands on the wheel, she looked at her engagement ring and wondered – should she take it off? She had to give it back to Ronan, it wouldn't feel right not to, but keeping it on was a way to stop anyone asking questions she didn't particularly want to answer. And it kept a distance between her and Nate, no matter what either of them wanted. Because she knew now, more than the day outside Snowdrop Cottage, that he had feelings for her too. She hadn't imagined it. But she did owe it to him and to herself to wait a while. A broken engagement wasn't something you moved on from just like that before leaping into something new.

She glanced down the row of vehicles. Nate's pick-up was already here and when she approached their stall – listen to her, *their* stall, as if that's the way it had always been – the look they exchanged was an acknowledgement that both of them were thinking about yesterday and last night. The way he looked at her was different, as if they'd peeled back another layer of their friendship, and she tried her best not to feel too giddy with the possibilities.

There was a lot of crossover as they worked – getting each other a coffee, helping with customer enquiries if the other was busy with someone else. They adopted a rhythm and a flow that felt natural. As the day progressed, it was even on the tip of Morgan's tongue to suggest to Nate a drink at the pub. She needed to thank him for fixing her shelf, for saving Marley, for being a friend. But instead, she stayed as they were, two friends working on a stall, not rushing into anything.

She'd just sold a Victorian tea caddy in turquoise when she noticed the wooden cart Nate had at the front of his stall. It had been hidden next to the table and a few other items that had since been snapped up. 'This is brilliant,' she told him. 'My niece has a similar one, pushes it around everywhere, knocking into the walls, making my brother-in-law cringe every time. Henry will have to repaint once Lily has grown out of it.'

Nate rested his hand on the handle of the cart, which was well-crafted and contained big, coloured cubes for stacking and hand-eye coordination. 'I gave a similar one to my best friend whose wife had a little boy. He loved it and sounds like he's doing the same as your niece. Either that or he stacks the blocks up and then charges at them to send them flying.'

'Maybe I won't suggest that game to Lily.'

Nate did a bit of rearranging at his stall now some stock had been shifted. But there were plenty of wonderful things left for Morgan to admire. She'd felt it was encroaching a little last night to really raid through what he had but here, it was different; it was what customers did, after all. She complimented him on the gorgeous duckboard painted in white that would be a wonderful addition to a contemporary bathroom, the bath caddy she could imagine putting across the tub and resting her Kindle on, the wooden blanket ladder that could hold at least three blankets, the block candle holder for tealights she could picture on the mantelpiece above a fireplace.

Morgan sold a couple of items to a woman who had a bag from the bakery stall, a bunch of bright yellow flowers presumably from Hildy's stall and another little bag filled with cookies from Sadie's pitch. 'You've done well today.'

'I love it here; you're all so wonderful. It's my favourite day of the week, market day.'

'Mine too,' Morgan told her, looking sideways at Nate, one of the biggest reasons for her liking being here these days.

When his customer went on their way, she asked, 'Will one more week be enough for you to sell everything?'

'I think so. I'll see.'

'So you might have to come back?' Her breath caught in her throat at the thought.

'It's a possibility.'

Possibility. She liked that word.

'When's your interview?' he asked.

She hadn't wanted to talk much about it last night in his workshop. 'This Tuesday.'

'Nervous?'

Morgan broke off the conversation to take payment for a beaded bag her customer said was perfect for her daughter who loved to play dress-up. She turned to Nate. 'I don't think so, at least not yet. I might be right before, though.'

'Listen, about everything I said yesterday...' He had his hands tucked into the pockets of his money belt as though he didn't know what else to do with them.

'I won't go repeating it if that's what you're suggesting.'

'I wasn't. I just wanted to say thanks for listening. And... well, you made me feel better.'

The way he looked at the ground, self-conscious because he'd bared his soul, was adorable. 'I'm glad to have helped. We both did our best, Nate.'

'I suppose we did.'

'We did. Both of us. In difficult circumstances. And if someone asked you, could you really say you could've done more? Other than stay with your mum twenty-four seven, I don't think you could have.'

He chuckled. 'Twenty-four seven would've driven her insane.'

'It would've done the same to my mum as well. She used to accuse me of hovering too much as it was.' She said it with fondness rather than anything else, remembering the banter, the smiles, the happiness as well as any sadness.

Their moment was interrupted by Sadie handing out freebies. 'These aren't mine – these are on behalf of Trina from the bakery stall.' She held out the tray of muffins for Nate and Morgan to take one each. 'She said these aren't very popular and she made too many. Please, take two, they're small.'

'Not going to argue,' said Nate.

'Me neither.' Morgan plucked two as well before Sadie went on her way to the next stall.

Morgan looked at the muffins. 'There's nothing small about these.'

'Nope, I'd say they're proper muffin size. Should we be worried that she's getting rid of them and making people take double portions?'

'Only one way to know.' Morgan bit into the fluffy, light, banana oat muffin at the same time as Nate did. 'I don't know how these aren't popular,' she said before taking another bite. She laughed when he bit half of his muffin in one go. 'Wow, sure you don't want to put it all in at once?'

When he finished his mouthful, he lifted up his second muffin. 'Challenge accepted.' And proceeded to put the whole thing into his mouth. But as he did so, a customer appeared at his stall and asked whether Nate could make one of the wooden bath caddies to order.

Morgan came to the rescue and did her best to talk to the customer while Nate turned his back as his face took on an odd purplish colour at the task of chomping down the muffin as quickly as possible.

'Let me take a note of your requirements,' she suggested to the customer, trying to ignore Nate behind her, doing his best to finish so he could take over his side of the stall again. 'Do you have them?'

The woman's brow furrowed as she leaned around Morgan. 'Is he all right?'

Morgan briefly turned to see Nate's eyes watering as she looked at him from the side but other than that, he was fine. 'Don't worry about him – late lunch,' she said as if that explained everything. Pen in hand, she wrote down the details the woman had recorded on her phone and read out to her.

When Nate eventually turned round as though nothing had happened, he thanked Morgan and took over telling the woman that of course he could make one to order but that the one he had here at the stall should be fine. He measured it to show her.

'I thought it looked far too big for my daughter's bath but it's the right size.' The woman seemed surprised but happy. 'My daughter loves a bubble bath. She's always reading too. Dropped her Kindle in the water last week; her husband was *not* happy, let me tell you.'

'There's a section for a book.' Nate pointed to the place on the caddy where the e-reader could be propped.

More than happy with her purchase, the woman went on her way.

'Enjoy the muffin?' Morgan asked, breaking into laughter until tears streamed down her cheeks. It wasn't long before he joined in.

'Don't ever let me do that again.' He swigged from a bottle of water. 'But I like that I make you laugh. Admit it: you're going to miss me when I'm gone.'

She couldn't deny it. Nate was leaving in a week. Which meant she was running out of time with him.

18

Nate had spent the last three days since the markets wishing he would bump into Morgan, but she seemed to have been keeping herself busy with whatever she was up to and perhaps that was a good thing. He'd heard from Bud in Wales that he had so much work on, Nate would be straight into it when he returned in less than a week, both with the jobs Nate had already booked in and the extras Bud had taken on when there was only one of him. He'd gone the extra mile too and had told Nate that he and his mum walked past Mrs Featherton's place a few days back, knocked on the door to check on her and had ended up going inside to share the red velvet cake she'd made. The two women had apparently hit it off, sharing baking tips, and were meeting up next week to bake a chocolate sponge together.

Nate walked over the humpback bridge on a summer's day that was unfortunately overcast and bereft of the usual brightness the time of year brought with it. But Branston was happily trotting along beside him and wagged his tail at the sight of Jeremy coming towards them.

'Jeremy, how are you doing?' Nate had got used to the way people in Little Woodville always had the time to stop in the street and ask after one another. Maybe they did that where he lived in Wales too, but he was usually so busy, he'd probably never noticed.

'I've been on the bus to Bourton-on-the-Water.' His enthusiasm bubbled away; there was colour in his cheeks. 'I'm glad to be back now, though. Stunning place but ridiculously busy.'

'I went with Mum once around Christmas. She loved the little shops.'

'I thought I could sit by the water and watch the world go by.' Jeremy harrumphed. 'Had a better time on the bus.'

'You're getting the hang of public transport by the sounds of it.'

'Have to: I'm selling the car.'

'You are?' He hoped Jeremy hadn't felt pressured; he hoped his talking about it the other day had been helpful rather than making him feel at all bad.

'It's time.' And actually he looked happy about it rather than anything else. 'I wouldn't have driven to such a popular village today so I wouldn't have got to go. Can't imagine what parking costs there, given the price I had to pay for an ice-cream.'

'Well, good for you. Where to next?'

'The world is my oyster on the bus,' Jeremy proclaimed. 'Might see where your dad wants to go.'

'He'd like that.'

Back at Oak Cottage, Nate went out to his workshop. Stock was depleting at a good rate despite adding to it along the way. It was strange to see the walls bereft of items stacked up and waiting to find an owner or purpose. He'd thought he'd be pleased to get to this stage but instead, he had an odd feeling, and rather than looking at it as an accomplishment, he was beginning to feel as though he might be losing something all over again. He ran a hand along the varnished blanket box, its beauty not lost on him. His mum would've loved it; she would've put all her blankets inside and probably rotated their use so she had an excuse to go back to the box and open and close it. He had no idea what to do with it now. All he knew was that it wasn't something he would ever sell; it meant too much.

And now his creative urge was gnawing at him again. Once he was back in Wales, he didn't have the space or the tools to do all of this. He needed to make the most of it while he could. He rummaged through some of the offcuts he had and found enough hard-wearing pieces to make a bird feeder that would put up enough fight against the elements to last. They'd had one in the garden a long time ago but never got round to replacing it when it broke. He measured, cut, lined up pieces, fixed things together until he had a feeder with a little roof that made it look like a miniature house with open sides to allow birds to perch but not bigger animals.

Outside, he took it over to the oak tree that held centre stage in their garden. His mum would approve of it for sure; she'd have enjoyed her favourite spot and watched the birds come and go. He found the branch he wanted, pretty sure the feeder they'd had when he was a boy had hung in near enough the same position, and he laughed to himself. He'd sneak some sort of bird food in the form of kitchen scraps onto it and see how long it took his dad to spot it.

Nate spent the rest of the day and early evening in the workshop, trying to take his mind off Morgan and the interview, a sinking feeling in his stomach that if she wasn't offered a job, she would've come over and told him by now. Wouldn't she?

He started work on a second bird feeder he could add to his stall this final Saturday and by the time he finished, it was growing dark, and when he went inside the house, his dad had already gone up to bed.

The next morning, Nate couldn't stand it any longer. He had to know. One way or the other, he had to find out whether Morgan had been offered a job in a place that felt like it was a million miles away.

It worked out well that Trevor had already asked to take Branston for a long walk so he could spend as much time with him before he returned to Wales. Jeremy was going too so getting rid of the car was not only driving the man towards public transport, it was getting him walking more, which could only be a good thing. His dad was nimble, Jeremy wasn't bad, but Nate swore his dad would be a lot slower at his age if he hadn't kept up daily exploration of the village and its surrounds.

Nate headed out himself at a pace and when he reached Morgan's home, he pushed open the gate to Forget-Me-Not Cottage. The postman behind him said a hello and Nate offered to take the bunch of letters and give them to Morgan. The letters felt like a prop that might help him enter into small talk rather than the real reason he'd come.

He knocked once, he knocked again. Maybe she was out and about. The sun was shining, it was a beautiful day and a group of kids had been playing Poohsticks on the humpback bridge, causing him to think about the first time he'd set eyes on Morgan Reese. It wasn't something he'd forget easily.

'Good morning, Nate.' It was Nel, who ran the pizza place on the high street with her husband André. She came walking up the path as Nate was peering in the lounge window, hands cupped around his eyes to get a better view inside.

'I'm not staking out the place,' he said awkwardly. 'Promise.'

She took some keys from her bag and jangled them in front of

him. 'These might make it easier. You been assigned the post?' She
noted the pile of letters in his hand. And before he could ask what
she meant by *assigned*, she was putting the key in the front door. 'I
got Marley. I'd say you got the easy job. I've heard he needs to learn
some more road sense. I'm paranoid he'll go missing on my watch.'

'I'm sorry, what are you talking about?'

'Morgan, she's asked me to look after the cat. Here he is.' Her
voice altered an octave as if the cat wouldn't understand her otherwise. She bent down and scooped the feline into her arms as he
met them at the door.

'Has Morgan gone out?' Nate was confused now.

Nel was obviously a tiny bit in love with the cat, the way she
kept rubbing her face against its fur. 'Morgan's away,' she told him
when he finally had her attention again. 'I thought you'd know,
with the markets and everything.'

'I don't know anything.'

She looked worried now. 'She's a grown woman but I think
when Elaina died, we all made it our mission to look out for her.'

'You were good friends?' He hadn't realised.

'We were. Elaina supported me when I was sick. I would've
done the same, but she loved that Morgan had come home for her.
Looking after Marley is the least I can do now.' She paused as if
remembering the purpose of their conversation. 'I'm sure Morgan
is fine.'

Nate was still confused. 'You said she's away? What do you
mean by away?'

'She's gone.'

'Gone where?'

'To Scotland.'

Nate had heard people say their heart sank at disappointing or
bad news but he'd never thought it was physically possible and yet

that was exactly how he felt now. It was as though his own heart had plummeted to the floor.

He passed her the batch of letters from the postman. 'Could you put these inside?'

'Sure. See you around,' she called after him, although he was already halfway down the path.

And he made his way home with a hollow feeling inside of him. Morgan had gone. She'd left, gone to Scotland to start a job and marry Ronan.

And she hadn't even said goodbye.

* * *

'What's going on with you?' Trevor asked when at midday, making bacon sandwiches for their lunch, Nate dropped two rashers on the floor and then proceeded to cut his finger as he sliced the bread in half once it was filled with much less bacon than there otherwise might have been. He'd insisted on doing some sorting in his dad's loft the moment he'd got back from the house because it meant he could take his frustration out on the things up there. He'd made a pile of things that his dad could look through before they went to charity shops or in the bin and stacked everything against the wall in the bedroom he was sleeping in. As it turned out, there wasn't as much up there as he'd feared but it had still felt cleansing to have a good go at it.

'Nothing's wrong.' Nate ran his finger under the tap and wrapped it in kitchen towel to stop the blood. Why did tiny cuts always bleed so much?

Nate had got a message from Jasper to say that Morgan had gone to Scotland and he didn't know anything other than that the stall was Nate's. Nate had no idea whether that meant he had it to himself next week, or whether he could have it forever if he wanted to come back here to Little Woodville. The message implied Jasper knew about as much as Nel did.

'If I'd done what you just did, you'd have me shipped off to the nearest old folks' home before I could argue,' Trevor pointed out as Nate found a plaster to replace the tissue.

He sighed and pulled out a chair at the table. Even that wasn't straightforward – the legs got stuck on the table's feet and it was a wrestle to get them free. He sank his teeth into his sandwich and he was halfway through before his dad said anything else.

'Was the loft terrible?' Trevor asked.

Nate had to smile. 'No, it wasn't. You saw the pile of things to go through, didn't you?'

'I did but I wondered if it was so awful up there, that's what's put you in this mood.'

'No, it wasn't terrible. And now it's done.'

'Thank you. I appreciate it.' But he wasn't going to let it drop. 'Son, what's going on?'

Nate gave him a look. 'Don't think I haven't noticed how much HP sauce you've put on your sandwich.'

'At my age, I deserve it,' was his reply. 'Does your mood have anything to do with a certain lady friend who came here one evening?'

'You knew Morgan was here?'

He bit into his sandwich, the HP sauce oozing out of one side. 'I'm old, not stupid. I peeked out after you'd made cheese on toast and saw you through the window. Don't worry, I didn't spy for long; I left you to it.' After another bite and wiping the sauce from his plate with a finger, he said, 'I figured if you had something to tell me, you'd tell me. If you didn't...'

'She had an interview for a job in Scotland.'

Trevor paused while he ate his mouthful. 'Everyone knew she

was moving there.' But he tilted his head. 'Never thought she'd go. Something seemed to be keeping her here.'

'Well, not any more. She's gone.' Nate sank his teeth into his own sandwich.

'But she didn't say goodbye to anyone.'

Nate hadn't thought anyone else would be as bothered as him. Nel had looked confused and concerned rather than perturbed, Jasper was obviously bewildered, judging by the tone of his message. Nate wondered – had she said goodbye to anyone? Or had she decided she wanted to leave without any fuss? Which he supposed had its benefits.

When he'd finished eating, he flipped the top back on the HP sauce bottle and took both plates over to the sink.

'Something must have happened,' said Trevor, still discombobulated at the sudden news that Morgan had left the village. 'I don't think she'd just up and leave the house, the market stall, Little Woodville.'

Nate sat down again. He'd sort out the dishes later. This wasn't just about his feelings; it was about everyone else's too. 'Perhaps doing it without much fuss was the way to go. And there's not much we can do about it now. What it does mean is that I should be able to take most of my wooden items to the markets on Saturday as I'll have both tables to myself.'

'You'll sell it all, I bet.' They went through what was left. 'I sneaked in there earlier today and I saw the blanket box. Your mum would've loved it.'

Nate let a breath go. 'You know, I think she would too.' He wondered whether his mum would've liked Morgan. But it hardly mattered now, did it? 'I won't sell it, though.'

'It's a nice memory.'

'Would you like it?'

Trevor thought for a moment. 'No, you keep it. It was between you and your mum. I feel it's something special for you.'

Branston made a funny sound from his basket – the dog was obviously dreaming but it had Nate laughing with his dad.

'I'll miss him, you know,' said Trevor. 'And you, of course. It's been good having you both around.'

'I've really enjoyed my time here. It's gone too quickly. You'll call me if you need me, won't you?'

'I've got plans, son. Jeremy has bus routes to goodness knows where, Gillian has already given me the date of the next card game which I'm invited to and Betty even said she'll teach me how to make something called a Bundt cake to take with me. Apparently, Gillian loves it.'

'How is that any different to a normal cake?'

'Your guess is as good as mine. So what's the plan when you return to Wales?'

'Work, work and more work.' He should be grateful; it would keep his mind from thinking about Morgan, likely with Ronan right now, starting their new life in Scotland. He should wish her well with the new job, but he couldn't quite dig that deep. Not yet, anyway. And besides, she wasn't even here to tell her as much.

'And you aren't going to worry about me, are you?'

Nate appreciated the directness. 'I can't promise that. But I give you my word I won't hassle you until it's necessary. You've got a good life here, Dad. I'd forgotten how much I loved this village myself. I shouldn't be surprised you never want to leave.'

When the phone rang, Trevor answered it to a flustered Betty at the bakery. He quickly handed the call over to Nate.

'You've tried unblocking the drain?' Nate asked her. It seemed the issue wasn't at the bakery but at their home in the en suite shower room and Peter had tried what he could to clear a blockage that was causing water to accumulate in the shower tray and start to spill over. It was the only shower they had and she was already catastrophising that it might get so bad, it would ruin the floor, leak through the ceiling.

'Can you help?' Betty pleaded.

'I'll come take a look. I don't have all my equipment with me, but I've got enough and there are a few tricks I can try.'

Trevor turned the kettle off as Nate ended the call. 'I'll make you a cuppa when you get back. You're in demand here.'

He pulled his boots on at the front door. 'I can try a few things – high tech stuff. Actually, do you have a wire coat hanger?'

Trevor headed to the bedroom and came back with one.

'I'll try this first, then there are a few other things, but I can get quite a lot of debris out this way.' He grinned at his dad's face. 'I wouldn't think too carefully about it if I were you.'

He was there and back in less than forty minutes. 'Coat hanger worked a treat,' he called out after Branston gave him a warm welcome inside the front door, wagging his tail back and forth.

'I don't want it back,' Trevor called from the kitchen. Nate could hear the kettle reaching its boiling point as he padded down the hallway.

'Don't worry, I left it with Peter so he can try it again if needs be. The job really needs high pressure water to give it a proper clean out. I told him I'd bring everything I need next time I'm here.'

Trevor brought the mugs of tea over to the table. 'You've already decided to come back soon?'

'I have. Is that all right?'

'Of course it is. Having you and Branston here is wonderful.' He gestured to the way Nate was toying with his mug. 'What's on your mind?' He knew the action meant Nate was thinking heavily. He'd done it all through exam time at school, the tea often going cold before he'd even drunk half of it, his worries lurking in the murky depths of the liquid.

'This is the first time I've found myself questioning my own arrangements. All the way out in Wales rather than being here, I mean. I'm not sure what's the right thing any more.'

'You know your mum fell in love with this village first. "Come and see it, Trevor," she said to me after she'd come here to meet a friend for a summer picnic. "You'll fall in love with it like I have," she claimed. And she was right. She loved Little Woodville. She loved this house, she loved you, she loved me. She knew we didn't have forever, nobody does, but despite her suffering, she treasured what she had and wanted to hold onto it. And she'd be telling you to do the same now. Memories of your mother are here but wherever you are, those memories will stay with you. You don't have to be in the village if that isn't what you want. You have a business in Wales, a home. Keep your mum in your heart and she'll never leave you. You don't have to be here to do that.'

But what if he wanted to be here? Was it possible that after all this time away, he wanted to return? He'd never felt the urge before, never.

'May I ask,' Trevor ventured, 'did Morgan have anything to do with you finally uncovering the blanket box after all this time?'

'You're so nosy.' But he was grinning from ear to ear. 'Yes, she did. She had everything to do with it. She even helped finish it.'

'I hope she charged for her time.'

'Sure, Dad.' He felt like the same little boy who'd sold those wooden coasters, his dad coaching him in what to say and what would be a fair charge for each of them.

'May I ask whether Morgan has anything to do with your doubts about a return to Wales?'

'You may ask,' Nate grinned.

Trevor knew he wouldn't get much more out of him. 'You'll miss your workshop when you go home.'

'I will. No room for one back in Wales. But that's okay; I think I'd work better here anyway.' Already, he knew he'd miss being able to head out there of an evening when he had a few spare hours.

'Not the same though, is it? You know, inspiration can strike at the most inconvenient times.'

'You want me to come home.'

'Nate, I would never ask you to do that. And I just told you to do what you need to, not to let me or your mother's memory be a deciding factor.'

'You'd love it if I said I was moving back,' Nate teased.

And Trevor was doing his best to pretend that wasn't what he wanted. He was a good dad, never pressured, never felt his son owed him. 'Your mum and I had the same approach to parenting. She always said we could give you roots and wings and if you chose to fly back here then so be it. And if not... well...'

'Let's watch this space, shall we? Not make any decisions now, let things unfold.'

In only a short space of time, he'd felt at home in the village in a way he hadn't since his mum died, as though he'd had to immerse himself in it once again and learn to be in the world where she no longer existed rather than avoiding it.

'If I did move back here, it'd be an upheaval. I'd have to sell my house and the plumbing business – my client base is worth a bit.'

'I'm sure it is. But I'd say you've got the start of a client base here already if that's a worry. You've got Sebastian, Betty, Jeremy and that's without advertising.'

'Except your word-of-mouth advertising, eh, Dad.'

They took the mugs over to the sink.

'I heard you fixed a shelf for Morgan too.'

'Not the same thing at all,' he laughed. 'But word sure travels fast.'

'She'll be back son.'

'I'm not so sure.'

His dad went over to one of the cupboards and pulled out peanuts, raisins, some kind of seeds and emptied them into a bowl before taking a block of lard from the fridge.

'That had better not be dinner,' Nate grimaced.

'It's a cake.'

'An edible one?'

'A bird cake.' Trevor unwrapped the block of lard. 'Don't think I haven't spotted the bird table – there were a few summer visitors, chaffinches at my guess, squabbling over whatever you'd put in there.'

Nate smiled. 'Do you like it?'

Trevor stopped what he was doing. 'I really like it. I'd forgotten we had one years ago and it was good to see the birds gathering around it when I was out in the garden. It brought back some very fond memories. And your mum would approve too.'

He thought of how he'd felt when he'd hung it from the branch, far enough in that it was on a strong part of the trunk. He could remember watching the birds with his mum when he was a little boy, her lifting him up so he could put food on the table for their garden visitors.

And as they laughed, making the revolting recipe that Nate thanked heavens wasn't going to be served for dinner, Nate looked out at the garden, all the space, the open surrounds beyond the back of the house, another part of the village he'd not really acknowledged until this visit. It was as though in the years since losing his mum, he'd had his eyes partially shut or at least his blinkers on.

He wouldn't say anything to Trevor. But in that moment, laughing with his dad, Nate made a firm decision.

It was time he sold up in Wales and moved back to Little Woodville.

This wasn't about the memory of his mum or about his dad and whether he worried about him being so far away. It wasn't about Morgan either because she'd left.

This was about him and what he wanted. And he knew at long last that what he wanted was to be here. In Little Woodville.

19

THREE WEEKS LATER

Morgan rubbed her eyes. She'd slept most of the day away and the sun shone in through the curtains as though nodding its approval at the major decision she'd made about her life.

Last month, she'd had a Zoom interview with the media company who were interested in her even though she'd told them that she no longer wanted to move to Edinburgh. She'd kept that little detail to herself; she hadn't wanted to tell anyone, especially Nate, in much the same way she'd wanted to keep her engagement ring on her finger to avoid having to explain. The company had then set up an in-person interview for a position in Cheltenham and had flown her up to Edinburgh to their head office to meet the management team. And not only had they offered her the position there and then, one with a full-time salary that would allow her to commute from Forget-Me-Not Cottage three days a week with two days working from home; they'd put her up for two nights in a luxury hotel and she'd joined them the next day for a team-building exercise.

Morgan had met up with Ronan before she left Edinburgh. She'd given him back the engagement ring over a dinner he'd booked and rather than look like a jilted party, she could tell he was doing really well. And that made her happier than ever.

Morgan hadn't returned to Little Woodville immediately following the interview, however. She'd taken the chance to go and stay with Tegan, take some time away which she very much needed.

Northumberland was everything Morgan expected it to be. Full of family banter, farmyard sounds and smells, unique experiences – never before had she woken to find a snout poking through her open bedroom window, which had scared the life out of her. Seeing Henry handle the pig and try to coax it back to where it had escaped from, Morgan realised the animal was scarily strong and after her extended stay, she got to see first-hand why there was the well-known phrase *happy as a pig in mud*. Her niece and nephew didn't mind the mud one bit, but Morgan had favoured climbing trees with Jaimie rather than helping out with the pigs, or giving Lily cuddles when she woke from her afternoon nap.

It had been quality time they'd all needed; it had been fun. Henry had given Morgan and Tegan every evening together to talk and that's exactly what they'd done, making the most of the days that might be shortening but were still a decent enough length. They talked about everything: their childhood, their parents, their losses, what they had left. But more than anything, Morgan had finally stepped away from her own life, her own goals and issues, and got to see and appreciate what Tegan had up here – her young family, the in-laws close by, the meals together that were chaotic, with voices tumbling over one another, yet comforting. The sisters had also discussed donating the profits they'd made from Elaina's market stall to charity in the same way Nate had. And they'd agreed that supporting an osteoporosis charity would be a fine way to honour their mum.

Marley leapt up onto the bed in Forget-Me-Not Cottage now as

Morgan looked out of the window. She'd purposely left the curtains open because she intended to have a quick nap after driving back from Northumberland this morning. But embraced in the cottage's welcome, she'd slept for longer than she'd intended.

Now she needed to get organised. She had a quick shower – the unpacking could wait – and as soon as she was ready, she headed to the pizzeria. She'd called Nel from Northumberland and given her an estimate of when she'd return to the village – luckily she hadn't had to say where she was because she'd had to leave a voice-mail – and she wanted to thank her for seeing to Marley for so long. Once she'd done that, she wanted to head over to the Snow-drop Lane markets and see Jasper, apologise to him for being so vague. But today, she'd be there as a customer rather than a trader. She still had items she needed to sell but the stock was dwindling enough that the cottage was no longer overrun and Tegan was coming again soon to help deal with the rest. Her next few weeks were set to be busy finishing the last of her freelance pieces and shopping for office clothes because she doubted the casual attire she wore around the house would work in a professional setting. She thought she might even make a start on sprucing up the cottage or thinking about how to redecorate when she got the opportunity, once the ownership was transferred to her name only.

Nel had been a good friend to Elaina and always kind to Morgan since her arrival back in the village. As soon as Nel saw Morgan come into the pizzeria, she came out from behind the counter, arms wide open for a hug that had Morgan feeling as though Elaina had had a word in her ear to look out for her daughter when she was gone.

Nel shunted them both towards the open doorway so they could stand outside but keep an eye on whether Nel needed to leap in and help André out.

'It's good to see you back... are you, back, I mean?'

Morgan grinned. 'I am.'

'For how long?'

'For good.'

Nel tilted her head in approval. 'Your mother would be made up to know you've settled here.'

'I think you're right.'

'Thank you for the flowers; they're gorgeous and filling our lounge with the most beautiful scents and colours.'

'I'm glad you like them. Thank you again; I mean it. I know I just upped and left but thank you for jumping in with the cottage and Marley.'

Nel squinted in the sunshine as they stood outside to appreciate the warm days that would soon be coming to an end with summer over. 'Coming to your place was an escape from the busyness of my own life, to be honest. André always fusses that I don't rest as much as I should.'

'I'll buy you dinner at the pub one evening to say a proper thank you.'

'Not going to say no to that... any time.' Summer always brought out positivity but Morgan sensed that even if it had been pouring with rain today, she'd still feel as upbeat as she did right now. She was back. Really back.

'I bumped into someone else at your place when I was looking after everything.' Nel held the door to the pizzeria open for a customer as they came out, box resting on their arms. 'Nate.'

'He'd have been expecting me to be at the final market session the week after. He was probably disappointed.'

Nel quirked a brow. 'He didn't look disappointed. He looked devastated. But I know you must have had your reasons for going and for doing it so quickly.'

She recapped on what had happened – the job interview and the position in Cheltenham.

'I'm so pleased for you.' But with customers milling, Morgan could see her attention was torn.

'You go inside; we'll talk more at the pub soon.'

She put a hand on Morgan's arm. 'It's good to have you back.'

Morgan went on her way, embracing the sunny day that was cooler than when she was here over a month ago, a slight chill on the air that hinted autumn was around the corner and necessitated the need for a cardigan over the shirt she'd teamed with jeans. She walked fast enough to get to the markets before closing but slowly enough to take it all in.

She paused at the top of the humpback bridge and leaned against the honey-coloured stone wall as she thought about Nate. He'd be long gone by now. Back to Wales.

She turned into Snowdrop Lane and meandered up towards the ground that hosted the markets every Saturday. Trading would have just finished so it was clear-up time. Hildy emerged from the front entrance as Morgan crossed the car park area.

'I thought we'd lost you!' Hildy waved enthusiastically, laughter lines prominent and proving the sense of fun that tended to be associated with the woman.

'Never,' Morgan laughed in her embrace.

'Are you back? For good or to pack up?' Her spirits diminished at the final suggestion.

'For good. I'm buying Forget-Me-Not Cottage, so you're stuck with me.'

Hildy pulled her in for a hug again. 'That's the best news ever!'

'Morgan!' Zadie from the second-hand book stall had appeared behind them and bustled in for her turn to hug the returning resident. 'Can't stop, got to go back for another box. You know what Jasper's like; he runs a tight ship. But we'll catch up. Soon.'

'Promise,' she hollered after her because she was already off. It felt unbelievably good to be able to finally let it be known that she wasn't going anywhere.

'You've been missed,' declared Mindy as she emerged from the markets entrance with a huge box in her arms. She didn't stop, the box looked too heavy, so she went over to her car.

Many more of these greetings and Morgan might well cry with the emotion of it all.

Sadie came out of the main entrance next, a big plastic container in her arms. 'You're back, great to see you!'

'Thanks, Sadie.'

'You missed my birthday cake cookies,' she grinned.

'Sounds interesting.'

'White chocolate chips, sprinkles... they sold out before lunchtime. I'll make them for next week.' She nodded her head to the container in her arms. 'Freebies inside if I can interest you; think there's some chocolate, some oatmeal and raisin.'

Morgan shook her head because she wanted to catch Jasper and at this rate, she wouldn't get a chance. 'I won't today, but next week for sure. I won't be working the stall but I'll come for a wander this way and see everyone, say a proper hello.'

'Great. See you next week.' Sadie hadn't been doing this long either and she was already as much a part of it as the others. Jasper had a good team; she wondered whether he organised stalls and traders according to personality or whether he'd got lucky with them all without much effort at all. Or perhaps anyone who was a market trader was naturally adept at being friendly and fitting in.

As Morgan went in through the front entrance to the markets, which was really just a very wide gap between two stalls, she could feel her mother's spirit with her. The breeze blew her dark hair lightly as she approached the stall that had once been Elaina's. She could see boxes piled up on both tables but any signage to let her know who'd had the stall for the day was already down with the packing up underway.

She was about to walk on and find Jasper but she froze when she looked again at the man behind those tables, facing away from her.

It couldn't be, could it?

He was bending down and that was why she hadn't immediately realised. But looking at him now, the well-fitted jeans, a bottom she'd seen bending over enough times, the muscular shoulder blades in a casual t-shirt and the tanned, strong neck as he turned in her direction, she knew it was him.

'I thought you'd left.' He put the box in his arms down on the table, pushing another out of the way to enable him to do so. 'Thought you'd taken the job.'

'I did.'

She was about to explain everything when he picked the box up again and pushed a wooden chopping board under one arm. 'That's me done, ready to go.'

'I can take something if it makes it easier.'

'I can manage.' Without another word, he left the stall and made for the entrance and the car park.

Had she totally blown it with him?

'You came back...' she stumbled as they walked, him pacing ahead of her. 'To the markets, I mean, to sell things.'

'Yup.'

Was that all she got? He wasn't making this easy.

'Are you still making things?'

'Yup.'

This was painful. 'Nate, would you stop and talk to me?'

'This is heavy,' he claimed and strode over to his pick-up.

'You're so frustrating!' Her outburst didn't do much to stop him arranging the box and the board in the metal tray before he pulled the cover over everything. 'And you're stubborn!'

'Any more insults for me?' he asked once the cover was secure.

She didn't say a word.

He pulled open the driver's door. Was he just going to leave?

But he turned, one hand on the top of the door. 'I don't like not knowing what's going on, that's all. You just left. Without a word. And Morgan...' He ran a hand across his jaw. 'I can't do this with you. I've told you that more than once.'

Before he could climb into the pick-up, she asked, 'What are you doing back here?' This time, she moved in front of him and closed the driver's door. 'Why won't you look at me, Nate?'

He looked then but only briefly. 'You know why.'

'No, actually, I don't.'

'How's the new job in Edinburgh?' he asked. 'That's where you went, isn't it?'

'I did go to Scotland, yes. But I haven't started the job yet.' She pushed her back against his driver's door, unwilling to let him get in, let alone drive away from her. She was about to tell him that the new job wasn't in Scotland, not any more, when he put his hands on the tops of her arms and moved her out of the way gently. She didn't have a chance to brace herself and refuse to move.

He climbed into the pick-up and started the engine. When he wound the window down to get some air circulating, she rested her hands on the top.

He puffed out his cheeks at her persistence. 'Where's your fiancé?' A hint of mockery mixed with a tone that sounded hurt, pissed off, delivered the question. But in that moment, he clocked the ringless fourth finger of her left hand.

'I don't have one,' she said simply. And still he said nothing. 'Oh, you're impossible, Nate. Maybe I can't do this either.'

She stomped away between parked cars so his pick-up couldn't follow her and when she emerged towards the entrance of the car park, she turned onto Snowdrop Lane.

But she hadn't walked much further when she heard a snapping of twigs beside her, followed by a swish of the bushes before Nate appeared, puffed from what was likely a sprint to cut her off. He'd never looked so good, even with the leaf on the shoulder of his t-shirt, a twig he yanked from his hair before he scraped a hand through it, the stubble that said *sexy* rather than *forgot to shave*.

He stood in her path, the puffing subsiding as his heart rate returned to normal. 'Would it interest you to know that I've moved in with Dad? For the foreseeable?'

She hadn't expected to see him today, let alone have him say something like that. 'You're moving back to the village?'

'Looks like it.' He stepped closer, forcing her to look up some more rather than have her gaze fixed on his chest.

'What about Wales? Your home? Your business?'

'Technicalities, Morgan.'

She looked down again, the stone near her shoe of sudden interest. This was real now. Both single, both in the village.

'What, you don't have anything to say?' he asked. When she still said nothing, he added, 'Well, that's a first. Now who's being stubborn?'

'I'm not being stubborn. I'm—'

But he stopped any more arguing by closing the gap between them and pressing his lips against hers firmly enough that she knew he meant business, softly enough that it took seconds to sink into the kiss she felt through every part of her body.

20

Autumn arrived with a pleasing palate of yellow, orange and red dotted around Little Woodville. As the nights drew in, the village took on a cosier ambience, there was a nip in the air, a crunch underfoot as leaves drifted across your path when you walked, and the stone of the humpback bridge appeared to glow in the lower light of the season.

The eponymous flowers of Forget-Me-Not Cottage were no longer on display given it was autumn, but Morgan's home didn't look any less beautiful. She'd redecorated the lounge already in a colour she knew her mother would've approved of – white with a very slight hint of lilac – but that was it inside because she'd wanted to work outside while the weather still allowed. And so she'd painted the shed and the garden bench in forget-me-not blue, the paint colour a way of keeping the theme going for the cottage even in winter, along with the artificial forget-me-not plant she'd found for the kitchen windowsill.

Morgan pulled on a chunky cardigan and took Branston for a long walk through Snowdrop Woods. She liked looking after him whenever she could; he was good company and had much better road sense than Marley. They had fun following their familiar route; she kicked through piles of leaves, and they ended up at the Bookshop Café where she made sure he wasn't going to traipse in mud. Luckily for the both of them, it didn't look like it – it might be a different matter when winter arrived, though.

She said her hellos to Sebastian and Belle, collected a hot chocolate and headed on up to the flat above the shop to see Nate.

Since Nate had moved back to the village, he'd lived with Trevor, but as well as Morgan and Nate becoming an item, things had developed for Sebastian and Belle too.

A few weeks after Nate and Morgan were seen out and about enough for the entire village to know they were together, they'd been in the Bookshop Café when Sebastian had turned the sign on the door to *Closed* a little earlier than expected.

'Whatever are you up to?' Belle had asked him as he'd headed towards her. She'd already got changed into a little black dress with silver, strappy sandals, delighted to be dressing up for once rather than wearing an apron with spatters of milk, chocolate, coffee and whatever other ingredients she'd used.

'I've got a problem,' Sebastian had said, causing Nate and Morgan to share a puzzled glance across the table they were sitting at. They were all going out for dinner to the local Italian restaurant this evening but Sebastian had wanted them here for coffees first. A peculiar request but they'd agreed to it.

'What sort of problem?' Belle had looked at him. 'Not the toilet at Snowdrop Cottage again. Honestly, you should probably replace all the plumbing in the cottage; who knows what will go wrong next.'

'Belle, I'm trying to say something here.' Sebastian had taken the cloth out of her hand and set it on the table before picking up both of her hands again. 'You're right to think it's a problem with the cottage.'

'I knew it.'

But he had put a finger on her lips before she could say anything else. 'The problem isn't the plumbing. The problem is that it's empty without you in it. Always has been, ever since you barrelled into my life, all bossy and making claims about it.' He had gulped; he was nervous, not something he usually was. He had a commanding, secure presence but in that moment, he had been anything but. 'Move in with me, Belle.'

Her mouth had fallen open but then a smile had crept onto her face before she flung her arms around his neck. 'Yes! Yes, yes, yes!'

'There's just one more thing...' He had pulled away and there had been no doubt what he was going to do when he had gotten down on one knee.

Belle's eyes had filled with tears and she had barely seemed to hear him say the rest: the proposal he'd clearly been working up to. She had put her hands to her mouth as he had opened a small, velvet box to reveal a ring that caught the light and gleamed.

He had taken her left hand. 'When I met you, I knew I'd met my match. You're the most infuriating, gorgeous woman I've ever laid eyes on, and I only want to do the future with you. I would've asked you to marry me long before today but we decided to wait and I'm done waiting. Will you marry me?'

Belle had been so emotional, she'd barely managed to say the word *yes* but as soon as she had, Sebastian had pushed the ring onto her finger.

Morgan, who'd been watching in amazement, had whispered to Nate, 'We're intruding.'

'We should sneak off,' he'd agreed as he'd picked up his jacket and her denim jacket. But as they'd stood up, Sebastian had stopped them.

'Where are you two going? It's dinner at the Italian, remember?'

'I think you two might need your own celebration.' Morgan had gone straight over to throw her arms around Belle. 'Congratulations, I'm so pleased for you.' She'd moved on to Sebastian next. 'Well done you.'

Nate had shaken Sebastian's hand and was hugging Belle as Sebastian grabbed his own jacket and Belle's coat. 'Dinner is still on, you two. You've become good friends and I wanted you to be witness to this.'

'I'm glad we were,' Morgan had smiled.

'Nate knew everything,' Sebastian had said with a grin. 'He helped me choose the ring. And Morgan, you got the size for me.'

Morgan and Nate had exchanged a look. They'd both kept it quiet from each other after Sebastian had sworn them to secrecy, but if Nate was anything like her, he'd have been itching to tell her. She'd found it hard to keep her mouth shut but hadn't thought Sebastian was going to pop the question tonight. She'd thought this was a meal between friends but saw now that it was a lot more than that.

'So this dinner tonight is a thank you,' Morgan had confirmed as Sebastian began to switch off the lights.

'Kind of.' Sebastian had helped Belle on with her coat.

Morgan had inspected the ring yet again. 'It really is gorgeous. Does it fit all right?'

'Perfectly.'

'Better than a wooden ring?' Last week, she'd pretended to Belle that Nate was going to try making wooden rings and sell them on the stall. As if. She'd almost laughed, especially when Belle hadn't questioned her measuring around her fingers. She'd done all four so it wasn't obvious. And then she'd had to keep a straight face when Belle started talking about wooden jewellery and how she didn't see much of it around.

'So much better,' Belle had replied.

'You do realise I was totally lying about Nate making wooden rings, don't you?'

'Well, now I do,' she'd laughed as they all filed out of the Bookshop Café.

'You still haven't told us what the dinner is if it isn't a thank you,' Nate had said as Sebastian locked up.

'You'll see. You'll all see.' And he had led the way along the high street towards the Italian restaurant. More sophisticated than the pizzeria and for a different clientele, it had been dimly lit, with a romantic ambience and as Sebastian had pushed open the door and they'd stepped inside to a cheer, it had all became obvious.

'This, my darling Belle,' Sebastian had announced, pulling her to him and into his arms in front of the crowd, 'is our engagement party.'

Belle had looked about to cry as she covered her mouth, overcome with emotion. And when she'd seen Gillian sitting at the back, Betty and Peter, Trevor, all of their friends and her parents who had flown in from Ireland, she'd rushed towards her family.

Sebastian had hired out the entire restaurant for the engagement party, sure of Belle's answer, as he rightly should be when they were so perfect for each other. Wine was poured, chatter filled the air, food was shared and good times and at the end, Belle came over to Morgan and Nate.

'Here...' She had held something shiny in her hand and Nate had put his hand out because she was holding it out to him. She'd placed a key in his palm. 'It's the key to the flat above the Bookshop Café. It looks as though I have another home. So it's yours, if you want it. I'll have my things moved out tomorrow, I expect.' She had been beaming. 'Rent is due first of the month, it's a good rate, it's quiet, food discounted downstairs if you can't be bothered to cook.'

Trevor had overheard. 'Oh, thank goodness, you're getting him out from under my feet. He's cramping my style.'

'And you've had too much wine,' Nate had said quietly as Trevor and Jeremy laughed at the joke.

Belle had told him, 'When me and Sebastian fell for each other, we could've easily moved faster but we both wanted time to get used to being together; we wanted to date first, take it slow. And I get the feeling you and Morgan might want that too.' She had squeezed Nate's hand with the key in his palm. 'That's a spare key, call it a prop for my suggestion, but seriously, I'll be out quickly.'

The engagement party had ended with toasts to the happy couple, Betty and Peter saying their goodbyes before they closed the bakery and headed off to see family overseas for three weeks, Jeremy declaring he was glad he didn't have a car and the responsibility of driving home. And as soon as they got the chance, Nate and Morgan had sneaked away back to Forget-Me-Not Cottage for some alone time.

Now, with Branston beside her, Morgan let herself in to Nate's flat and the dog headed straight for the kitchen for a thirsty gulp from his water bowl. Nate had moved in a couple of days after Belle had handed him the key and he'd been getting sorted ever since.

'I'm back,' she called out. She took a sip of her hot chocolate, much needed after a long walk.

Nate emerged from the bathroom in a cloud of steam, his bottom half wrapped in a fluffy, white towel. Morgan didn't think she'd ever get over quite how hot her boyfriend was. That, and good with his hands. She almost blushed at her own thoughts.

'Sorry I'm running late.' He came and kissed her on the lips, moaning at the same time at the deliciousness of it. 'I had a job for Clover at her cottage. That husband of hers left her, the kids, and a mess with a bodged, DIY shower. The unit was practically hanging off the wall. Sorted quickly but then I had a job for Barbara at the church, or rather an inspection and a quote to sort the heating out.'

'They'll need that come winter.'

'Sure will. I couldn't turn the work down when she asked.'

'Of course you couldn't.' She watched him approvingly. 'Good job I made the dinner last night and stashed it in your fridge.'

'I'd forgotten that,' he smiled as he dashed to the kitchen and put the oven on. 'My mouth is watering thinking about it now. Exactly what I need after a busy day.'

She'd made a cauliflower cheese, not for the first time, and it didn't taste exactly like Elaina's but between her and Nate, they'd come up with a recipe that was theirs. A quick warm in the oven would get the cheese on top bubbling away and she'd serve it with a salad.

'You're staring,' he grinned, one hand on his towel as though he thought it might fall at any moment.

'I am not.' But her sip of hot chocolate barely hid a grin. 'Well, maybe a little bit. I'm still getting used to seeing so much of you.'

He stepped forward to kiss her again and she almost dropped the hot chocolate, wishing she didn't have it because she'd like to drag him towards the bedroom right now. His forehead against hers, he breathed, 'I'm a bit knackered. Please tell me we're not meeting anyone at the pub tonight.'

'Not as far as I know.' They often did, whether it was his dad, or Jeremy, Sebastian and Belle or anyone else. 'I'm too tired to venture out again. Getting up and out to an office three days a week is exhausting.' And she'd rather cosy up here anyway.

He put a hand against her cheek before taking a diversion into the bedroom, where he pulled on a pair of jeans. She put a hand on his chest, his skin still damp and warm from the shower, before he lifted a sweatshirt over his head and down over his torso.

Belle had been right to offer the flat to Nate. This way was much better than rushing into anything, even when Morgan had a whole cottage to herself. This kept it new, exciting, and now he wasn't at his dad's, they at least didn't have to worry about being interrupted. It had been a bit like being teenagers again the times she went there to see him and they had to be on their best behaviour.

Nate put the dinner in the oven and prepared the salad while Morgan finished her hot chocolate in the lounge. Branston had curled up on the rug already, uninterested in expending any more energy. A lamp gave a soft glow to the room which had Nate's bottle-green sofa and armchair as well as a couple of side tables in a rich dark wood that had made their way from Wales, taken from the house he'd sold quickly enough.

It looked homely in here already and Morgan spotted the new addition in the lounge as Nate came into the room. 'When did you bring that over?' It was the blanket box he'd made for his mum, blending in so well with everything else, she hadn't noticed until she was facing this way. 'It looks perfect in here.'

He wrapped his arms around her from behind, his damp hair against her cheek as he nuzzled her neck. 'Take a look inside.'

She went over to the piece she'd helped to finish and opened it up. And there it was: the denim and caramel lambswool blanket her mother had adored, the one he'd taken to the dry cleaner for her yesterday as he'd insisted he was going that way.

'I wanted to keep it here for you if that's all right.' He took her in his arms when she came back to him. 'You can take it home to the cottage if you like but I thought maybe it was a part of you that you might like to have when you're at my place.'

'I think I'd like that.' She kissed him once, looking deep into his eyes with the promise of more later when they both had some energy between them.

'How about we put on a movie?'

'You read my mind.'

He rested his forehead against hers. 'It's cold enough to sit beneath the blanket too.'

Smiling, she went and got the blanket from the box and took it over to the sofa. 'This wouldn't have been such an effective surprise in the height of summer.'

'No, we'd have sweltered underneath that.'

'I wouldn't have cared as long as I was with you.' She looked back at him with a knowing smile until he came over to her.

Nate pulled her down onto the sofa with him, both laughing, both of them still too busy with each other and suddenly not too tired at all when the oven timer pinged to tell them dinner was ready.

Neither of them were all that interested in the movie or the food. At least not for a while.

They had each other, both of them back in Little Woodville. And that was what really mattered.

ACKNOWLEDGMENTS

A big thank you to all my readers who have read and enjoyed *Christmas at Snowdrop Cottage* and sent so many messages or shared social media posts to say how much they loved the story. Because there was so much love for Little Woodville and its residents, I decided that a second book had to come and *Summer at Forget-Me-Not Cottage* was born. I hope you all love it as much as the first book in what is now known as the Little Woodville Cottage series.

Thank you to the entire team at Boldwood Books. It's an absolute pleasure to work with you all! This is my third brand-new release with Boldwood and I hope there are many more to follow.

I'd like to thank Tara Loder, my former editor with whom I discussed the idea for this book and the continuation of the series. Tara had so much enthusiasm for my stories even when the doubts crept in. And much gratitude to Caroline Ridding, editor extraordinaire, who stepped in and took over the editing process. It was quite possibly the hardest edit I've ever had to work on but the book is so much better, of course!

Research nowadays is a lot easier thanks to technology and I'd like to acknowledge Parkinsons.org.uk for their up-to-date website which I used when I was putting together Nate's mother's story. All mistakes are my own but I hope what I've created is a realistic character and perhaps some awareness of osteoporosis and what it might be like to face such a diagnosis.

And last but in no means least, thank you to my husband and

my children... to my children for always being proud of me and to my husband for the same and also for his unwavering support. And of course the lunches he makes me so I can continue my writing – if he wasn't cooking, I'd be eating beans on toast every day...

Helen x

MORE FROM HELEN ROLFE

We hope you enjoyed reading *Summer at Forget-Me-Not Cottage*. If you did, please leave a review.

If you'd like to gift a copy, this book is also available as an ebook, large print, hardback, digital audio download and audiobook CD.

Sign up to Helen Rolfe's mailing list for news, competitions and updates on future books.

https://bit.ly/HelenRolfeNews

Why not explore the New York Ever After series

Helen Rolfe

Helen Rolfe

Helen Rolfe

Helen Rolfe

Helen Rolfe

Helen Rolfe

Helen Rolfe

ABOUT THE AUTHOR

Helen Rolfe is the author of many bestselling contemporary women's fiction titles, set in different locations from the Cotswolds to New York. Most recently published by Orion, she is bringing sixteen titles to Boldwood - a mixture of new series and well- established backlist. She lives in Hertfordshire with her husband and children.

Sign up to Helen Rolfe's mailing list for news, competitions and updates on future books.

Follow Helen on social media:

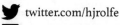 twitter.com/hjrolfe
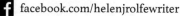 facebook.com/helenjrolfewriter
 instagram.com/helen_j_rolfe

Boldwood

Boldwood Books is an award-winning fiction publishing company seeking out the best stories from around the world.

Find out more at www.boldwoodbooks.com

Join our reader community for brilliant books, competitions and offers!

Follow us
@BoldwoodBooks
@BookandTonic

Sign up to our weekly deals newsletter

https://bit.ly/BoldwoodBNewsletter

Printed in Great Britain
by Amazon

29663041R00152